About the Author

Unity Dow, recently appointed Botswana's first female High Court judge, has a long record as a human-rights attorney. She co-founded the Women and Law in Southern Africa Research Project and is a member of International Women's Rights Watch, an advocacy organisation. Judge Dow was the plaintiff in a ground-breaking legal case in which Botswana's nationality law was overturned and that led to passage of legislation through which women were enabled to pass on their nationality to their children. She has also written about the link between the Convention on the Rights of the Child and children's legal status in Botswana. She lives with her family in Lobatse, Botswana.

FAR AND BEYON'

Unity Dow

aunt lute books
San Francisco

First Edition

10 9 8 7 6 5 4 3 2 1

Aunt Lute Books
P.O. Box 410687
San Francisco, CA 94141

First published December 2000 by Longman, Botswana (Pty) Ltd
This edition published in conjunction with Spinifex Press Pty Ltd,
North Melbourne, Australia, 2001

This book was funded in part by grants from the California Arts Council, the
National Endowment for the Arts, and the San Francisco Arts Commission
Cultural Equity Program.

Edited by Christopher van Wyk (South Africa) and Deborah Doyle (Australia)
Typeset in Times by Claire Warren
Cover design by Deb Snibson

Library of Congress Cataloging-in-Publication Data

Dow, Unity.
  Far and beyon' / Unity Dow.
    p. ; cm.
Originally published: Botswana : Longman Botswana, 2000.
Summary: A Tswana mother, grieving the loss of two sons to AIDS,
embraces traditional magic, while her remaining son and daughter
increasingly reject her beliefs.
  ISBN 1-879960-64-8
  [1. AIDS (Disease)—Fiction. 2. Death—Fiction. 3. Grief—Fiction. 4.Mother
and child—Fiction. 5. Sex role—Fiction. 6. Brothers and sisters—Fiction. 7.
Botswana—Fiction.] I. Title.
  PZ7.D7525 Far 2002
  [Fic]—dc21
                              2002020651

Dedication

For daughter Cheshe, son Tumisang and daughter Natasha.

Trudge not, through life, leaving ugly gashes.
Tiptoe not, through life, leaving half-formed impressions.
Tread gently, lovingly and purposefully; leave graceful heart prints.
Love the Earth, for she loves you so.

More mogolo go betlwa wa taola, wa motho o a ipetla.
    The essence of self is carved by oneself; only the essence
of a diviner's bones is carved by a human hand.

*And in memory of Nancy Dean Dow, for leaving graceful heart
prints all over the place.*

Unity Dow, May 2000

Acknowledgements

There is a circle of people in my life: to some I am related by blood, to others by shared rhythms; all are my friends. It is an ever-expanding circle. May it never shrink! To all of them I say thank you for participating in the creation of an environment that made this book possible. I wish, however, to paint a few of them in rainbow colours, not so that others might be outshone, but rather so that the beauty of the whole may be emphasised.

My parents, Phiri and Malefshane, beautiful and beautifying people, who taught me that a needle is as important as a pressing iron, for both will give perfection in equal measure.

Peter, my husband, who listens to me, even when any sane person would hum to shut the chatter out. Thanks for reading early, very early, and yelping with encouragement.

My siblings, especially Lesang and Tiny, thank you for reading early and nudging me on. My daughter Cheshe, also for reading early: *Ja phala, ngwanaka.*

Christine Bussmann, Maikano Platte, Thomas Platte, Mmaphefo Fergus, Phil Fergus and Miriam Hirschfeld, for reading and then promptly cheering me on with words of encouragement. And Christine, for you an extra brush stroke in lilac, for being honest and forthright in your comments.

Pat Mora, thank you for hearing very little and believing a lot. May you find no cure for your optimism!

Cathie Dunsford and Susan Hawthorne, thank you for your advice and particularly for massaging a dream into reality.

PROLOGUE

The sun was going down and it sprayed the sky with a burst of colours. Different hues of purple, pink, blue, silver, grey and gold. A fragment of cloud changed shape: a cave formed. A tangerine pink lined the cave, which looked warm and inviting, in pink velvet. A place to roll around in softness and love.

She looked deep into the cave and saw a baby girl with a soft face and a pug nose. Her little legs were drawn back as if she were just about to kick out, as babies do. The beauty of all that she saw got mixed up with the pain and she did not know whether to laugh or cry, and she did both. Through her tears she went on watching. There were more swirls of colour, the baby melted away and in her place a kitten was formed. The kitten melted away leaving behind a wisp of cloud, a tuft of gold inside a pink cave. Then the cave began to drift apart and all that was left now was one golden piece of cloud framed in silver. She searched the skies hoping for another sign, but all she saw were shapes that had no meaning for her. Grey was slowly taking over, but a stubborn, murky pink remained. Anxiety turned into hope, and she stilled her heart not to hope too much lest she jinxed her hope.

When the sun came up, the woman emerged into wakefulness. She wriggled slightly for comfort then lay still again as she felt an ache spreading through the lower part of her body. She reached out and felt the tiny bundle next to her. She smiled with triumph as the memory of last night came back to her. She had brought a baby into the world: a beautiful little girl who will help her in the home! She will call her Mosa, for *mosadi*: woman. She will protect her and nurture her. She will teach her the ways of women, and she will

1

watch her grow into a beautiful woman. She will send her to school so that she will not be as ignorant as her mother. Then she will not have to depend on a man for her survival. She will get married. But out of love, not out of need. Yes, she will find a handsome, kind man who will love and protect her. They will have beautiful children and they too will grow into adulthood. Until then, though, she will keep a watchful eye on her. This precious, precious daughter of hers.

She drew the baby to her, placing the tiny mouth on to her nipple. The mouth and the nipple were a perfect fit. Of course the nipple had done this before, but it did not have to coax the mouth. Life flowed from mother to daughter and love flowed both ways, a busy three-way street kept going by one tiny heart and one large one beating not in tandem, but definitely in harmony.

Pain mixed with love and hope and anxiety, and joy came spilling out and soaking her pillow. She fell back to sleep with the baby attached to her, a different kind of attachment from the one of the past nine months.

CHAPTER 1

This morning the sun rose, hesitant and apologetic. A wind howled from the north, swirling and whirling and picking up anything it could along its path. Plastic bags, pieces of paper, leaves flew through the cemetery. Women flung their shawls quickly over their faces. Men squeezed their eyes shut. A whirlwind formed and charged across the group of mourners then took off, still spinning and collecting more debris, beyond Monamodi village and into the plains.

There was a chill in the air, and the sun did little to challenge it. It seemed content with hiding behind a small cloud, which spat at the mourners and vehicles and on the coffin too, leaving wet, bruise-like marks all over. It was not supposed to rain today. But then death is not supposed to claim a strapping man in his prime. A little dusty, a little wet, a slightly dark beginning to a day.

Not that Mara really cared about how this day would turn out. It was not as if she could ever look back and marvel at its beauty. Only the brutish arrogance of nature would fling this kind of day in her face, on this day of all days.

She felt numb, stiffening as each handful of earth hit the coffin. Having thrown in her own handful of earth, she staggered away from the grave. She heard the piercing wail of the very person who was causing all her misery. The words of the first diviner came to her as she tried to close out the wails, the hymns, some of them bordering on jovial, and the chanting of the priests from her mind.

"I see a thin woman entering your home as if she belongs there, yet does not quite belong. She must be a relative, or perhaps a friend?" the diviner asked with a frown of concentration as he tried to decipher some meaning from the bones.

Before Mara could answer, the bone thrower shook his head in deep thought and concern at what his bones were telling him. He looked up at her and said, "Pick them up and breathe life into them."

Mara collected the eight small pieces of bones, and, cupping them in her hands, blew into them.

"Say after me: 'I ask you once more'."

"I ask you once more," chanted Mara.

"Tell me what troubles me."

"Tell me what troubles me."

"What is eating me and my family?"

"What is eating me and my family?"

"Who is scattering us?"

"Who is scattering us?"

"Who is killing us?"

"Who is killing us?"

"Now throw them," he ordered.

Mara threw the bones and they scattered all over the floor. One bone, which looked more like a piece of hard plastic or ivory with intricate engravings, jumped away from the rest and fell with its point facing westward. Mara drew in a sharp breath. Although she could not interpret this, she was shaken, because she knew only too well that west is the direction of sunset: the place of darkness and death. Hopelessness. Nothingness. The end. She stifled a scream.

The diviner looked up sharply but said nothing. Then, muttering to himself, he turned back to the bones. He began to recite a long and impressive praise poem begging and demanding of the bones as if they were his close friends and confidants. They were special bones he had inherited from his great-grandfather. They were bones that had unravelled the problems of countless families and individuals long before the diviner or Mara was born. They had spoken through the centuries and would no doubt speak one more time today. He expected truth from these bones and there was no doubt in Mara's mind that he would get it. Her only fear was that she would not be able to cope with the truth. She was afraid to know. She had suffered much but had all along feared to learn the identity of the person behind her suffering. She knew that strangers had no reason to bewitch people unknown to them. The truth will no doubt tear apart a friendship, a family link or an intimate relationship.

4

The truth will not bring peace, she thought.

Mara was jolted to the present by the call for the last prayer. She had missed the filling-in of the grave even as she sat there facing the men heaving and scraping with their spades. Suddenly she became aware that her face and body were covered with a fine layer of dust from the same earth meant to cover her son. She felt slightly buried and for a moment wished that she were completely buried. For a moment she was not sure whose funeral she was at: Thabo's or Pule's. Of course it was Pule's: Thabo's was at least eight months ago. She tried to remember Pule as he had been before he fell ill. He had been a strong, confident boy who had always been keen to give a helping hand around the home. But that picture was pushed out of her mind by the most recent one: the picture of a young man reduced to a bag of bones and glazed eyes.

Is there randomness to suffering? Mara asked herself. Or is it well ordered? Does it go on forever in an unending line, or is it a circle?

Before this latest death, Mara had been sure that she at last had the witchcraft under control, but now she realised that she was still in serious trouble. The latest diviner, the sixth one since the nightmare had begun three years ago, had seemed like he knew what he was doing. It was not until the last days of her son's illness that Mara came to finally accept that the boy was not going to make it. Hadn't this latest thrower of bones removed the entire creature, the sejeso, from his chest cavity? She had seen it with her own eyes, with all its tentacles intact. Had there been another creature in there that the sangoma had missed? Or perhaps the sejeso had given birth to a young one just as the diviner was sucking it out: who could say? Or perhaps the sejeso had already sucked the life out of him by the time it was itself sucked out. Outwitting evil is not easy, as every Motswana knew all too well.

But Mara knew that speculating on what had probably gone wrong was not going to be of any use now. What was important was to find an even stronger diviner to protect herself and the remaining members of her family. She tried to force her mind to the present: to be part of the burial of her son.

But her mind flew ahead. Should she go further afield in her search for a diviner? A Zimbabwean perhaps? They were reputed to be particularly good. It was not going to be easy, but the least she could do was try. Stan, her eighteen-year-old son, was slowly but surely rejecting the ways of his tradition. And Mosa, her precious, precious only daughter, had, at the tender unmarried age of nineteen, moved out of the house to live with a man out of marriage. She had shown such great promise at both primary and high school, getting good grades and leading all kinds of school clubs. She had been the chairperson of her high school's debating team, the editor of the school newsletter, a member of the school's National Vision Club. In fact she had shown interest in reading and writing even before she started school, at the age of six. Then she had dropped out of school, amid whispers about a pregnancy, an abortion and an unsuccessful traditional cleansing. Mara was worried about her children and wanted to protect them. She was, however, feeling increasingly helpless. Without a husband to help, she had to shoulder all the family problems alone.

Twice Mara had nearly been married. First, to the father of her first two sons, but tall, handsome Simon Thuto had died in a mining accident in neighbouring South Africa, which had claimed at least twenty-five other men. The wedding itself had been postponed on at least two occasions because Simon could not get off work at times convenient to both sets of families. And then the accident happened.

Then along came Serati Lalang. But his promises for a life together had fizzled out, two children later, when he decided to marry a woman of his mother's choice. Mosa was three years old, and Stan a year and a half. Serati paid the four cattle stipulated by custom and carried on with his life without so much as a glance back. Thus both Stan and Mosa could not remember their father. The payment had severed all links, and under customary law, no obligations to the children existed. The cattle had been given to Mara's eldest brother, Maruping, to rear for the two children: a woman could not take control of cattle. The same brother had taken control of the few cattle the siblings' grand-parents had owned. Occasionally, there were murmurs of disapproval from Mara and her other siblings about the way in which he dealt with the cattle under his control, but generally everybody agreed that taking care of cattle was a big task, and they always forgave him.

As she considered a diviner from Zimbabwe, she wondered how a Zimbabwean diviner, no matter how good, could reach her ancestors. What language would he use? Could his bones talk to foreign ancestors? No, she decided: there was no way she was hiring a Zimbabwean.

The ignorant white doctors claimed that her two sons had died of AIDS-related diseases. An even more ignorant nurse had suggested that the poor housing, lack of a father figure and long illnesses had led to the problems and to the rift between Mara and her daughter. The nurse had sat there, in her superior, white uniform, talking this nonsense. Mara had listened, not wishing to contradict someone in a government office; after all, she was hoping for extra food rations for her sick son. At the end of this nonsense from a Motswana child, Mara could only shake her head at all the woman's stupid ideas: didn't she realise that that was exactly what the person bewitching Mara wanted everybody to believe? How could everyone be so stupid? The white doctors she could excuse, but the nurse was simply unbelievable.

That was the price that parents had to pay for giving their children education. Education was good. It opened up doors for the children, giving them opportunities to earn money and to live a more comfortable life, to work in an office from where they could issue orders from behind a desk. But it also gave some young people strange ideas.

The grave was completely filled now, and she heard the wailing of her relatives as a hymn washed over her:

Go swa go tlaa apesiwa ke go sasweng.
　　Death will be enveloped by life.
Go bola go tla a apesisiwa ke go saboleng.
　　Rot will be enveloped by freshness.
Lerole mo leroleng.
　　Dust to dust.
Molora moloreng.
　　Ashes to ashes.
A go bakwe leina la morena!
　　Praise the Lord!

The last prayer finally ended, a chorus of "Amen" rang out from the crowd, and everyone seemed to move and speak at once. Life, then death. Another circle was completed. The wind had calmed down. The sun reclaimed the day. The cloud floated off, leaving a clear, blue sky.

Old friends and relatives greeted each other with good cheer while still pretending restraint, resulting in pockets of hushed whispers and stifled laughter: a bubble of joyous sadness. The solemn moment was over, and Pule's death was already behind most people present. The ones who had wailed and fainted now slapped the dust from their clothes, and all the mourners made their way back to the yard, to the food waiting in warm pots.

Struggling to her feet, Mara saw a hand reaching over to support her. She stiffened: she would not be touched by one who pretends friendship while full of ill-will. She looked up and saw her sister, Mma-Nametso, reaching for her. She allowed herself to be helped towards a waiting bakkie and obediently got in. Neither of them spoke, and their eyes did not meet as they settled into the seat. Mara felt, rather than saw, her two remaining children brush past her to climb into the back of the van, a Toyota belonging to an uncle. Again her mind went back to that first diviner who had made everything so clear to her.

The diviner, looking at the bones, addressed Mara: "I see a woman you like and trust. She comes through your big gate."

"I have only one gate," interrupted Mara hesitantly, not wanting to disagree, not wanting to contradict the bones. For a second, she even thought that perhaps she did have a big gate.

"It is a big gate, is it not? Or is it a small one?" the diviner demanded curtly, as if he were a bit angry at the interruption.

"Yes," said Mara. It was in fact not a gate at all but a wire mesh fence that had long since collapsed. But yes, the entrance was big enough to pass for a big gate, she told herself.

"Well, there is a thin woman who comes to your house often and laughs with you, but her heart is not full of laughter. Her heart is bad. It is full of envy. It is a grey heart."

Mara looked puzzled. Who could it be? And why would anyone be envious of her? She was poor and unmarried; her previous partner was so abusive that she was happy when he took up with another woman and left her. She had a badly paying maid's job. She owned no cattle and no goats, and, as she was fond of saying, if she had an itch, she would have to use her teeth to scratch it because she had no tools to do even that.

"But I am a poor woman with nothing for anyone to envy. I do not understand why anyone would be envious of me."

The diviner looked up and with a wry smile said, "Why are you here? Just think. What made you come to consult me?"

"Well," Mara began, "things have not been going well for me recently. My employer has been rather harsh with me, demanding that I work longer hours and complaining about my work. She says I am lazy, and she claims I steal from her. Her children show me no respect and . . . her husband grabs at me in the kitchen . . . well, that is not really important . . . My son Thabo woke up one morning last week with blisters all over his body. You know: the burn of the ancestors. Also, one of his fingernails was cut whilst he was asleep. And a bit of hair was missing from his head: shaved off. Since then he does not seem to be interested in anything. He used to love football and was in the school team before he went to university. He was a first-year student at the university and was very clever. I hoped that one day he would help me get out of this poverty. He . . ."

"Exactly my point," interrupted the diviner. "Someone can see that you will be out of the poverty soon and that someone has dark thoughts about you. She is now working against your future. Even your employer has bad thoughts about you. I can see all of it here. There might even be a man involved. Perhaps a man you trusted is now being made to turn away from you? Perhaps . . . mmm: I have to consult the bones again."

"Are you saying Mma-Pako my employer is bewitching me? She is not related to me. She has much more than me. Surely she would have no reason."

"No; I am not saying that. Your employer has hardened her heart against you because of the other bad woman's witchcraft. This other person is closer to you. She has sneaked in firewood from the *moomane* tree, the tree that makes those who use it for firewood quarrel."

"I know the tree," Mara said softly.

"The woman has sneaked it into your firewood pile. She has also buried leaves from this tree on the path you take every day, to make your employer annoyed with you whenever she sees you. You must be careful what you burn for firewood. But more importantly, you must stop using the gate you normally use to enter your employer's yard. And you must promise to start work earlier than before so that the bad spells are not awake yet. Just before sunrise is a good time, even if it means sweeping the yard whilst waiting for your employer's family to wake up. Get there before the sun warms up the bad powers and makes them potent. You will notice a change of attitude from your employer if you do that."

"Mma, mma: we have arrived; we have arrived. Are you feeling alright?" Mara's daughter, Mosa, said, giving her mother a gentle shake. Mara returned to the present and realised that they were back at home. Had anyone spoken to her during the ten-minute ride from the graveyard? It was quite possible, although she had not heard anything. She looked up: her eyes met her daughter's, and she saw sadness and despair. She wanted to reach out to her, put her on her lap and offer her a breast. She felt a tug at her womb, the first and safest of homes this daughter of hers had ever known – that anyone had ever known. She forced out a slow breath, and with her eyes told her she loved her. She hoped Mosa had heard.

People were milling around the entrance to the yard, waiting for their turn to wash their hands. Some were already seated inside the yard, most of the men on the few chairs and all the women flat on the dusty ground, their legs stretched out in front of them. Some of the men who could not find chairs were squatting on one heel, others were seated on bricks or makeshift chairs.

A woman who had a bandaged leg was the only female seated on a chair, standing out in a sea of scarved heads. A man approached the woman; there were whispers, explanations. Then he moved on. Another approached: more explanations. She rolled off the chair, careful not to hurt her bandaged leg. The man took the chair and walked off. Now there was order. Mara took all this in as she got out of the van.

There was chattering everywhere, and loud laughter. For these people the funeral was over, as if Pule were somehow not dead any more. Mara saw a relative, whose wail had been loud and persistent less than an hour ago, laugh and hug a friend. Greetings were exchanged and the health of family members was asked about.

"And how are your children?" a voice asked.

"Two are dead," Mara answered to herself. She walked to the tub of water to wash her hands like everyone else. She knew the importance of this ritual. The bad luck and darkness surrounding death must not be brought into the yard. Death had to be kept out. That was why the tubs were outside the gate. As she walked to the centre of the group of people washing their hands, everyone moved away. She did not look up but felt their watching, sympathetic, appraising eyes.

Mara knew that the loss of two children so soon after each other was bound to raise questions about her own role in their death. The speculations from the watchers would be numerous. Did she kill them? Did she hold them with her heart for some bad deed they had done, refusing to forgive them, thus causing their death? Did she try to bewitch some powerful person and receive her own medicine back twice over? Did she displease her ancestors in any way? Perhaps her sons were born already marked with bad luck because of something she had done. Perhaps they had been breech births and were now marked for life.

Mara bent over the dish to wash her hands. From this position she could see only the feet of her watchers, and it occurred to her that she would be able to recognise her tormentor even by her feet. They had been that close. She looked for her amongst this world of mostly torn, scuffed and ugly shoes; an ugly toenail that badly needed trimming; dusty, laddered pantyhose. But her tormentor was not there. She straightened up and again without looking at anyone walked into the yard. Still she could feel the burning eyes. The clusters of greetings turned into a blanket of silence.

From nowhere her sister appeared and once more supported her as she walked slowly through the seated crowd to her tiny, two-roomed house with its corrugated roof. She knew it would be unbearably hot in there, and after six days of not being allowed out except to the pit-latrine, she hoped that one of her aunts would suggest that she be allowed to sit outside. But this was wishful thinking, and she knew that: as the main bereaved person, she was expected to stay in one room until the final hair-shaving and clothes-washing ritual on the day after the funeral.

All day a trail of people would come in to say their greetings as they left, smelling of meat, lips shining with grease despite the pretence at sadness. Well, to be fair, not all pretence, but still, the lowered voices, the searching looks, the pursed lips were more an act than anything else.

As Mara sat down on the mattress she had been using as both bed and seat for the past week, she heard the voice of her younger father in the yard, commanding everyone to sit down for the official communication about the cause of Pule's death. Immediate silence: everyone was curious, as always, about what the family would tell the public at this *tatolo*, the last speech, to confirm that it was all over. It did not matter whether the cause of death were a car accident or old age: there was always speculation about what the family would say. After all, a seemingly innocent traffic accident could have resulted from the fact that a family belonged to a religious sect that demands sacrifices. No one expected the family to tell the truth about the cause of death, but people were always curious to find out how far from the truth the family would go.

"People of my tribe," Uncle Bonoso began, "you have just buried your child. Your child died after a long illness. That long illness is the cause of his death. Thank you. In addition, I announce porridge. Please wait to have some."

Although everyone had heard the uncle, his words were not meant for the women – who sat separated from the men – and so an aunt repeated the exact information for the benefit of the women. Tradition demanded the division, and the curse of AIDS could possibly be attributable to failure to adhere to this and many other traditions. An elderly man had taken it upon himself before the announcement to order women venturing to the men's side, and vice versa, to get back to their side. Young people were the biggest offenders, and the old man shook his head in dismay, trying to get them to see the folly of disregarding tradition. Were they not satisfied with the ever persistent drought? Would they never learn? The transgressors responded with sneers and a cynical shaking of heads before dragging their feet back to where they belonged.

Mara had not expected any other explanation for the death of her son. Thabo, too, had died from "a long illness". The murmuring that followed was to be expected. Vague words such as "long illness" always meant something was being hidden. Mara thought she heard someone say the word "AIDS", but she could not be sure. In any case, she could not imagine anyone being courageous enough to utter that dreaded acronym, especially at a funeral: "this disease", "the radio disease", *"phamo kate"* or "the disease that has a short name" were the more acceptable synonyms. She was tired and stressed out, and needed some peace and space, some rest.

The clatter of spoons and plates told her that food – sorghum porridge, samp and beef – was being served. Once again the noise level went up: relatives, neighbours and friends asking about each other's health and their children's, commenting on each other's weight and offering congratulations for being fatter and therefore happily married whilst chastising, for all to hear, the people considered to be over-weight or too thin. The sizes of behinds were commented on, and unsolicited advice was offered about whether they should be reduced or fattened some more. Behinds were good-naturedly patted and bellies poked. Sexual innuendoes were exchanged and there was much laughing. Some discussed politics, others football. Information was swapped about recent births, deaths, illnesses and weddings. Some whispered in detached groups as gossip and scandals were passed on. These were the rhythms of village life.

Even from the confines of her room, Mara had a clear picture in her mind of what was going on outside. She knew that as the food was being served, people would be keeping a keen eye on the amount of meat coming their way. Neighbours would be questioned about the number of cattle killed, hoping that at least two had been slaughtered. Seswaa, shredded beef, served mainly at funerals and weddings, was a speciality that seemed to bring out the worst in both the servers, who wanted to keep as much as possible in the pot for themselves, and the guests, who never seemed satisfied with the amount on their plate. Sharp, angry looks and soft mutterings of disapproval were the only indications of the conflict, but one could never miss it. Mara knew that the one cow slaughtered for the occasion would lead to some tensions, but this did not bother her now. She was hot and frustrated and wanted everyone to leave her alone. She wanted to plan her next move in her quest to protect her family, and she wanted more time with her two children and her grandchild.

She closed her eyes and tried to shut out the noise. Her mind wandered once more back to that first visit to Rre-Dichaba, the first diviner, who had begun the complicated diagnosis of her family's ills.

"Who then is behind my problems?" Mara had asked anxiously. "And can you counter their powers? I do not want anybody dead, but

I do not want my family hurt either."

"A thin woman of the colour of the bark of the moretlwa bush. Dark, but not too dark. She laughs a lot. Yes, I see laughter but it is a sinister laughter. You laugh with her and she is counting your teeth. She plans bad things for you, and you are blind to her plans. You have a good heart, a white heart, and a female heart. She has a black heart, a heart that wants to kill. Her heart is full of envy. She has a beige heart; she wants what others have but she covers it with her laughter. You must know who the person is." He looked up at Mara for confirmation.

She shook her head slightly, not wanting to contradict Rre-Dichaba. "I have no idea who it is. There is no person like that in my life. I have no one fitting that description."

Rre-Dichaba fixed his eyes on Mara and declared, "I cannot give you a name, although I can see it right here. You will see her when you are ready to confront the truth. Until then you will continue to deny the obvious."

The diviner once again looked at the bones. Shaking his head with apparent regret and sadness, he said, "Pick them up again, for I see a very bad future for you. I see clouds gathering, lightning; I see a sandstorm, and I see you in the centre groping for your way. I see sand in your eyes, and again I see the woman's back walking away from you. And you are there alone. Yes, I see a bad future. Let's hope your ancestors can take pity on you and help you. I do not see your children. Mmm: where are they? I see vague images. Are they crying or are they calling for you? This is heavy stuff. Your case is a tough one. You must pray to your ancestors and your God. Only they can help. Pick them up, breathe into them and throw them. Let me listen to them one more time."

Mara picked up the bones and entreated them to tell her the truth. She chanted after the diviner:

"I ask you once more."

"I ask you once more."

"Tell me what troubles me."

"Tell me what troubles me."

"What is eating me and my family?"

"What is eating me and my family?"

"Who is scattering us?"

"Who is scattering us?"

"Who is killing us?"

"Who is killing us?"

"Where are my children?"

"Where are my children?"

"Are they in danger?"

"Are they in danger?"

This time the bones fell in a totally different pattern. The engraved one was closest to her and she was relieved that it was not pointing to the west. She desperately wanted to know if that had any special significance, but she was too scared to ask.

Rre-Dichaba's voice was slow and deliberate, and he spoke with concern. "You are surrounded by bad luck and ill-omens. You need a thorough cleansing. I will give you something to put in your bath, every day for seven days, and then you have to come back for another consultation. You also need something to help you with your job. A small herb to sprinkle in your employer's food or tea. Do not put too much, or she might taste it. And remember, do not use the gate you normally use to enter your employer's yard. I will give you something to sprinkle at the old gate. When the moon is insulting women, the very last sliver, only after that may you use the gate again. But you must wait until after then. I will also give you herbs for your family. You must burn them in the house and have the whole family inhale the fumes. If you have a lover, you must keep away from him for seven days; otherwise, any of his powers, from his own doctor, may neutralise the ones I am creating for you. Do you understand? That may hurt you or him. It is not good for powers to meet like that unless properly planned."

Mara nodded and proceeded to receive the various herbs. Occasionally, the diviner bit off bits from the roots and herbs, and chewed on them. With the amount of root and bark and herbs all around him, this was a way of checking the type of medicine he was prescribing. He handed her a lump of putty-like medicine, black and oily. What if it contained human tissue? Mara wondered, as a smell akin to rotten skins hit her nostrils. She was somewhat alarmed. It was common knowledge that the best traditional medicines did contain some skin or other human parts. The occasional disappearance of a schoolchild was ample proof that traditional medicines were

15

occasionally still being made with human parts. Most people preferred not to know too much, and Mara was no different.

Mara thanked the man and stood up to leave. At the door, she looked back at the diviner, took in his ample frame and was disconcerted to see a frown on his heavily bearded face. She had hoped for a look of encouragement.

But that was three years ago. Since then a lot had happened. She had finally accepted that her best friend, who her children had always called, *mmane* – "young mother" – and who they considered their second mother, was bewitching her and her children. It had been a painful realisation that had buried her in melancholy and depression. Later, as she had moved from diviner to diviner, and from prophet to prophet, she had found out that other people were also bewitching her or her children, but the hurt of that could never be compared to the pain brought on by the realisation that Lesedi was an enemy. After all, it was because she was in a weakened state that later evildoers were able to succeed.

Mara remembered how at first she had been reluctant to accept that Lesedi was bewitching her. When Thabo first took an interest in football, it had been Lesedi who had brought him a shirt she had bought at a jumble sale on one of her frequent visits to Gaborone. Lesedi had somehow known that Thabo would appreciate the blue shirt with the large number 7 printed in gold on the back. He was the envy of his friends for months as he strutted around in his special football shirt. Indeed, Lesedi's special place in Mara's family, just like Mara's in Lesedi's, dated back to their respective first pregnancies. Although they had grown up in the same village, they had hardly noticed each other until they met at a wedding and started comparing notes about their pregnancies. They had laughed nervously as they speculated about what childbirth would be like. After that, a strong bond was created between them. They shared laughter and pain. Mara was like a sister at Lesedi's wedding, just as she had been like a sister when the marriage ended in divorce. They took care of each other's children. Mara did not want to believe that an old, trusted and very close friend was responsible for her misery. Then Lesedi had arrived one day, as usual bearing a gift, this time for Pule. As she approached, she seemed hesitant and unsure. Her arms were folded,

16

which had seemed strange and awkward to Mara at the time. Lesedi had a way of swinging her slim arms as she walked in a way that caused her whole body to sway as if with pride. Then, as she came into the yard, she unfolded her arms and Mara saw a trickle of white powder drift from her left palm. Mara saw it because one of the diviners had warned her to watch her best friend's left hand. He had warned that evil would flow from it. Seeing this, Mara then accepted the truth as told by the diviners. As Mara's eyes bore into her friend's left hand, Lesedi extended her right hand, in which nestled a tennis ball, and called out to Pule.

"Pule, come and see this. This is for you. Mr Wilson, over at the Dutch Reformed Church Mission Hospital, gave me a couple of old balls, and I saved one for you." She said it with a smile. But Mara was sure she had seen hesitation in that smile. Pule came charging, ready to receive the ball. Both his hands were extended to show gratitude, but Mara pushed them away. The ball hit the sandy ground, bounced once and stopped dead between the two women. Pule was old enough to know when to leave without being told to do so. He beat a hasty retreat. Something happened between his mother and her friend, and he could tell it was something major. There had been no sharp words, no screaming. Lesedi, however, immediately understood the charge. After that, there was a silent closing of hearts. Coldness came between them, and visits to each other's homes dried up. A part of Mara still ached for the lost friendship. No one was able to fill the place left by Lesedi. She not only missed what she had had with Lesedi; she missed Lesedi's children, and the strong friendship that had existed between them and her own children. Sometimes she tried to believe that perhaps Lesedi had not bewitched her deliberately; after all, sometimes evil goes where it is not directed. But even then, she could not get around the fact that Lesedi was directing evil, even if not deliberately to her. And of course there was the white powder that had floated from her left hand. That could only mean that Mara or her family was the target of the evil. When she went back to the diviner to report the incident, there was a knowing nod from the man.

Outside, people were leaving. Some came in to her to say their greetings. These were acquaintances and distant relatives not close enough to stay on for cleaning up but too close just to leave without saying their goodbyes. Mara acknowledged them and murmured a soft *dumelang*: hello, in response to their searching eyes. Her eyes brimmed with tears, but she hid her face, lifting it at brave but brief intervals. She sipped from her pitcher of murky water, filled with herbs and spices from a diviner, for fortification.

Mara heard and felt a howl rise from deep within her womb, crashing into her heart and charging up her throat – but it did not escape; instead, it rushed into her head, filling her ears and smashing into her brain. She shut her eyes and felt her eyeballs throbbing against her eyelids. And still her brain was flooded with the howl that would not escape. Her womb tightened, feeling both full and empty, and inside it she felt fear rattling. She reached for her pitcher. Can one douse fear with medicated water? Can a hot, steamy howl be calmed by water? She felt a sudden urge to rise from the mattress and march out of the door, out of the yard, out of the village, to just walk and walk and walk. She wished she were younger: then, perhaps, she could replace the fear in her womb with a baby.

Nunu, her three-year-old grand-daughter, kept trying to take a sip from the pitcher or making loud and embarrassing observations that grandma was drinking dirty water.

"This child is just as talkative as Mosa when she was this old," an aunt observed.

"And looks just like she did, too!" another added.

Mara saw a wasp angrily battering itself against the window pane, wanting to come in. Why would you want to come into this hot box? she wondered. You have the wide, wild world to roam free. Fly away: there is only baked sadness in this room.

Of course the wasp was too angry to listen, and continued to fling itself against the pane, buzzing furiously until somebody outside squashed it against the window. Will its mother feel a howl inside her at the death of her offspring? Mara asked herself.

CHAPTER 2

Stan was glad to be going to bed in his quiet, comfortable room. Even his usually resilient, stout, muscular legs were aching from too much standing and too little rest. The shower felt good, and he was now feeling refreshed. Like everyone else, he had hardly any sleep at all for the past two nights: what with the wake, the skinning of the cow, the cooking of the meat and the digging of the grave.

Digging the grave had been the toughest part. The boisterous young men, drinking and swapping stories about girlfriends, football and the love triangles on the TV soapies, had been too much for him. They were preparing his brother's grave, but they could have been digging a stormwater drain, for all the emotion they put into the task. He knew he had behaved the same when he was a hyena, digging a grave before. Hyena, he thought was indeed an apt name for these nocturnal grave-diggers. The amount of meat reserved for them in payment for their special services after the funeral matched the name perfectly. They had worked by the lights of a van; hard work made lighter by the beers sneaked in. Stan and the younger boys were not offered any, of course. The older men knew about the drinking that went on, but as long as the hyenas were discreet, all would be well – of course they never left any signs of their drinking; indeed, perhaps graveyards were the only places in the country without litter.

No one would ever dare drop a can or a plastic bag there: you can never be sure with the dead, so you just did not disrespect them. And there was always the living to deal with. Leaving beer cans in a graveyard could be just the kind of excuse some old men were looking for to give some youths a public lashing.

"Stan, please stay one more night," his mother had pleaded. "You cannot be off so soon after your brother's funeral. What will people say?"

But Stan had decided to come home to sleep in a clean and comfortable bed. He hoped his mother would understand. He had tried to explain that another night by the fireside with the rest of the men would have been too much for him. The exhaustion was not only physical; it was emotional.

At the graveyard, Stan had watched his mother and sister from a distance. The female family members and close relatives tossed the handfuls of earth into the grave as their way of saying goodbye. But when he was offered a spade to do the same, he quickly stepped back. He knew that he was expected to be amongst the first to fill in his brother's grave, that it was an honour, not a chore. But after the experience of Thabo's funeral, he just could not stand hearing that haunting sound of the dirt as it hit the coffin; instead, he waited until there was more earth in the grave before he helped fill it.

He watched his mother being led to toss in her handful of earth, so frail that it seemed as if the smallest breeze could blow her away. He had wanted to go to her, to hold her. But he also wanted to be held by her, to be comforted by her. But he was the only man left in the family, and he had to be strong. He felt the pitying eyes around him. So rather than go over to be with the two women who were closer to him than any other, he watched them from across the hole that was swallowing up his second brother.

Perhaps due to fatigue, his mind began to wander. With the beautiful hymns filling his ears, he had the sense, for a split second, that he was watching his own funeral. He shook his head, and breathed in and out slowly. Fear gripped his heart. He felt lost and without an anchor. Adrift. Perhaps to prove to himself that he was still alive, he grabbed a spade and shovelled a few loads of earth into the grave. Feeling a bit more in control, he handed the spade to another waiting man and the chain continued. As he stepped back an older cousin grabbed his shoulder and gave it a gentle, reassuring squeeze. "Thank you," Stan's eyes responded, grateful for that brief moment of human contact.

He looked around, searching for his sister. She had moved away after the tossing of the earth and was now singing with the crowd, tears streaming freely down her cheeks.

Stan looked away as if to get a bearing on where he was and what he was doing there. All around him were fresh graves. His mind was all over the place, in search of comfortable thoughts. Fresh graves. Can a grave really be fresh? How can death be fresh? Fresh: not spoiled, not stale, not rotten, not musty. That was what Ms Valley, his English teacher, had read out from a dictionary hardly a week before. He looked at the not fresh fresh graves, and noted the dates of birth. Young people who had died prematurely. One or two were the graves of people he had known, maybe not personally, but at least by name. He had known about their long illness, their death and their funeral. Fresh: Looking or appearing youthful, Ms Valley had explained. Not any more, thought Stan. By the time they had ended up in a fresh grave, they had long lost their freshness. Fresh: Not fatigued; vigorous, energetic. Stan himself was not feeling fresh.

Two rows away was Thabo's grave. Two people were standing next to it, talking, and one of them, a young man, was leaning against the metal frame around the grave. Stan was overcome by a sudden anger. He strode over to push the man off his brother's grave. *How dare he?* But he came to his senses before he could carry out this rash act; after all, he too had been leaning against someone else's grave. The young man meant no disrespect: on what else could you lean at a place like this?

The call for the last prayer was made, and the crowd came closer for the Lord's Prayer, recited with a fervour by all:

Raetsho yoo, ko legodimong,
Our Father, who art in heaven,

Even the young man who had been leaning against Thabo's grave now had his arms folded and his head bowed.

"It is done, Stan, my brother's grandchild," Bonoso Selato, one of Mara's uncles, said as they walked towards the waiting cars and vans. "Accept what God has done. Take care of these three women left by your ancestors under your guidance. Be a man and be strong. God tests us in different ways. Be strong." The old man tugged at his rather short jacket as he walked. The jacket had seen better days and had clearly once belonged to a much shorter man. Uncle Bonoso walked without the aid of a cane, but his gait suggested that he might have found one useful. His hair was black except for a streak of white. During happier times, Stan and his brothers secretly called him Old Man Streak.

Stan did not respond, afraid that if he opened his mouth a wail would escape. I do not know how to take care of three women, he wanted to say. Uncle Bonoso continued, "Your grandfather was a brave man. You are the spitting image of that man. You bear his name and you must bear his courage, my child. Your heart is full of sorrow, but you must not let the sorrow turn into bitterness. Be strong, old man."

Stan slowed down to allow the man to go ahead, but Uncle Bonoso slowed down too. "Yours is a heavy responsibility. To be the only man is a heavy job. But you will manage, old man. You are strong. And we will always be there to hold your hand. Go on: the van is waiting. Remember: your heart will grow soft with time; it will not bleed forever."

Still, Stan said nothing; instead, he listened to his heart hammering loudly within his chest, afraid that if it went on like this it would surely stop beating. He walked over to the waiting van and climbed into the back. Amongst several relatives there was his sister, and she, too, looked as if she were concentrating on keeping her mouth shut.

"Pule has been buried well," an aunt was saying.

"Yes, you are right: he has been buried well," a cousin agreed.

"There were no arguments; there was no shame. Yes, we have buried him well." The cousin looked at Stan and Mosa as if inviting them into the conversation. Stan ignored her, and Mosa, too, was pointedly looking away from the talking women.

Stan felt a pressure from his sister's shoulder, a call for a connection beyond just the physical. He responded with a little squeeze against his sister. He wanted to talk about Pule, the brother who had taught him how to play football on the dusty patch in their front yard, not Pule the corpse. He wanted to remind his sister Mosa about how they had fought as children, for the privilege of being piggybacked on their brother's back. How he, Stan, had argued that being the youngest, he should get more turns. How Pule had always been at pains to give them equal turns.

"The Selato family always bury their kin well," the first woman intoned.

Both brother and sister rode in silence, a fifteen-minute journey that felt like an hour. Mosa was thinking about the piles of books she had inherited over the years from Pule. Pule had had a knack of persuading teachers, especially expatriate teachers leaving the country, to hand over all their old books to him. He was an avid reader, collecting books about almost every subject, and Mosa had taken after him in that way. Recently, she had found herself re-reading *To Kill a Mockingbird* by Harper Lee, a book that had been one of Pule's favourites.

At home, like everyone else, they washed their hands before entering the yard. Stan scooped the water with his hands from the male tub, noticing that the tools for digging and filling the grave had already been offloaded and placed next to the tub. Is it my duty, he wondered, as the surviving male in the family, to place these spades there? There is too much to learn under such trying circumstances.

The rest of the day was spent in a frenzy of activity. Feeding the hyenas and older men, and the cutting and hanging up of leftover uncooked meat for drying. By the time he left the yard for the Bana-Ba-Phefo High School, where he lived with Mr Mitchell, an American mathematics teacher, it was already early evening. He was so exhausted that the five-kilometre walk had seemed much longer than usual. He said hello to the night watchman and a couple of students at the gate, and hurried on. He thought he had seen the watchman earlier on at the funeral, but he could not be sure. He had seen some of his classmates and quite a few of his teachers. Mr Mitchell had been at the funeral as well. He was genuinely grateful for their support, but he was not in the mood for sympathetic looks. He took a dark footpath to the teachers' quarters, avoiding the centre of the school: he knew that it being a Saturday, there was bound to be some kind of entertainment activity for students. He could see students milling around the dining hall, which was also used as the entertainment hall on weekends.

Stan had hoped that the funeral would bring some sense of closure, but, lying on his bed, looking at the ceiling, he knew that there were many unresolved issues between members of his family about Pule's death. He had hoped that some emotional closeness would have occurred, but his mother was hardly available to him or to his sister, Mosa, for that matter. All those female relatives surrounding her as she sat in the small, hot room made it impossible for her to be with her children. Stan had felt uncomfortable to stay in the room any longer than was expected for a man. As for his sister, she had been occupied by all kinds of duty during the day.

Even as he regretted not having spent time with his mother and sister during the day, he was glad for the peace and quiet. Mr Mitchell had tried to coax him out of his room to watch a football match on television, but he declined the invitation. His body and mind badly needed rest, and he needed energy for the ceremony of the following day. He knew he would be doing little in the way of work, but he still had to be there. He and Mosa would only be receiving a small piece of black cloth to pin to their clothes as a mark of their bereavement. Did anyone still look at or care about this little token of bereavement? He didn't think so.

His mind did not rest, wondering and wandering. He remembered Modise, a friend from his childhood days. Modise was a *letlhomelwa*: the child born immediately before him had died in infancy. As a mark of this special status, Modise had sported a small tuft of hair at the back of his head whereas the rest of his head was shaved clean. Stan understood that the special condition of having lost an older sibling rendered the afflicted child fearful and irritable and gave him a weak heart. Stan had been careful around Modise, making sure not to agitate or frighten him in any way. Spotting a *letlhomelwa* child always brought a murmuring and some tiptoeing around the afflicted child, and any new member of the circle of friends would be immediately warned.

"He is a *letlhomelwa*: be careful with him," an old friend would whisper.

"He has my clay cow. What should I do?" the newcomer would whisper back.

"Wait until he loses interest in it."

"But I want it now!"

"Do you want his heart to stop?"

"No, but I want my cow back!" On the verge of tears.

"If you demand it back from him I am leaving right now!"

"But I want it back." Now in tears.

"Shut up; shut up, please. He is a *letlhomelwa*. Do you want to kill him?"

24

Now remembering, Stan thought, Yes: we had thought Modise, the *letlhomelwa* child, very special. He had been allowed to grab their playthings from them with impunity because they were under strict instructions not to upset him. But most important of all, they could not frighten or startle him. Thus, if they were approaching him from behind, they had to warn him in advance. Of course none of them had wanted to kill Modise. Playing hide and seek with him had been a particular challenge. He always won because for fear of startling him and causing his heart to stop, his friends had to announce their hiding place before he stumbled upon them and got startled.

Stan and his friends had always taken special care not to make Modise cry – which he was always threatening to do if he did not get his own way.

His mother tried everything to settle him. At night, as he lay sleeping, she placed pieces of grass over his ear and whispered to him that his sister had died and was with the ancestors and would not be coming back. But this did little to settle him and make him less fearful.

Looking back, Stan decided that Modise had just been plain spoilt.

Yes, Stan recalled, there was a time when a tuft of hair, a piece of black cloth, a black dress, a black apron, brought responses from others. This was long before people, fresh people, started losing their freshness, long before they started dropping like maize kernels out of the hands of a greedy man and ending up in a fresh grave. Sometimes the responses were not positive, as in the case of a widow's black dress.

Stan remembered how, as children, they feared widows, believing that these women brought misfortune and death. Death was rare then. If a widow walked through a herd of cattle, the owner was doomed. Once, Stan had gone to the borehole to water some goats, and a widow had come for water. The group of kids scattered, afraid they might come into contact with the black dress. When the widow asked one of them to help her raise the bucket to her head, there were no volunteers. Stan went forward with fear gripping his heart. He held his side of the bucket and heaved in tandem with the widow. The bucket balanced perfectly on the woman's head, and he believed that he was already dead, thinking, if he were, death was not that bad after all; there was no pain. Then he looked at his friends, who were staring back at him mesmerised: was it his face? had he broken out in a sudden rash of spots? He felt his face, and it was dry from the forbidden swim in the bilharzia-infested water, but otherwise it felt alright. He had responded out of pity for the widow, but now he might be the one receiving pity if he started growing warts all over his body. He stepped back, still half expecting to fall down dead. The widow said, "Thank you, my child. May you grow and have white hairs."

"Thank you, ma'am." Might as well collect a blessing: God knows, he needed plenty right now.

Clearly, his friends did not think he was going to live to be an old man.

Later, he told his mother about the encounter with the widow, and she responded that nothing bad ever came from an act done with a good heart. He felt better, but still it was days before he stopped examining himself for some deadly disease.

That fear of death was not as ever present as had been the case when he was younger. He sat next to widows on buses all the time. He would still not go out of his way to touch one, but if contact were made, he would not lose sleep over it.

He thus did not expect his classmates to treat him differently simply because of the black piece of cloth he would have pinned to his left sleeve for the next six months. A few years ago, the teachers might have been kinder and classmates might have offered to do his duties for him. Not any more. The black cloth was a symbol, the importance of which was quickly fading away amongst the youth. Too much death was deadening emotions. And, some would argue, starting a gout epidemic with the continuous slaughter of cattle.

Stan tried to rein in his mind. Why was it galloping all over the place when he needed rest? He picked up a car magazine and flicked through it, trying to force his mind into idleness. Finally he fell asleep.

CHAPTER 3

For Mosa, Pule's funeral had helped focus her attention on living. On triumphing. On doing more than just surviving, which, she decided, she had been doing for months. After months of drifting, she felt she needed to find a way out of her personal crisis. The last days of Pule's life, the coming into the family of Nunu, the realisation that her mother was struggling to survive emotionally, had all come together to force Mosa out of what she was later to see as self-absorption.

As her brother's coffin was lowered into the grave, she promised herself that she was going to live her life to the full, if that was still within her power; to reach out to her mother, brother and niece, so that they would survive as a family. She realised now how she had needed them these past months.

During the past three years or so, Mosa felt that her mother had not been there for her. Now she realised that her mother could not possibly have been there for all of them. She had been stretched thin by the demands of the living, the dead and the dying. If anything, it was a miracle that she had been able to cope at all. Mosa felt that she was selfish not to have appreciated all this before.

She made a silent and solemn promise that she would take care of little Nunu, the new addition to her family. She watched the young child now, who seemed puzzled, clinging to some cousin or aunt who had taken the child from Mara, who seemed to have turned into stone. She knew that Nunu would be both a blessing and a responsibility, but she was already proving to be a joy. She had never really thought much of the child before. It was strange to have this little person, coming and going with her mother, in their life. Then

Nunu's mother moved to another town and Nunu had stopped visiting altogether. Mosa had not particularly missed her; she had hardly known her then. Then the child was brought at Pule's insistence during the last months of his life and had stayed ever since. Mosa had not seen the striking resemblance between father and daughter until after the father's death. Perhaps she had really never looked at the child before. Now she wanted the best for her and was prepared to share mothering duties with Mara. She knew her mother would have to go back to work soon and then Nunu would need her even more. She needed that responsibility, and felt prepared for it.

"I must go back to school! I must go back to school!" she screamed to herself. She knew that the promise was easier made than fulfilled, but she was determined to go back and learn. She missed the sprawling, ugly compound, where there was always something to do.

Her eyes fell on Stan standing on the other side of the grave. There was a moment that she thought he was about to bolt, just take off and run. Then he steadied himself, shaking his head as if to clear it. What disagreeable thoughts are coursing through your brain, dear brother of mine? she wondered. With an aggression she had never seen before, he grabbed a spade and shovelled two or three spadefuls of earth into the grave. Then his energy evaporated as quickly as it had come, and he seemed to slump and deflate. He put the spade down and turned away while the men continued filling up the grave.

A young man who had a deep baritone led the mourners as they sang *"Nkosi Sikelela iAfrica"*: – "God Bless Africa". His body swayed to the music and he tapped his foot rhythmically. Mosa loved this hymn, and joined in the singing and swaying, tears streaming down her face. The rest of the crowd picked up the mood, and the song rang out loudly and beautifully across the graveyard and beyond.

Nkosi sikeleli Africa.
   God Bless Africa.
Maluphakanyisw' Udumo Lwayo.
   Let her fame resound.
Yizwa imithando yethu.
   Hear our prayers.

Nkosi Sikela iAfrica.
It seemed as if God hardly listened these days.

As far as Mosa could recall, it was not until recently that the hymn had been sung at funerals. She would never have considered it a funeral song. But of late, it was proving to be very popular indeed. There was something about its words, its tune, the rhythm that gave a beautiful harmony to any crowd that sang it.

With her eyes, Mosa sought out her mother. Most people had moved away from the path of the dust as the grave was being filled, but she had not. Two aunts sat with her, shielding themselves from the dust with their shawls, but Mara seemed oblivious to the sand swirling around and settling on her. What is dust when you have lost a son? Her face had acquired a reddish film from the earth. One of the aunts leaned over and whispered something to her, but she did not respond: not a nod, not a shake of the head, not a movement. What could the aunt say of any importance, in the face of the loss enveloping a mother burying a second son within twelve months?

Could she possibly survive another death in the family? Mosa wondered. What if I am next? Could she survive another funeral? From where Mosa stood, her mother looked like no more than a tiny bundle of dusty rags. A fragile bundle that could be lifted by the wind and carried away. Although her mother had always been a small woman, it seemed as if she had become even smaller. And there was a porous look about her these days, Mosa thought. A lack of solidity.

Se o nkadimileng sone,
    What you have loaned me,
Fa o re ke sebusetse,
    When you say I must bring it back,
Ke ntse ke kere, Golokile; golokile,
    I will keep on saying, It is fine; it is fine,
Leso le fa le tshabega.
    Even though death is feared.

Mosa found that as long as she took part in the singing, her mind did not wander too much. But the hymns themselves led her along many paths. Were they ready to return to the Lord what He had loaned them? Why did the Lord demand so much?

*Motho yo o tsetsweng ke mosadi, o malatsi makhutshwanyane
mo lefatsheng.*
A person born of a woman has few days on earth.
*O tshwana fela le bojang, jo bo thunyang mosong,
bo segwe maitsibowa.*
He is like the grass that blooms in the morning and gets
harvested in the afternoon.

As the hymn picked up in tempo, Mosa could not help but ask,
Why did the Lord have to demand the return now? Could He not have
been more patient? Why two brothers, and in such quick succession?
But lamenting was not what was going to get them out of the deep pit
of despair that was threatening to bury them as surely as two graves
had buried her two brothers. She resolved to be strong for herself, her
mother, her little niece and her remaining brother. Strength, she
decided, would have to start with facing reality and accepting truths
none of them had been prepared to face before. Strength can come
only from honesty, she told herself. Honesty can come only from
strength, another part of her brain countered. A circle, without
beginning or end. I will have to force an entry, she resolved.

"Africa is held together by circular rhythms: almost an ideology,"
she remembered Mr Mitchell once saying almost out of the blue. He
explained that when he had first come to Botswana, he was struck by
the randomness of things, what he had thought then to be a total lack
of order. "No straight streets, no neat rows of houses. No symmetry."
But he had since changed his mind. The symmetry, he believed, was
in the circle of things, of words, of gestures, of houses, of clusters of
houses. "Even the handshake, with the extended right hand, the left
hand clasping the middle part of the right arm, the four arms forming
an eight of sorts. The clasping hands, rotating and clasping. The
greetings: the one who begins has to end, to complete the circle. Yes,
to understand Africa, you have to understand that it is powered by a
circular rhythm." Mosa remembered being engaged in many long,
philosophical discussions with Mr Mitchell just before she had
dropped out of school. He had been her mathematics teacher since she
entered Bana-Ba-Phefo High School at age fifteen and had always
treated her with respect, as if she were an adult. She felt that amongst
the many teachers she had had, Mitch, as everyone called him, would

be the most sympathetic to her plight. Perhaps she could enlist his help in her attempts to get back to school.

Mosa forced her mind back, and by the time the priest called for the final prayer, her face was dry and a look of resoluteness had crept into her eyes. She had made promises to herself that she was determined to keep.

As she rode back to the house in the back of the van, she was grateful for the physical closeness of her brother. She wanted to hold Stan's hand but felt restrained. There were thousands of tear dams threatening to collapse and start a flood at the slightest opportunity, and she could not afford a relapse into grief. I need to be strong, she kept telling herself. And she and her brother were not alone. There were all these chattering relatives who felt compelled to give a commentary about how the funeral had gone and kept offering their sympathies. She wished they would just shut up, but she knew they meant well, trying to offer some comfort.

"At times like these, one's sympathies go out to the breast that gave milk," one woman said with a sigh.

"Yes. And to the mouths that shared the same breast," said her companion.

That night, Mosa went to bed early. First she tried to coax Nunu into sleeping with her, but the child preferred to share a bed with her grandmother. There will be plenty of time, Mosa decided. Exhausted, she fell asleep almost immediately, not stirring until the following morning, when the yard began to fill up with relatives for the head shaving and clothes-washing ceremony.

There was one item of clothing that would not be washed. She had kept Pule's baseball cap secretly hidden away in her clothes trunk, and no stranger's hands would be touching that cap. She recalled how Pule had saved and saved to buy the cap at the annual village trade fair. Its visor bore the letters MU, for Manchester United, Pule's favourite team, in bold lettering. He had treasured the cap and had always washed it very carefully. She knew only too well that if her mother or any of the relatives discovered her secret, she would be reprimanded for encouraging death back into the yard. But in her trunk and in her heart, her secret was safe.

Mosa spent the day thinking of ways to get back into school. She was certain that she needed to finish high school if she hoped to get anywhere in life. She also missed the various extracurricular activities she had been involved in. She missed her classmates, even the not so nice ones, like Khumo, the class bully. She particularly missed the competitive atmosphere generated by tests and quizzes. She had not forgotten the beatings and harassment that were part of school life. But still, she felt school was her passport to a better life. As she cooked and washed and dusted, her mind went through all kinds of schemes for how to regain entry to school. After twenty days out of school, one automatically loses one's place. She knew that she could not just go back, declare that she had been pregnant and expect to be re-admitted. Government policy was that a student who had had a child should remain out of school for a year, after which the young mother had to be re-admitted to a different school. This policy was meant to protect the good students from the influences of the girl who had gone astray. The dishonoured student was then expected to keep the secret of motherhood from her new fellow students.

Mosa was not prepared to make public the reasons for her having dropped out of school. If she did, she might have the police knocking at her door and demanding explanations. She knew of a girl who was arrested after having an abortion. The poor girl had gone to the hospital, and a nurse had recognised the evidence of an incomplete abortion. The nurse had called the police, and a nightmare had begun for the young woman. By the time she had been cleared of any criminal act, she had lost her place in school and had been publicly humiliated.

In any case, it was Bana-Ba-Phefo, the only high school in her district, she had to get back into. The high was really a combination of junior-high and high school, and she had attended it, like her two brothers before her and her younger brother after her, since she was fifteen. It offered three streams of junior-high classes to students from Monamodi village, and eight streams of classes to high-school students from both Monamodi and nearby, smaller villages. Most of the high-school students from neighbouring villages lived in the school dormitories. Thus another school for Mosa would mean boarding at another village in another district, and the closest was at least fifty kilometres away. There was no way that her mother could possibly afford this: she had to get back into school, and that would have to involve some deception of sorts. Truth was not going to get her where she wanted to go.

By the end of the day, as she finished washing up and delivering borrowed pots and cutlery to neighbours, she still had not come up with a scheme. She saw a tired, gaunt, poor woman with five children living in a hot box, and knew that was herself she was looking at in ten years unless she got back into school.

CHAPTER 4

By the afternoon of Pule's funeral, there were only a few dozen people from the three hundred or more who had attended the funeral. These were close relatives whose job it was to clean up after the big feast, and to prepare for the following day's hair-shaving and clothes-washing rituals. As had happened many times since Pule died, six days ago, yet another meeting was called. It seemed to Mosa that someone always had a major suggestion to make. There had been meetings about the funeral program, the coffin, the date of the funeral, the cow to be killed. Meetings, meetings, meetings. How is my mother coping under all the pressure? she wondered.

"Should the obituary mention that Pule had a daughter, even though he is not married to the mother?"

"Should we kill the cow at your uncle Maruping's cattlepost, or should we kill the ox at Gabane?"

"What about the coffin? What kind of wood? What colour?"

For six days, unending questions.

Mosa went into the house, and informed her mother and the seven women in there, mostly older, widowed women, that a family meeting was being called to discuss the hair-shaving and clothes-washing ceremonies to take place the following day.

Mara already knew what would be discussed. The family would have to elect the person who would do the shaving. This was simply a matter of confirming what everybody already knew. So the consultation was a mere formality.

The real problem was that Mara wanted little Nunu's head to be shaved as well and was expecting some resistance to this: the deceased's three-year-old daughter was not really a member of the family.

Because the room was small and hot, the meeting was held in the doorway, partly inside the room and partly outside. Most of Mara's assembled relatives – seventeen uncles, aunts, cousins and siblings – were sitting just outside the room, in the shadows cast by the dipping afternoon sun. Once again, bare heads were raised and scarf-covered heads sat on the ground. Men do not wear a hat in a house or when in a meeting, and women do not appear without a head scarf at a family meeting. But as during the day before, the exception was Mma Bakang, with her bandaged leg. But not for long, though: a young man came and stood next to her. He said not a word, but the gesture spoke volumes: she rolled off the chair, grimacing in pain, and took her place on the ground, where her gender belonged.

Mara moved closer to the door in response to a call by an aunt, who reminded her that "The meaning of words is in the face." The three camelthorn-acacia trees in the yard boasted long, slim patches of shade, and the earlier, intense heat had subsided somewhat. How she wished she could stand up and walk towards those trees, to stretch her legs. She had had to endure sitting in one place for what seemed like hours. She was not looking forward to this meeting. It was going to demand firmness and resolve from her, and she was not sure whether she was strong enough. She saw her daughter walk over to one of the trees and sit down. She would pretend not to be listening to anything said at the meeting. But Mara knew she was ready to take in every word. This girl will never lose her curiosity, she thought to herself.

"Child of my uncle, children of my tribe, you whose totem is my totem, today's job has been finished," Uncle Mmopi began, startling Mara to attention. "It went very well, but we must now talk about tomorrow's tasks so that the task of burying our son must finally be concluded. Burying a person is more than just putting his body into the ground, as you all know. I do not have to remind you about that. The ancestors are looking at us and want us to do the right thing. We must agree, so I ask you, 'Who is the razor's holder?' " He looked around as if inviting comments, but then went on to ask, "Do we all agree that the hand that must hold the razor is the hand of Maruping, Rra-Ranko, the brother to Mara and the uncle to Pule?" He glanced from face to face, searching for dissent without really expecting it.

Everybody looked around to confirm that they were in agreement, and a small, bald old man with slits for eyes piped up, "Yes, we all agree. The razor's hand is the hand of Maruping. The last time Modise was only standing in for him because he could not himself do the job. There is no doubt that the razor is his and the shaving ritual is his responsibility." His wife would, of course, do the actual shaving.

Uncle Mmopi turned around to Maruping. "This, my nephew, is your job as Pule's uncle. You have done a good job since this whole business began, and you must now perform the last ritual for your nephew. We understand that you work far away from home and that you work for people who seem to be Paul Kruger's brothers: that abominable Boer who was a slave driver, who killed many of our ancestors and stole our land. But you must try to make time for your family responsibilities as much as possible. The ancestors demand it."

Maruping, Pule's maternal uncle, had spent the night of the wake at the head of his nephew's coffin. He had kept dozing off as Mara and the same close female relatives who had shared the room with her lay around the coffin. The room had been cramped and hot, but duty was duty. Had the nephew lived to marry, he would have had a host of other responsibilities. The head shaving was his duty, and he had no complaints about it. One could hardly complain that there was only one moon. Or that the sun rose in the east.

The discussions went on for a while amongst the men, with most of them repeating what had already been said. Having exhausted the topic, Mmopi called upon the women to comment, and they all chorused their agreement.

"Mma-Ranko, wife of Maruping, your husband holds the razor, and so you know your job," a woman said. "Remember, Mma-Ranko, you will bring a razor, sugar, milk and tea to be brewed tomorrow. Do not forget the beer, please."

Everyone present knew that Maruping and his wife were having problems, with Maruping routinely battering Mma-Ranko. But for tomorrow's ritual, they would co-operate, and no one doubted this. It was also quite possible that the job would give Mma-Ranko a night's rest, because Maruping was unlikely to do anything to jeopardise the performance of the important task at hand. The ancestors would be watching, and only a fool would let anything interfere with a ceremony like this one.

At the end of the more than twenty minutes of discussions, it was agreed that in accordance with custom, the shaving ritual was the responsibility of Maruping.

"Child of my brother," Mmopi said, addressing Mara, "now comes the second question. Who does the razor face? The razor is glinting, ready to do its job; Maruping is holding it: who does it face? I want to hear the answer from your mouth. Say it clearly so that we can decide it here and now. Again, child of my brother, I ask you, who does the razor face?"

Mara looked up at her uncle, her uncle's son, really, who had inherited the right to the position of head of the Selato family a long time ago. As such, he presided over all major family discussions, and acted as adjudicator if and when frictions occurred amongst members of the extended Selato family. A brother who sold a cow without reference to his siblings might find himself having to explain to his unhappy siblings, with Uncle Mmopi presiding. Mara regarded the older man before answering. When she did speak, her voice was clear and without a tremor, but the effort was evident in its uncharacteristic high pitch. "The razor faces me and my two children, my uncle. It faces us alone, but I want you to also remove the bad luck of death from Nunu, my son's daughter. I know that the child does not have any rights in this family, but she is the child of my child, and she brought great joy to my son during his last days. You cannot leave her with the bad luck of death. You must shave her head as well. Not to shave her head would be to kill her. If you do not shave her head, you might as well take the same razor and slit her throat. Please."

Mara's words hung in the air as everyone considered their implications. A few had expected her to say it, but for most it came as a complete shock. They had all heard the anguish in Mara's voice, but they knew that what she was asking for was not easy to grant.

The silence was broken by Uncle Bonoso, known for his compassion and kindness. "Mara, child of my young father, please do not think with your heart; think with your head. Do not think with your womb, for your womb has been wounded and wants to be re-filled. Think with your head, I implore you. We know that your heart is red with grief. We know that your soul is like rain clouds before a storm. We all know that your womb has been split open and two children stolen from it. Our hearts drip blood in sympathy. But you must look beyond today and consider what you are asking us to do." The old man lowered his head, as if in prayer, and muttered, "The ancestors of Selato, come to our aid. *'Nkosi Sikelela iAfrica'.''*

Another man explained, "You cannot have a child who is not yours be part of a ritual like this. What about her mother? This is not our child. We have not married or even betrothed her mother. The child cannot be ours if the mother has never been our bride. How can we have a motherless child? What will her mother's people say if they find out? Surely they will take us before the customary court. Surely our ancestors will be displeased. What about her mother's ancestors? Mma-Pule, you ask for the impossible. You really ask for the impossible." There was more than just surprise: a touch of fear, fear of unleashing the displeasure of God and the ancestors.

But Mara was not swayed. Little Nunu had to be part of the shaving ceremony, and she believed it with every fibre of her body. To leave the child unshaved would give her bad luck, which could even result in her death. Mara had to have everyone see it her way.

"Children of the house of Selato," she said, "listen to me, and listen to me well. Nunu is the child of my child, and you all know that. I know her mother was not betrothed in accordance with our custom. I know she was not married to my son. I know that she was not a part of this family in the eyes of custom. But this child came to us because the ancestors demanded that she be brought into the house of Selato. Pule was very sick at the time, and the ancestors talked to him almost every night, demanding that he bring the child here. Pule would wake up shaking and sweating, with one story, night after night. Night after night, he saw his grandfather, that is, my father, sitting on his horse, you know: the black one, the one he named Morolana, after the yellow desert marigold. He described the horse, even though he could not possibly remember it from seeing it as a child. He was a toddler when it died. Surely you see how important this is. Pule had numerous visits from his grandfather. Once, even his grandmother came, and she, too, begged him not to abandon his child. He would shake and shake with fear that unless his child came to live with us he would not get peace from the ancestors. Mma-Nnana can confirm this. Nunu is a child of this family because this family's ancestors demanded it. I cannot go against the wishes of the ancestors. It is now your decision, but don't ever say I did not warn you. You have to choose. Who do you want to please: the neighbours or the ancestors?"

Mara looked up at each member of the family in turn, pleading and challenging with her eyes. It was a long speech for her. She felt the howl in her brain, the fear rattling in her womb; her heart was hammering. In–out; in–out: she tried to breathe, but her lungs refused to comply.

"Where is the mother of this child, anyway? And where are the parents of the child's mother? Why have they allowed the child to come here?" an elderly relative wanted to know, eyes clouded over with cataracts and breath thick with the smell of tobacco.

Then, amid all the gruff and hoarse voices of the men, a squeak: "Mma-Pule, Mma-Pule," called Nunu, pushing through the men to her granny. "I want to sit on your lap, but I am not a baby. Do not say I am a baby, Mma-Pule." The child raised her voice just high enough for everyone to know that if she were not assisted promptly, she would throw a tantrum and disrupt the meeting.

Nunu's bold entry disrupted the gathering, and she was picked up and passed over the thicket of bodies around the door until she reached her grandmother's lap. As she perched there, she pouted her lips and started swinging from side to side, challenging anyone to call her a baby. She could not possibly understand what was going on, but her actions affected everyone. Her tiny face was the spitting image of her late father's, and many who were watching her wondered whether they could possibly refuse her. What reasons could they use to accept her as part of the family? A young man pulled playfully at one of her toes, and Nunu gave him a broad smile as she nuzzled in her grandmother's lap. For some, that tiny face won them over, but it would not do to simply agree. They had to have a proper and full discussion; after all, there were the ancestors to consider.

Mara explained that Nunu's mother was a South African who was working in Botswana for a short time when she and Pule met. She had been living away from her family for years, so there really was no one close by but herself to discuss the little girl's welfare. She agreed to bring Nunu to be with her father, Mara explained, and would not mind if her hair were shaved to mark the death of her father. She had not even attended the funeral herself. Perhaps she did not know about Pule's death; perhaps she had returned to South Africa.

"Do you realise that shaving this child's head will give her mother inheritance rights? A child cannot be a member of the family unless the mother is, and a mother cannot be unless she is married, and a married woman has the right to inherit from her husband," a cheeky female cousin said. She was given a sharp look for speaking before the women were given permission to do so, and for bringing up the issue of inheritance. How dare she be so crude as to speak of property so soon after a funeral? the looks were asking in silence.

"I realise that," Mara said wearily. "Pule died leaving nothing, except this child. Nunu's mother knows that. There is no property to inherit. That is not the issue: please."

"But how can we shave the child's head without cleansing the mother?" another voice asked. "If the child goes through the ceremony, the mother should undergo a cleansing ceremony to protect her from ill-luck. We cannot protect the child only to endanger the mother. The two go together: you cannot do one and not the other. This is not a simple matter, Mma-Pule. Please do not think with the breasts that fed Pule; think with the head that raised him."

"Saebo, Nunu's mother has no interest in our customs. She says she does not believe in them and would not agree to the cleansing even if you offered it to her," said Mara. This was only partly true. Saebo had only once said to Mara that she did not think the diviner they were then consulting had the power to cure Pule, but she had not said anything more.

No one at the meeting believed that anyone was stupid enough to refuse cleansing after a partner's death. Even a South African from the bright lights of Johannesburg would not be that naive. To do that would be to court disease and possibly death. They merely let Mara's assertion go, assuming that Nunu's mother would have arranged and paid for her own cleansing privately. To discuss it further would be to implicate themselves should Nunu's mother suffer some illness later on.

"May I say something, older father?" said Mma-Maria, an ample woman who had a reputation for being level-headed and to the point. She was a staff nurse at Molemo Government Hospital, and was respected for her education and position. Seeking permission to speak showed her understanding of her position.

"The way I see it, the ancestors have spoken; otherwise, this child would not be here. I was here a few weeks ago, when my brother, Pule, weak as he was, called me over and made me promise not to abandon his daughter. His exact words were 'This is my blood. Do not throw it away. In her veins runs the blood of the Selato family. She is your child. If I die, I will not rest unless you take care of her.' I remember that voice, and I see this face, and I say we have to shave her head. Not to do that would be to invite a misfortune to befall the house of Selato." Mma-Maria's voice was loud and firm.

There was silence for a few seconds and a hint of confusion. It was not expected that a woman should take a definite position so early in the discussions. Mma-Maria should have made her point carefully and tentatively and have waited for the older men to decide the issue. Her disregard for protocol was, however, understandable under the circumstances. It was clear that she was not going to leave the decision to chance. What to do now: rebuke her? ignore the disrespect?

"I think we must now conclude this matter," said Uncle Mmopi with a rather wistful look in his eyes, rubbing a hand over the knob of his stick. The knob had become shiny from many of these rubbings. He was older than sixty years, but exactly how old no one was quite sure. "It is not an easy matter, and we may one day regret the decision. But I see no other way. The child must be part of the shaving ritual. She is a Selato. The ancestors called her here, and it is their wish we will be honouring. Is that the agreement?" He looked around, his pointed chin appearing sharper than ever and his jaws working as if chewing on something.

The meeting responded with agreements prefaced with caution and warnings. But Mara had the decision she wanted. Nunu's head would be shaved. In–out; in–out. At last her chest was responding to her commands. The howl in her head died down; the rattling in her womb grew fainter.

She looked down at the child, and managed a wry smile as she brushed off sand from little Nunu's hair.

From where she sat, with the other girls, Mosa marvelled at her mother's strength. She would never have thought she had it in her to argue about anything. She had looked so defeated and frail at the graveyard. Indeed, it is correct, as the saying goes, 'A mother will hold a knife by the blade to protect her child.' Mosa was playing a game of cards with a cousin and was losing. The cousin stormed off in a huff, angry. Mosa begged her to come back, promising to play more seriously. She needed the game as an excuse to sit where she was. Openly listening would get her into trouble.

"Mara, child of my aunt's child," Mmopi continued after some time, "I have to bring up another matter. Why have your ancestors forsaken you? Where is your God? Why has God turned his back on you? Your children are dying. You have lost your old sparkle. You are a shadow of your old self. There is a wind blowing through your house. There is sadness and death. Why? Have you tried to find out why? You will excuse me for asking this straight out, but it is my duty. Child of my aunt's child through your mother, I am your uncle and your father. I must ask."

"My uncle Mmopi," began Mara, "in honour of your late father, who I loved very much, I will address you in his name, for it is for him that you play this special role in my life. I have no hope of light. As you know, the one who waits for the moon waits for darkness, for the moon can rise only with the night. I wait for darkness. I am in darkness. But I hope for light. My house is the house of no hope. When the last ploughing season started, I buried Thabo. Now I have just buried Pule. Mosa does not listen to me, and Stan is getting all kinds of strange ideas. When will it stop? Will it ever stop?" One lone tear rolled down her left eye and dropped on to Nunu's head. The little girl, fast asleep, was unaware of her grandmother's anguish.

Mosa played the wrong card, losing yet another game. She had to agree with her mother's assessment of their relationship. She made a silent vow that things would change for the better.

It was agreed that the Selato ancestors were greatly displeased and that there was a need to appease them. It was decided that the matter would be discussed the following day, after the shaving ceremony. Everyone was tired after fewer than two hours of sleep. The wake had continued until four o'clock in the morning. The three priests had done a fantastic job of preaching all night and keeping everybody singing. But the lack of sleep was beginning to have an effect, and everyone agreed to a postponement of the discussion about appeasing the ancestors.

CHAPTER 5

Mara had spent a relatively peaceful night. Fatigue had enveloped her as soon as she had had her evening meal, and she slept with very few dreams and no nightmares. The inevitable coming and going of the older women during the night, as they went for their night pees, did not disturb her too much. After having shared the room with them for seven nights now, she was used to their nightly needs. She was woken up by light seeping through the small front window. The dead wasp was still stuck to the window pane; perhaps its mother did not know that it was dead.

The sun was just about to rise, but she could hear the sound of relatives assembling outside. She stood up, peeped through the window and saw the big water pot boiling: tea was being prepared. A woman came into the house, carrying a traditional grass broom, and informed her that the ritual sweeping of the yard would start soon. The woman then turned to the assembled crowd and informed the women that she was "announcing the broom".

She proceeded to sweep the room, and some of the women stood up and joined her, sweeping the yard from different points. There were lots of women, and very soon the 120 square metres of dusty ground were swept clean. All traces of Pule were gone. No footprints; no cigarette butts; no beer cans; no odours. Nothing. As non-existent now as the piece of cloud that showed itself at his funeral.

"Mma-Pule," a voice called, "here is your water for your bath."

Bathed, she changed into a blue summer dress. She had lost a lot of weight recently and had a sad longish face, but she was still a strikingly beautiful woman. Her eyes suggested easy laughter, and her gestures were slow and gentle. Laughter, though, which used to

43

bring a twinkle to her eyes, was long gone.

Nunu had woken up early, as children are apt to do, and had attached herself to Mosa, who had already given her a cup of tea and a piece of *phaphatha*: home-baked bread. Mara went to the pit latrine and came back into the room to wait to be officially called outside. A relative came in and informed her that the elders were waiting outside and that it was time for her to join them.

Mara emerged from the house. The sun had risen rather fast. No hesitation today, no apologies. Even though it could not have been later than nine o'clock in the morning, the heat was already baking the dusty yard, chasing people to the shady trees. Mosa and other girls were already serving the forty or so relatives with breakfast of tea and *phaphatha*, walking back and forth between the fireplace and the two groups of men and women. Some boys were playing football in the yard, occasionally being called to bring firewood. If any of the girls thought it unfair that they were working while their male age mates played, they didn't let on: they were just going through the ritual of life, without comment or question.

The men were seated at the men's fireplace, although the fire was only smouldering. The women were sitting under the biggest of the camelthorn-acacia trees, in front of the house. The two groups were within earshot of each other, so the division was more ritual than actual. As Mara approached the group, one of the women stood up to go and inform the men of her presence. She could have just called them from her sitting position, but that would not have been considered polite. The men came over to join the women, and some of them left their chair behind. The responsible wives leaped to their feet and hurried over to get the chairs. The men sat down. Bare heads high; scarved heads low.

Mmopi's wife announced the washing of Pule's clothes. The women stood up to do the job. The men went back to their fireplace, and once again, scarved heads rose and carried the chairs. There was order. An old dance, choreographed centuries ago, was being re-enacted. Had the men carried the chairs, it is quite possible the wives would have been offended. Years ago, one of them had come back from South Africa with a Malawian husband who was so in love with her that he helped with all manner of wifely duties: carrying his own chair, helping her carry water and sweeping the yard. Even to this day,

44

the tellers of the story get goosebumps when they think of that man, bending over with a broom, sweeping the yard. His wife was utterly embarrassed. Of course, he had long ago stopped that foolishness, and had even started to occasionally beat her, like most other men did. Love had long evaporated, leaving behind marriage.

Mara would, of course, not be doing any of the washing. But she had to point out all of Pule's personal property. She consulted with Stan about a few items, but on the whole, she was able to collect the items unassisted. Pule had used very little of them during the last months of his life. He had lain in bed most of the time, in shorts and occasionally a T-shirt. The human smell that Mara was hoping for was largely absent. All would still be washed and packed away in a tin trunk for six months before being given out to his brother, sister and some close relatives, at a special ceremony.

The family had decided on six months instead of the usual twelve. This was to accommodate the ancestor-appeasement ceremony. Of course, it could not be held in a house that was in mourning.

The washing took a good two hours, so it was not until noon, with the sun as hot as ever, that the shaving ceremony began.

The shaving took place in the middle of the yard, on a spot where there was no shade and under the watchful eyes of everyone present. Mara walked from the shade to where Mma-Ranko sat waiting. Mara would be the first to have her head shaved. She sat down under the hot sun as everyone watched from the coolness of the shady trees. Mma-Ranko removed the razor blade and the bar of soap from their wrappers and lifted them up so that everyone could see they were new. Mma-Ranko knew that the honour of performing the ritual carried with it the danger of being blamed for witchcraft. Hair, like nails and footprints, was a very easy way of getting at an enemy. Her movements had to be careful and slow so that she could not be accused later of doing something underhanded like hiding a piece of hair.

Mma-Ranko wet the hair, lathered it with the soap, and began. Mara's hair began to fall off in clumps as the razor moved over her scalp, from front to back in straight rows, leaving in its path a smooth line. Every time a clump fell off, Mma-Ranko carefully picked it up and put it where everyone could see it. Soon, Mara was as bald as the soccer ball the boys were kicking about, and Mma-Ranko gently pushed her head forward for everyone to see. She washed the smooth head and dried it in gentle, deliberate movements. Then she opened a bottle of Vaseline and tilted it for all to see. The top was smooth; it had obviously never been used before; never been touched. Mma-Ranko applied a dab of Vaseline to Mara's head and offered her a sip of traditional beer from a gourd on the ground next to them. With this done, Mma-Ranko brought out a small, black apron that had been sewn that morning. Mara put it on – to be worn for the next six months. To the assembled guests, Mma Ranko finally announced, "Your daughter has been shaved."

There were satisfied nods from the watchers, and Mma-Ranko gathered the hair into one bundle, making sure to pick up even the tiniest of clumps. She handed the hair to Mara, who took it, together with the water, and walked to the pit latrine to dispose of it.

The apron caused some mutterings of disapproval from some relatives: wasn't Pule too old for Mara to be wearing an apron? But Rre-Namane, a diviner, had advised that it was a signal that Pule, like Thabo before him, had really died in infancy, because they had both been marked at birth by displeased ancestors. Some relatives were not convinced that this was in accordance with culture, whereas others were happy to go along with a man knowledgeable in these matters. Some argued that the apron was only to inform others of Mara's bereavement and that the age of the child was hardly relevant.

Mosa was, as usual, intrigued by the ever changing practices and what she perceived to be a lack of consistency. There was always an argument about what the real tradition was and what an adaptation was. With every adult claiming to be an authority, there was not always consensus about what constituted the real cultural practice.

Nunu was next to be shaved, but she refused to go near Mma-Ranko. Why should she willingly submit herself to a stranger waving a razor?

"You can sit on my lap while Mma-Ranko shaves your head," her grandmother told her. But the little girl squirmed and protested.

"We'll look like twins," Mara promised, and the child was comforted. She would like to look like her grandmother, and that made her sit still. She was, however, disappointed when she did not get an apron. But she did get something else: a black-cloth necklace that she was to wear until it broke off; otherwise, it would be cut off at the clothes-distribution ceremony in six months' time. The three-year-old was happy to get the attention and when she was given her hair to dispose of, she marched proudly off, aping her grandmother. That her father was dead did not seem to have occurred to her yet.

The two siblings were next. Mma-Ranko shaved their heads as efficiently as she had done with the first two. She then pinned the pieces of cloth on their clothing. Each was offered a small sip of the traditional beer. The ceremony over, the bucket of beer was passed around.

As the sun dipped to the west and the shadows lengthened, the clothes were removed from the lines and were packed away in a huge tin trunk. Also packed away were Pule's favourite coffee mug, his Nike shoes and his books. The shoes were his favourite possessions. Mosa remembered how proud he was when a teacher gave him the shoes after he had impressed everyone during a soccer match against another school. When soaking in water was not advisable, as in the case of the dryclean-only suit and the shoes, there was thorough scrubbing and brushing.

Mosa felt that with the washing of hands the previous day, the sweeping of the yard, the shaving of heads and the washing of personal effects – all intended to wash away the bad omen brought by death – her brother's essence had been washed away. At the end of all this, there would not be a smell of Pule anywhere.

Mara, too, thought of this as she cast her eyes around the yard. She caught Mosa's eye, and was certain they were thinking the same thoughts. They would never again get a whiff of Pule's cigarette-scented breath. Mara had found the hidden cap. She and her daughter had the same yearning to preserve something of Pule, something to touch and sniff at in private, but her beliefs were too strong. It occurred to her that even though she had hated Pule's smoking and that they had fought about it all the time, she would miss the smell it had given his breath. Not that he had smoked much during the past few months: smoking had brought on such a fit of coughing that he had finally given it up.

Mara looked around in the hope of finding an old cigarette butt, but the yard sweeping had taken care of that. She felt an immense sadness come upon her. There was that howling again, thundering through her head. Her arms tightened around her grand-daughter sitting on her lap, and the child, startled, let out an unexpected shriek of annoyance. Mara loosened her grip on the child, and urged her to run off to join other children.

Proud of her bald head and the new necklace, Nunu needed little encouragement to go and show off. A few kids teased her about it, but a stern lecture from an adult solved that problem. Still, one whispered to Nunu that she was special only because her father was dead. None of the adults responded to that, deciding that ignoring the episode would be better than trying to intervene.

Mara thought of the trunk and that it would remain sealed for six months, ever present and conspicuous in that small room; indeed, she would have to use it as a table for the next six months. After Thabo's funeral, many nights she had had these dreams that the trunk with its possessions was Thabo's coffin. She would wake up sweating from these nightmares, in which Thabo would be begging to be let out. Even during the daytime she would imagine that she could hear some movement from within. These dreams stopped only after a special prayer meeting by the Twelve Apostolic Church of God. She hoped that Pule's spirit would be more restful.

The men would let the fire burn for another two weeks, and another circle would be completed. Most of the female relatives were packing their blankets, moving back to their homes. Her sister, Mma-Nametso, would stay with her for two more weeks. With the cramped sleeping quarters, she would like to tell her that she would be okay, that it was okay for her to go. But she could not possibly do that. Her sister would be failing in her duty, and Pule's spirit would not settle unless everything went according to tradition.

For at least a month, she could expect to receive visitors who had not been able to attend the funeral, coming to pay their respects. Some would bring a bit of money to contribute to the funeral expenses; others would bring sad faces and low voices. Whatever they brought, they would remind her of her loss, and her heart would become even heavier with grief.

Later, Mara noticed for the first time that the only mirror in the house that had been covered for the past six days was now facing the room, as it had done before Pule's death. Mara walked over to it and saw that it had escaped the cleaning. Could it still have the smell or touch of Pule? There were many fingerprints on the surface, and Mara hoped that at least one set was her son's. She put the mirror on top of the wardrobe to protect it from cleaning: it would be her secret link with her son. He might have left no smells or footprints, but he just might have left fingerprints. And of course he left Nunu.

Mosa and Stan were mostly peripheral to the events of the day. But still they did not try to sit together or talk to each other any more than was strictly necessary. They threw furtive looks at each other, but neither had the courage to make the first move. They circled each other in a day-long dance that must climax one way or the other.

CHAPTER 6

"*El Niño! El Niño!*" Mara cried with dismay. There were promises of rain. Rain clouds gathered, thunder rumbled and the smell of rain filled the night air, but then nothing. The climax failed to come, the clouds dispersed, the heat came back with a vengeance, and Mara thought, Oh, this *El Niño*, whatever it is!

This was the middle of summer: the season of thousands of annoying bugs, bloodthirsty mosquitoes, fat and fast and frightening spiders.

Summer: the season of nervous breakdowns, according to traditional beliefs. True enough, thought Mara, the fat woman who lived three homes away who suffers yearly relapses has had to be admitted to Molemo Government Hospital. She would be transferred to a mental hospital as soon as transport was secured. The relapses always came with the first flowers of the new season.

Summer: the season of howling winds, of whirlwinds with snakes in the centre of their swirls. The season of lightning sent by witches, which could strike when not one puff of cloud was visible.

Summer: the season that marked the end of the old year and the beginning of hope for the future. Mara was, however, without hope.

It was the season of rain, with the promises of renewal and new beginnings. If the rain did not come, it was the season of despair and hopelessness. It was the season of celebrating the year's achievements or of despair at hopes unfulfilled and targets unmet. Mara felt that there was nothing to celebrate and plenty to despair about.

It was the season when everyone looked up with hope for rain instead of down at flickering fires. It was the season of heat from above over which there was no control. It was the season of waiting.

And for the ones without patience, it was the season of suicides.

Looking through the open door, Mara noted that not everything, however, waits. With amazing abandon and incredible optimism, a few trees were already flowering. The syringa tree in the neighbour's yard: flamboyant as ever. The wind carried the smell of the flowers to her, and her nose sniffed eagerly for more. She had always had a greedy nose for the aromatic trees and flowers around her, but she herself would never plant a syringa tree: it brought bad luck, and killed everyone and everything around it. It was not called *mosalaosi* – the one who remains alone – for nothing. It killed everything around it, if you dared nature enough to plant it. She knew of a woman who planted a *mosalaosi* just to get rid of her troublesome husband. Years later, there were still whispers about that. The people who pointed out the obvious fact that he had died from falling off a house whilst thatching it were reminded that the man had been experienced in his trade and had had no record of accidents. The *musunyana* bush showed bits of green but was bristling with white thorns. The *moologa* trees, up on the hill behind her, were ash white and radiant. There were bursts of yellow and sprinklings of purple.

There was sensuality in the way the trees swayed back and forth, especially in the afternoon, when they cast long, gentle shadows around themselves. And then there was the quiet dignity of the *morula* tree, standing tall and big and almost eternal. Surely there was some wisdom there.

There was the smell of passion, as plants filled with anticipation and flowers burst out with sexual abandon, for flowers are about sexuality and reproduction. The desert plants, guided by an inner clock, expect the rains, and they get ready for them, not waiting, for it is said that he who waits for the moon waits for darkness. If the rains do not come, the plants will shrivel and cut down on their leaves so they will need less water.

Do they, too, suffer nervous breakdowns? Do they hear my despair as I cry, *El Niño*? Mara asked. She was sad. But still, summer, she thought, was about promise. About new possibilities. The saying Let the year that loves-me-not pass, for the next may well love me, was precisely about hope. So she was a bit happy as well. But can one laugh in anticipation of happiness? She was happy for the promise of renewal, and sad for her loss, which weighed heavily on her, no

51

matter the time or place, no matter the beauty around her. She promised herself that she would learn from the trees. She would not wait for the moon: she would act now, when there was still light, not later, when there would be only the promise of light. For promises are not always fulfilled. Not even by nature.

Later, the summer night was filled with the neighing of donkeys, the barking and fighting of dogs in heat, the crowing of roosters, the shrill of night crickets, and the chanting and praying of some religious sect somewhere in the distance. The moon was threatening to turn night into day, and was almost succeeding. Mosquitoes were relentless, and bugs were flinging themselves into the fire and sizzling as they died. The sounds, smells and sights and passions of summer.

Mara tried to force her mind to stay with more optimistic thoughts. She forced herself to imagine a body of crystal-clear water, to imagine soft blues and gentle purples. To imagine rainbows; wide plains of golden grass peppered with yellow desert marigolds; beautiful, plump cattle grazing . . .

"The rain will come," she whispered to herself. The sun will cool down. The bugs will go away. Spectacular sunsets will appear. The moon will swell up into a vibrant orange, and hope will return. But Thabo and Pule will still be dead.

With these conflicting thoughts and daydreams of optimism and despair, Mara fell asleep. It had been two months since Pule's funeral, and she was due back at work the following morning.

Mara had not been to work since Pule died, and was actually looking forward to getting out of the yard. As a newly bereaved woman, she had been confined to her yard, and was allowed only limited and necessary visits outside. She had, for example, been allowed a visit to the clinic to collect a packet of aspirin when her throbbing headache showed no sign of ebbing. When, however, she had wanted to attend a community meeting about a proposal to build a pre-school, her older relatives advised against it. A woman who had just lost her son cannot be seen mixing with strangers in the streets.

When she left for work the following morning, she felt a new sense of purpose, even if it was to go and pick up after other people. She was leaving behind her poor, sad house and looking forward to her employer's more lavish one. She was also looking forward to seeing

52

Sanki, Patrick and little Emmanuel. She remembered them as beautiful, full of laughter and healthy. She needed a happy environment, and expected to find it as she made the beds, washed the dishes and cooked lunch for a family so near and yet so far from her own.

She was sad that Nunu could not be there to share the day with her. But there were limits to how far one could expect even a good employer to bend and accommodate. She had to ask a neighbour, Mma-Sadibo, to watch the little girl until Mosa came back from school. For Mma-Sadibo, the arrangement was convenient because she had a grandchild the same age as Nunu: Rati and Nunu could play together in the yard while her old Singer sewing machine rattled away as she made dresses for sale. Thus the arrangement with Mara was mutually beneficial.

Mara had not wanted to be stern with Mosa about telling her to hurry home after school. She was back in school and back at home, and Mara did not want to spoil that in any way. She was treading gently, where Mosa was concerned, until a comfortable balance could be struck between the two of them. She was pleased that Mosa seemed to genuinely care for Nunu, and she did not have to remind her to feed or wash the child.

Her employer, Mma-Sanki, had been very understanding about her need for compassionate leave. Two months was fairly long for an employer to tolerate, but Mma-Sanki was a special person indeed.

Mara had left the employ of Mma-Pako a year ago, when the demands of taking care of her own family had proved impossible to combine with the very onerous demands of working for Mma-Pako and her brutish husband. Mma-Pako had made it very clear that she would not tolerate Mara's absences from work. As she had angrily explained on many occasions, she had young children, was working herself and was not willing to risk her husband's demand that she quit her job to take care of the family. It was clear that although Mara worked for the whole family, she was considered to be Mma-Pako's assistant, and any absenteeism on Mara's part meant more work for Mma-Pako and her oldest daughter, Pako.

Mara knew it was not fair to blame Mma-Pako; after all, often when she did not come to work, Mma-Pako's husband beat her up, leaving the bruises there for Mara to see. The man was a bully who instilled terror in all members of his family. The only person he seemed to have respect for was his mother. Perhaps that was because she never saw anything wrong with his behaviour. It was whispered that one time Mma-Pako reported to her that Rra-Pako was spending nights away from home, she responded that her son knew all about women long before he met Mma-Pako. She saw no reason why Mma-Pako would attempt to restrict his son about matters she seemed to be performing very poorly in. "When your wife offers you stale porridge," she said, "you have the right to go next door to find out what the woman there is cooking." The two women hated each other, and the hatred spilled out into the house. The result was an unhappy household made up of a mean grandmother, an angry mother, ill-mannered children and a terror of a father.

Mma-Sanki was a more pleasant boss to work for. In addition, her husband did not try to grope Mara when he found her alone or make suggestive remarks about her behind. She was happy that Rra-Sanki left her alone, and the children were polite and helpful – as helpful as children raised knowing that there is hired help to pick up and clean after them could possibly be. She was happy that Mma-Sanki agreed to give her the two months off, and accepted her offer of a stand-in maid during that period. She looked forward to taking back her job. She was even looking forward to the six-kilometre walk that would take her from her poor household to the more affluent house of Mma-Sanki.

As she walked into the house, she was met by Emmanuel: little Emma, with his broad grin and a mouth full of oversized new teeth. Of course he had not bothered to brush them yet, but that did not deter him from flashing them to the entire world. He was a sweet, loving boy, and Mara loved him dearly. He was about the same age as Nunu, but the two had never met: so near, yet so far, thought Mara.

The boy had some sensational news that he could not wait to tell her: "Aunt Mara, we have rats. Did you know that? We have big, great, sharp rats. Big things! Really sharp!"

"Well, good morning, Emma. Where are your manners? Aren't you going to greet me first? You have not seen me for weeks!" Mara teased.

"Good morning, but we do have rats. And Daddy does not want the neighbours to know. I think he thinks they are dirty. What do you think?" Emma asked. If his father did not want neighbours to know, Emma was practically announcing it for all the world to hear.

"Well, I hope we do not have any rats, because then we will have to have them killed, and they sure will stink up the place," Mara said.

Emma's face fell, and his lips curled up as if he were about to cry. "You cannot kill them: they are sharp," he said, holding up his fist with the thumb stuck out. To him, everything was sharp. The water pipeline bringing all the dust to the village was sharp. The big, ugly, rumbling bus was sharp. His friend, Tom the firebug, was sharp. Even the skinny dog from God-knew-where was sharp. Mara noted that very little had changed in the way Emma viewed the world since she had been away. She also remembered that "sharp" had been one of Pule's favourite words as well. Later, "cool" became the word. She was sure that Emma would discover "cool" just as he had discovered "sharp": what with his Gaborone cousins bringing new slang whenever they came to visit.

As later became obvious, they did have rats in the roof. Mara had never seen rats before: mice yes; rats definitely not. Mara mused about development and what it brought. First it brought cockroaches. She remembered when she was a young girl and had never seen a cockroach because her family had not had enough food to feed the creatures. Or at least that is how she had figured it at the time. There had been no extras. In addition, they had had no extra room to share with the creatures. A school friend, however, had been proud that her family had cock-roaches. Her mother was a nurse and her father a clerk in the post office. Between the two of them, they had earned a decent income. They could feed their family and their cockroaches. They had had a kitchen in which the roaches could roam at night whilst the family slept peacefully in their bedrooms. That a whole room could be devoted to cooking and the storing of food had been a novelty to the young Mara.

Now, even Mara had her own cockroaches. She still had no special room to keep them, but she did have them. It seemed that modern cockroaches were not too particular about sharing space with house owners. The proliferation of pit latrines in the village was primarily responsible for the growth of the cockroach population: poverty no longer earned one the privilege of a cockroach-free environment. Now Mara could boast even bigger roaches. Some say they came all the way from Cape Town, on the southern tip of Africa. Others argued that they had come with the American Peace Corps

Volunteers, who had formed a large contingent of expatriate teachers since the mid-1960s; after all, weren't things bigger and better in America? It really did not matter where the nasty creatures had come from: they were clearly here to stay.

Now her employers had a new symbol of prosperity: rats! It turned out that the rats were living inside the roof, in a badly constructed septic system. Mara was not even sure whether the creatures had a Setswana name; she imagined they did, but could not remember ever hearing it. Emma announced breathlessly that at night they scampered and scuttled about, frightening the daylights out of all the children. Even Emma, who claimed that the rats were sharp, was not too keen that they lived inside the ceiling. Rra-Sanki called some people on the telephone, and they came in a sharp little truck. Two men in overalls crawled into the roof and put poison in there. Everyone hoped that the rats would die and not smell for too long. But by that time, Emma had found something else to occupy his ever roving mind.

The rat frenzy was good for Mara. Such a relatively minor but exciting problem took her mind off her own more serious ones. She had an appointment with yet another diviner that evening, and was thankful for the diversion.

She went about the rest of the day as cheerfully as she could, under the circumstances. Emma demanded her attention, and she secretly wished that he, too, were in school, like his older siblings. When it was time to knock off for the day, she was exhausted and hungry. By then, the rest of the family had come back home: the children from school and the parents from work. She had neglected to eat, and would have loved a cup of tea with a peanut-butter sandwich, but was too embarrassed to fix herself this simple meal. Mma-Sanki, however, was a very kindly and sensitive person. She had noted Mara's forced smiles and obvious effort at being cheerful for the children. And that Mara had not eaten.

"Mma-Pule, please do fix yourself something to eat before you go, or better still, why don't you have my food? I ate off Rra-Sanki's plate at lunchtime; I will not be needing mine," Mma-Sanki said as Mara dried and put away yet another plate. There never seemed to be an end to dirty plates in this house.

"Thank you. I think I will have some tea and bread. Can I make you some as well?" Mara asked, hoping for a no. Making tea for her boss, nice as she was, was always a performance. She insisted on a tray, covered with a tray cloth, and set with warm milk and special cups. The clay teapot had to be specially heated, because pouring the hot water straight from the electric kettle into a cup was not acceptable. Making tea for Mma-Sanki would definitely mean at least another half hour before leaving for home.

"No, thank you, my dear: Sanki will fix me a cup later on."

Mara tried not to be too obvious about her sigh of relief. Ten minutes later, she said goodbye to the Masasi family. She was off to her home and her meeting with the diviner. As she walked along the narrow footpath, dodging dog poo, her thoughts were already with her two remaining children. She thought of Stan, constantly shuttled between poverty and plenty. Robust and healthy looking, clearly well fed and focused on his schooling. The longer he had stayed with his teacher benefactors, the more he seemed to distance himself from her beliefs. He had never said anything specific, but there was no doubt that he had not agreed to come home this weekend with any great enthusiasm. Then there was Mosa, young and confused. She had dropped out of school and then moved out to live with a boyfriend. Or at least that is what she thought.

She expected to find brother and sister sitting together but not talking, as if they had nothing in common. Stan would be flipping through a sports magazine, and Mosa would be sitting reading some book or just staring out blankly. Mara knew that the source of the distance between the two siblings had multiple causes.

Stan was in school, and had a life and a future. Mosa, although she had just gone back to school, was desperately trying to settle back in after dropping out. There was a level of embarrassment on the part of Stan at his good fortune – and some jealousy on the part of Mosa. She seemed to be searching for something elusive, trying to make sense of her surroundings but without success.

The recent tragedies had only helped deepen the rift. The two had not come together in grief but had been further estranged. It had not helped that Stan had attempted to force a discussion about AIDS after the death of the first brother. Mosa had ended that discussion with a clear statement that of course her brother had died from having sex with a woman who had recently had an abortion. In the announcement was also an assignment of guilt: Stan had been a friend of the girlfriend's cousin, and ought to have known and warned their brother about the abortion. Mara, although she shared Mosa's beliefs, would have preferred that Mosa let Stan have his say. She believed that only through hearing her son's views could she begin to get him back to thinking rationally. That, however, had closed all discussions about that particular matter. This was more than a year ago, before Mosa's own whispered abortion.

CHAPTER 7

It pleased Mara that after Pule's funeral, Mosa stayed home and that she was able to get herself re-admitted to school. How she managed the latter was a mystery. Mara believed in education and was prepared to do everything within her power to keep Mosa in school. Even with the crazy ideas the educated youth seemed to get, education was still a good thing and offered better choices for the future.

During the six or so days leading up to Pule's funeral, Mara hardly spoke to her two remaining children. There had been no privacy, and she had not had the strength to say anything anyway. She had known even before Pule's death that Mosa was angry for some reason her mother could not understand. Her decision to go and live with her boyfriend had been out of character. Now that Mosa had moved back home, Mara was hoping to have a chance to discuss that, and more, with her.

As she walked along the path, she wondered whether it was the doing of the *moomane* tree that had pushed her daughter from her. Stan, of course, went off back to Mr Mitchell's house immediately after the funeral. She was hoping for some family talks tonight. Some laughter perhaps, a consolidation of the family. She had been trying to tread gently around Mosa, not to push her too hard, not to demand too much of her. She was hoping that this weekend would be different. The diviner's family-strengthening divination and treatment were aimed at setting the tone for togetherness.

Even as she hoped for the best, she was expecting a gloomy welcome from the threesome. She was therefore pleasantly surprised to find Stan telling Nunu about his latest exploits with Mr Mitchell and friends. Nunu was sitting on her uncle's lap, listening open mouthed, saliva dripping over her bottom lip: a tiny waterfall that would never generate any rainbows, but still no less beautiful, thought Mara.

Mosa was sitting on the ground, a smile playing on her lips. Mara gave a tentative wave because she did not want to interrupt the story. She sat down and listened.

"It was a long weekend," continued Stan after a brief smile and a nod at his mother. "David was there. And Lone, Stony, Nana, Bill, Mmamane, Richard and six others and myself, in two Land Rovers, two Land Cruisers and one Toyota Hilux four-wheel-drive. We were all itching for some serious punishment. So what do we do to satisfy this need? Did we walk through coals, Nunu? Lie on nails? Whip our backs with sjamboks? Did we do that, Nunu?"

"Nooo, Uncle Stan," cooed Nunu. "No, no, Uncle Stan: do not be silly. Of course you did not. Tell me what you did, Uncle Stan, please!"

Mara concluded that this was not the first story this evening. The two had a rhythm going, which had come with some practice.

"What we did is wait for the hottest month of the year: December, and during an *El Niño* year, and we got into these four-by-fours and went north. Behind us we were leaving comfortable beds with mosquito nets; TV sets; fridges; and houses with strong brick walls."

"What is Al Mimo, Uncle Stan? Do you really have a soft bed at Uncle Mitch's house? Can I lie on your bed one day? Do you have ice pop in the fridge?" asked Nunu, her eyes wide with wonder.

"Do you want me to tell you about the bed, or do you want me to tell you about the trip?" teased Stan. "Okay, I have white sheets . . ."

"No, no: I do not want to hear about your sheets. Even grandma has sheets."

"Okay: back to my story. Where was I? Alright. To make sure we received the worst punishment ever, we chose Kubu Island in the Makgadikgadi Pans as our destination. Do you know where that is? Of course you do not. The promise of blistering heat was particularly attractive. The fact that it had rained rather hard in the Boteti area meant that we could expect to be stuck in the pan, further increasing our discomfort."

"Do you think Mr Mitch is crazy? Do you think you are a bit crazy because you have been staying with white people?" Nunu asked in a whisper. "Grandma Mma-Bina says white people are crazy. She says they have strange ways and that you will end up like a white man.

Then, then, maybe you will speak through your nose and maybe you will become an albino. Do you think so, Uncle Stan?"

"Yes, of course I am stark-raving mad. So now I will tell you how crazy I am. Yesterday I . . ."

"Why are you not telling me about the trip now? Why are you not telling me about Al Mimo? I want to know about the trip. Grandma, make him tell me about the trip. Grandma, make him! make him! make him!"

Mara smiled but said nothing. She was enjoying the exchange, childish as it was. The paraffin lamp cast a muted light over the three. From where she was sitting, Mara saw only silhouettes of her two children but her grand-daughter's face she could see clearly. They were happy and relaxed, and the sight gave her hope for them as a family.

"You have to promise to listen without interruptions. Can you promise? Alright: we left at 7.30 in the morning and headed north. You know where north is?"

Nunu pointed a small, confident finger.

"Good: you are the smartest niece I have."

"I am your only niece," asserted Nunu proudly and with a hint of challenge in her voice.

"Like I said, you are clever. After twelve hours, we reached Makgadikgadi Pans. We had of course stopped for a picnic, fuel, to pee, and one flat tyre."

Nunu giggled at the thought of all of them relieving themselves by the side of the road.

"As the sun set behind us in all the magnificence of a true Botswana sunset, we were pleased that all was going according to plan, when we hit the first set of problems. Did you know that we have the best sunsets in the world? Well, maybe not the whole world, but we have great sunsets. You must never forget that when you are grown up and living in London."

"I am going to London, Uncle Stan? London is where the Queen lives with Cinderella. And they have seven dwarfs. And they live with Princess Diana. She is a princess, too, like Cinderella. And they live in a big, big house. That is what Keba says. Keba goes to school, and she says so. The teacher told her. And the pussycat went to London to see the Queen too."

Mosa and Mara tried to stifle their giggling.

"Do you want to tell me about the Queen? I can finish my story later." Stan was trying to hide his amusement. Mosa and her mother were laughing openly now. "Don't mind some people who laugh at things they do not know anything about. Your aunt and your grandmother do not know anything about the Queen and the seven dwarfs and all those princesses. Tell me about the Queen."

"But I have told you. They all live in a big house. Now tell me the rest of the story, please, Uncle Stan. I am going to close my mouth shut, shut, shut." Nunu set her mouth in a pout, bringing more giggles from the two women.

"Alright, then. As we were driving through the pan, one of the Land Rovers got stuck. We all jumped out of our vehicles, ready to push, and immediately our poor noses caught this horrible smell. It was soda ash, and it smelled like sewage. Like a big pile of rotten eggs. Some of the boys, I tell you: their noses couldn't take it and they ran back into the cars pinching their noses, trying not to breathe. Did I ever tell you about my nose? That has to wait for another story. The ones with stronger noses began to push, but then suddenly there was this cloud from the only patch of grass for kilometres. The cloud charged, and in no time everyone was jumping and hopping and scratching. I tell you, Nunu, those mosquitoes were the size of small chickens . . . Okay, maybe not that big, but they were big. They kind of collided with you. If you smashed your hand against one, there was a big splash of blood – and whose blood was that, Nunu?"

Nunu gave a confused little shrug.

"Your blood!"

"Uncle Stan!" the poor child said, jumping in her uncle's lap.

"Luckily, rescuing the Land Rover did not take so long. Did I say luckily? Well it is true that there were some amongst us who were not too keen on punishment and found themselves on the trip due to pressure from friends.

"With Isang leading the way, we finally reached camp. Everybody was excited. The younger boys and girls were hoping that one more vehicle would get stuck; the mothers were anxiously hoping that the threatening clouds did not turn into rain; and the fathers were being their daring mindless selves, charging forward with no worries whatsoever. The teenagers, like myself, were just cool. You would've loved it, Nunu. Perhaps your grandmother will let you come with us next time. Do you think you would like that?"

"Yes, yes, Uncle Stan!" she cried, clapping her hands and rocking with excitement.

Stan looked at his mother before going on. "Finally we reached camp, and tents went up in minutes. It was soon obvious that Kubu Island is the home of mosquitoes from hell. They were the biggest, most vicious, daring mosquitoes in the world; well, perhaps south of the Equator."

"Where is the quator, Uncle Stan?"

"Don't worry about where the Equator is. The point is that these monsters were huge. They were bloodsuckers of impressive proportions. Naledi and Nana tried to cook a quick dinner, but it ended with bugs in the pot and a few in the kids' mouths."

"The mosquitoes were like monsters? You lie, Uncle Stan! You lie!" Nunu was now standing up, almost hopping about. "You fed the children bugs, Uncle Stan? Do you think you are crazy, like Mr Mitch?"

"No, we did not feed the kids bugs, and if you had been there, I would have made sure no bug ended up on your plate. You believe me? Of course you believe me. You are my favourite only niece, remember?

"Then, the first day, the sun was a big ball of fire in the sky. All around us there were waves of heat. The air was salty; it stood still and burned into us. No shade could protect anybody. Richard suggested that perhaps the reason these bare patches were called pans was because you could fry in them. Well, we did fry. In the afternoon, a rain scare. The clouds gathered and the heavens rumbled and the wind blew. After a few sputters, however, there was quiet, and the mood improved somewhat. The beer and wine helped to calm things down. The more reasonable amongst us, especially those of us too young to drink, suggested that we go back home, but the older people did not listen to this advice.

"Second day. A long, thick line of sand, like a train, charged across the pan. It was magnificent but also frightening. There was so much sand that if you were sitting on my lap, I would not have been able to see you. We left our tents to sit on rocks, but soon centipedes and scorpions were popping up from everywhere. The kids screamed, the teenagers played music and the parents drank more alcohol.

"The third day was the calmest and most pleasant. By this time, we had learned to live with the mosquitoes, to tolerate the heat and tp chew on sand without complaining too much. On the fourth day we headed home with intentions of going back in winter. After the trip, we consulted guide books, and guess what they told us, Nunu?"

Nunu gave another shrug.

"That visits to Kubu were not advised during the summer months. Next time, we will read the guide books and ask people who know better. And perhaps next time your grandmother will let you come with us."

Nunu looked expectantly at her grandmother.

"But Nunu, the place is like a magical place: the baobabs, the rocks, the expanse of land around it; it is just unbelievable. There is the suggestion of ghosts and other beings that we as human beings cannot see. The howl of the wind promises or threatens creatures from another world. The place makes you think of swamp things, spirits, ghosts, *belerutang*, *kgogela*, UFOs and other things that we cannot explain. You would love it. Any questions, little one?"

Of course, Nunu had plenty of questions. She had been fascinated by the story. But as Mara listened to her son's fantastic tale, she realised that he was communicating with her too. Stan was trying to give them a glimpse of the life they did not share. He was also trying to tell them what made him happy, choosing to talk to them through Nunu because it made it easier for him. Mara looked at this strange son of hers. He had always been different from the other boys, had always seen beyond the obvious. He had always been a sceptic. She had believed Mosa to be the same. The two had shared a special bond as young children, but over the years it had been broken. Mara hoped that it was not too late for them.

CHAPTER 8

Mosa continued to lie there long after Stan had stopped his tale of wind and mosquitoes. They were waiting for the traditional doctor. Her own thoughts about the matter were unclear, but she was more inclined to go with her mother than with her brother: she felt they needed someone to intervene to break the mood of sadness in the house.

As they waited, they listened to the radio. A woman who had an assumed American accent was talking about the dangers of AIDS and was advising listeners about how to avoid the dreaded disease. The speaker kept switching between Setswana and English. Mosa thought the speaker's explicit language was inappropriate for a national radio station listened to by all ages. She was not against public education about AIDS, but she did not understand why that had to necessarily mean making listeners uncomfortable. When the Motswana/American voice began talking about erections and condoms, she looked over at Nunu, reached over and switched the radio off. Her mother mumbled something to the child about preserving batteries for news later on. Mosa thought she saw a flicker of a smile on Stan's face; he seemed to find her mother's excuse rather funny. She decided that she would challenge Stan about that one of these days.

With the radio off and Nunu breathing gently next to her, Mosa's mind went back to when she was younger. She remembered what a good storyteller Stan was even back then. For some reason, as they grew older, they grew apart. Stan's moving into the school compound to live with a succession of teachers had not helped to bring them closer either. They went to the same school, but they hardly interacted. Her dropping out of school under a cloud of scandal had not helped either. Mosa wanted back some of the closeness they had once had.

Mosa remembered how she and Stan, the youngest of the four children, had spent many late afternoons at their grandparents' lands, on a favourite rock, counting the colours of the sunsets or finding animal shapes in puffs of cloud. On a lightly clouded day, the colours of the sunset would increase progressively as the sun went down. Then, if the western horizon was clear while the eastern one was cloudy, they might even have what they had named a false sunset: an illusion that the sun was setting in the east. One day, sitting on their rock, watching the sun go down, Stan turned to her and said, "It's ridiculous!"

"The sunset is ridiculous?" she asked.

"No, it's stupid that Setswana has so few names for colours." He pondered the reasons. For Stan, everything had to have a reason. "Perhaps it is because we live in a desert and we have so few colours in nature," he suggested. "Look around: all you see is green and pale-yellow grass; few flowers."

Mosa argued that that could not be the reason. "In a good year, there are plenty of flowers with a variety of colours to have deserved some names. And surely there is enough variety of colour in bird life to have warranted someone coming up with names to describe them. What about the sunsets? The sun sets every day and gives off these colours every day."

"Why would a society limit itself to red, blue, white, yellow, brown and black to describe the world? Why is there no name for purple? For burgundy? How can we have only one colour for both blue and green? That is crazy! Why do I have to use English words to describe a sunset in Botswana?" Stan asked in exasperation.

"Do you see anyone suffering because there is no word for purple?"

"Or for maroon, or burgundy or violet or lime or . . ."

"Have you ever counted the names describing the colour of cattle?" Mosa asked. "The names are so specific they tell you the sex of the animal as well as the various colours on the animal. Some even tell you where on the animal the markings are. Perhaps because there is no purple cow, no one bothered to come up with a name for that colour."

"I guess you are right, but it bothers me whenever I have to use some foreign word because no Setswana one exists. I particularly hate Afrikaner words. Those people corrupted our language. They corrupted more than our language." Stan was getting worked up.

Oh, no, Mosa thought: here comes another long discussion about the Afrikaner. She quickly suggested that perhaps they should be going down to help with the evening chores. After all, they were on the rock on an errand to collect melon slices placed there earlier to dry. Then there was still the drinking water to be strained to get rid of tadpoles and other small lives before the two could relax and wait for their last meal of the day. Sitting on the rock any longer might well earn them a slap from their mean aunt. Their mother never hit them and was forever being criticised for being too soft on the children. But their childless aunt Rinah would lash out at any opportunity. Their nickname for her was Ali, after Mohammed Ali. How she was their aunt was a mystery to them. She had arrived one cloudy day with a battered suitcase, wearing a funny, pink, frilly dress, and had never left. She was a member of the family through some unclear link long lost in South Africa. Something to do with a great uncle who had married a Xhosa woman whilst he was working in the mines. Because he already had another wife in Botswana, he had decided that it suited him best to keep the Xhosa woman in South Africa. He himself had died in a mining accident. Aunt Rinah was somehow a descendant of the relationship.

An uncle, Rich, who came and went as he pleased, and always had kind words for all the children, whispered that Rinah was always mean because she had blood problems. According to him, she had too much blood because she had no children. "A woman has to have children; otherwise, her blood does not circulate properly, and then she starts having headaches, and she becomes a pain for everyone." So Mosa and the other children knew that Aunt Rinah was not to blame for her mean disposition. They disliked her and felt sorry for her at the same time, hoping that she would have children soon. Dodging that swinging right hand in time was not always possible, and they had to admit that she landed more slaps than she missed.

One day, Mosa asked Uncle Rich whether he could help Aunt Rinah in the matter of the children. "Just one child," she pleaded. Uncle Rich laughed so much that he rolled around the ground, much to Mosa's confusion. Surely Uncle Rich knew Mosa's interest in the matter. Surely he was a compassionate uncle and wanted the meanness to the children to stop. But when he finally stopped laughing, Uncle Rich announced that he would rather help a mouse-trap to have babies than Rinah. "Yes, I would take my chances with a mouse-trap any day, before I venture there, little Moose-Moose." This left Mosa confused. She had thought that poor Auntie Rinah needed a man and children, and that somehow her uncle would be instrumental in providing or helping in the getting of the children. How this would be done she was not too sure. But she was smart enough to know that this was somehow a secret matter not to be discussed openly. Being ten years old was a difficult age, she decided. It seemed like just as she began to understand some things, new areas of confusions emerged. She was just hoping that Uncle Rich would be happy to help.

Seeing his little niece's morose face, Uncle Rich set down the milk bucket and explained. "Look," he said, "you have nothing to worry about. Rinah is fast approaching the age when she cannot possibly have children any more. So her blood will cool down soon. Then, only two things could possibly happen: she will either love all of you and be the best second mother you could ever hope for or she will get really mean and all this will seem like child's play. So there is no point worrying now, because either real worrying still lies ahead or there will be nothing to worry about soon. Come and help your Uncle Wealfy milk the cows. And really, little one, I cannot help. She is my sister. A man cannot help a sister have babies. Come: you will understand one day."

As Mosa skipped behind her uncle, trying to puzzle out this nugget of wisdom, Aunt Rinah's high-pitched voice tore through the air. "Rich! I don't want you taking that girl milking the cows." From the doorway of the house, she had been watching the two huddling together, and guessed that Uncle Rich was putting all kinds of useless ideas into the child's head. "She has enough boy habits as it is, and does not need some travelling idiot to come here and confuse her even more."

In response to all this, Uncle Rich broke into a silly little song and grabbed the little girl's hand, and off they went, skipping into the foliage, on their way to the cattle kraal.

Only years later did she understand. Uncle Rich, the rich man, the wealthy man, had his own brand of wisdom. That may explain that although his real name was *Mohumanegi*: poor man, he insisted that everyone call him Uncle Rich. On his really happy days, which seemed to be brought on by his smoking his specially rolled funny-smelling cigarettes, he called himself Uncle Wealfy.

"I am Rich and Wealfy," he sang. "Call me Uncle Wealfy and you are my friend. Moose-Moose, am I not your Uncle Rich?"

Sometimes he called himself Uncle Not, for 'Not Rich'. He was a funny one, Uncle Rich. And kind: whenever he came home, he brought sweets for the children, and a generous peppering of new English words and phrases picked up during his travels. There was the time when his favourite expression was "peace and trankility in the nation" and he was always demanding that he be given some "peace and trankility in the nation". Or telling Rinah to give the children some "peace and trankility in the nation".

Later, he spoke incessantly about leaving to go "far and beyon'." During his far-and-beyon' phase, he told Mosa that although she was a girl, she would definitely go far and beyon' – with such seriousness that Mosa knew he was not just being his funny self. He was telling her something. "Yes: you have quick sense of plenty knowledge," he said, using yet another of his English expressions. "You will go far and beyon', Moose-Moose." Mosa had wanted to go far and beyon', although she was not certain she knew what it really meant.

The mouse-trap talk was just one the many subjects Mosa remembered that seemed to have another meaning beyond just the words. There was the time, for example, when she overheard Mma-Naledi and her mother Mma-Pule talking in hushed tones about how Rra-Naledi had lost his axe. Mosa had been watching the malt, drying in the sun to make sure that the chickens did not eat it. Stan had left to do some "boy" thing somewhere in the neighbourhood. He had wanted to sit and help his sister watch the drying malt, but he did not want to risk killing a rotten bird with his slingshot, as happened to all boys who sat around girls. And keeping chickens from malt was one of the surest ways for a boy to kill a rotten bird.

Mosa was bored and drawing figures in the sand as she guarded the malt against sneaky chickens. She overheard the two women whispering with concern about poor Rra-Naledi's lost axe.

"And since when?" Mma-Pule asked.

"Oh, let's see now," said Mma-Naledi. "Close to a year."

Mosa knew that she was not supposed to be listening. Whenever they huddled like that, it meant they were discussing a secret. But she was puzzled. Only that morning, she had seen Rra-Naledi chopping wood with his axe. Concerned by the sadness in Mma-Naledi's face,

Mosa ran out of the yard, through the scattering chickens and over to Mma-Naledi's house. She weaved her way through the huts and disappeared behind one of them, where she retrieved an axe. She half carried, half dragged the axe over to the two whispering women, and presented it, exhausted but relieved.

"What is this now, Mosadinyana?" her mother said, a bit taken aback and coming out of her whispering world of secrets. "You are going to hurt yourself. Put that axe down. What are doing with it, anyway?"

Now it was Mosa's turn to be surprised. Instead of praise and congratulations, she was met with confusion and a mild rebuke.

"But, but, Mma, this is Rra-Naledi's axe. Mma-Naledi just said he had lost it. Look: it is not lost; it is right here." Her look of triumph had meanwhile crumpled into confusion.

The two women looked at each other and then burst into laughter.

"*Ao*, Mma-Pule, what are you going to do with this child of yours?" Mma-Naledi asked laughing and crying and shaking her head.

"She is just a clever little girl. Let us thank her for finding the axe. Mosa, thank you for finding the axe. Please return it to its place. And do not tell Rra-Naledi that we thought it was lost. Mma-Naledi is just confused." Mma-Pule winked at Mma-Naledi.

Mosa got the distinct feeling that there was a deeper meaning to the talk of the axe than was apparent in the words. She felt dismissed and left out. Her mother's trick of making light of the matter had not worked. But she knew that trying to find out more about the mystery of the missing axe that was not really missing would not lead any-where. She dragged the axe back – more slowly now – and put it back in its place. She wanted to ask Uncle Rich what all this meant, but he was away on one of his travels.

Mosa always looked forward to Uncle Rich's return. This was not just because of the sweets and the stories he brought home – although these were special treats. It was also because of two special items he owned: the beautiful black bicycle – Black Magic – and the radio. During Uncle Rich's absences, the bicycle hung from the rafters in the middle of one of the huts. Uncle Rich had made a special seat for Mosa and when he was around, she sat behind him, holding tight as he rode along sandy roads, singing and laughing and telling her all kinds of stories and answering her many questions. Uncle Rich never said to her, "Whose child are you?" when she asked him questions. When Uncle Rich was away, Mosa would fall asleep with the bicycle hanging from the rafters, giving her dreams of her holding on to him as they rode among the stars and over the moon. She woke up wishing he would return soon.

One day, Uncle Rich announced, "Moose-Moose, you are tall enough to ride Black Magic. I am going to teach you today – everything from riding to patching tyres."

"Uncle Rich!" was all she could say as she felt both the fear and excitement streaming through her.

"Oh, no: you will not teach the child these things," Auntie Rinah said with a stomp of her foot. "This child has a boy soul as it is; she doesn't need you teaching her how to ride a bicycle – or patch a silly tyre." She tried to get Mara to join her in her protest.

But Mara simply smiled and said, "Let the child have her fun with her uncle, Rinah. If we stop her getting on to that bike, she'll simply find some other "boy" thing to do.

The day was spent with Mosa pedalling furiously through thorn-bushes, skidding across paths and tumbling on to gravel. By the end of the day, she had bruises and scratches on elbows, knees, nose; everywhere. But she could ride a bike and fix it.

After the riding lessons, Mosa's dreams about Black Magic changed. She no longer dreamed that she was holding on to her Uncle Rich. She now dreamed that she was riding the bicycle herself. This had become a recurrent dream since then, a dream that always left her feeling positive and optimistic. A riding, flying, gliding dream that always made her wake up with a smile.

Until the last time she had the dream, when a frightening twist was added to it. That was the night she had found out that she was pregnant. As usual, she pedalled around the stars and over the moon, gliding through puffs of cloud, catching a glimpse of the legendary man pulling the thornbush. But this time there was a difference. She dreamed that she had ridden all the way up to the sun. She felt a burst of heat; the front tyre melted into nothingness; and clutching her mangled, one-wheeled bicycle, she plummeted back to earth. She woke up just as she hit the earth, sweating and shaken and lying awake the rest of the night.

Her beautiful dream had been eluding her since then.

The radio was another of Uncle Rich's magical items. He never left the radio behind, so it was only when he was around that Mosa got to listen to it. It gave them music, stories and news. Uncle Rich listened to the news morning, noon and evening. It was as if he could not get enough of what was happening in other parts of Botswana as well as in the rest of the world.

Through the radio, Mosa learned about wars in other parts of Africa; shootings in the United States of America; prisoners somewhere who were on a hunger strike. She also learned about malaria outbreaks in the north of Botswana. It seemed to her, if the radio could be believed, that there was always some army man taking over some country somewhere in Africa. And severe starvation on the continent where she lived, which, according to the news, was not a particularly great place to be. She learned that she was in the Third World, but there was never a mention of where the other two worlds were. Uncle Rich did not know much about these worlds either. But he thought India or China might be a Fourth World. He was not sure, he said. He suspected though that calling Africa the Third World was probably an insult.

"It is just my suspicion, Moose-Moose. From the way they say it. I do not know."

In South Africa, where her friend Magdalene's mother took care of beautiful white children, there were some blacks not happy with their lot. It seemed, from the little she had understood, that these black people thought they too should be running the country. Mosa tried to work out in her mind why these black people would want to run somebody else's country. Why didn't they just go back to their countries? It had not seemed fair that people like Magdalene's mother would want to take over the white man's land. A particularly difficult character, she gathered, was a man called Nelson Mandela. It sounded like putting him in prison had not entirely shut him up. She often found the news very confusing indeed, and asked Uncle Rich about this.

"Oh, Moose-Moose that is our land. They took it away, Moose-Moose. They took it away."

Mosa was happy that except for Ali's occasional slaps, her part of the Third World, whether this was an insult or not, was peaceful. No one seemed keen to take it away from her. And although she had to blow at tadpoles to stop them from swimming into her mouth when she was having a drink of water, no one was dying from drinking dirty water, as happened in some faraway countries in Africa. This was even though a nurse once came to their school and told them that they had to boil their drinking water. That had sounded like the most ridiculous advice ever given by a government official. The parents had listened politely, but had laughed as soon as the nurse had packed up her little bag and left. Yes, she figured: the world out there was a particularly tough place to live. She was happy to be where she was – except that she did want to go far and beyon'.

Rinah did not think it proper for Mosa to be so interested in the news. She muttered grim warnings about irresponsible mothers and uncles who allowed a young head to be filled with half-truths about a sick and unsafe world. Aunt Rinah did not always believe the news. For example, she did not believe the stuff that had been said about Palestinians and Jews, because Israel was a place in heaven, and Jordan was a river Moses or Jesus had to cross. She was certain one of these two holy men had at some time crossed that river, and she was certain that no one could possibly know what was happening at those places unless that person were in heaven. Even someone able to speak through a radio to people far away from him could not possibly have the power to report what was happening in Israel. On this particular occasion, she demanded that the radio be turned off. In response, Uncle Rich picked up the radio and moved to another patch of shade.

"Come, Moose-Moose. Come and listen to why this country is the best place on earth to live. Even if there are those who will not give you peace and trankility in the nation."

Mosa followed her uncle, keen to hear about the West Bank and Israel and Jordan and a man called Arafat. The radio seemed to always have a story about a difficult man somewhere. There seemed to be fewer stories about women, difficult or otherwise.

A few metres from the quarrelsome Aunt Rinah, the two acquired some peace and tranquillity, and listened to the news. Mosa did not understand all of it, but she was more inclined to believe Uncle Rich's interpretations than those offered by Aunt Rinah; after all, it was his radio, and he knew how to operate it. Everybody else could get only an angry hiss from the thing if they dared touch its knobs and buttons. On some days, the radio remained mute no matter how much turning and pressing its buttons received. Uncle Rich, on the other hand, just had to cradle it and turn its dials this way and that way and it came to life. Sometimes he put it on his lap, like nursing a baby. He opened it and popped in some batteries. He always knew when someone had been fiddling with it, and that never pleased him at all. This was because if someone else touched it, it hissed at him as well.

It was around this time – she was nine years old, Stan eight – that she found Sis' Koki's ANC card. She sneaked it out of the hut to consult Stan about it. She explained to Stan that Sis' Koki could be in trouble because this was evidence of her being involved in political activities in South Africa. Sis' Koki was a domestic worker in South Africa, and had come home on some urgent and secret mission. Barely literate in the English language and hampered by the bad handwriting on the card, the two ended up confused after trying to figure out what the card was all about. It was full of abbreviations and references to weeks.

"It says here 'Para 1, Gravida 2'. I think that has to do with the military. You know, para-troopers and the like. Maybe 'gravida' has to do with grenades and other military stuff," Stan suggested. Stan's friend Michael, had an older brother who had joined the newly formed Botswana Defence Force, and was using the little information he had learned from his friend to try to understand the ANC card.

It seemed that activities and projects were measured in weeks. Stan suggested that perhaps the whole thing was in code and that one had to be a member of the ANC to understand the message. News about the ANC was always whispered, and it was not uncommon for a young man to suddenly return from the South African mines, where he had been working, and suddenly quietly take up farming. These sudden returns were somehow related to ANC trouble. So when, a week later, Sis' Koki announced for all to hear that she was off for her ANC appointment, Mosa waited to be alone with Uncle Rich. She asked him about Sis' Koki and the ANC. It turned out that Sis' Koki's ANC, or Ante-natal Clinic, was quite different from Nelson Mandela's ANC, or African National Congress. Mosa breathed a sigh of relief to learn that her corner of the world would not be upset by any political activities after all. She also learned that Sis' Koki was going to have a baby.

After three months, when Mosa had almost forgotten about the baby, Sis' Koki went off to another ANC meeting and came back with a baby. A beautiful, pink little thing with black ears and soft, black, curly hair. Her mother named her Nnana.

"I must shave her head," Aunt Rinah said.

"Leave the hair: it is beautiful. Do not shave the baby," Mosa pleaded.

"Whose child are you? Your tongue is too long," Ali snapped.

It seemed to Mosa that "Whose child are you?" was a question asked almost daily of her, even by her mother, whenever she asked too many questions.

But Mosa could not stop herself: "Why does she have a ribbon on her belly button?"

Her answer was a slap from Ali. Ali's payment was an angry look from Mara, who in turn received a retort from an aunt who had come to visit.

"What are you going to do with this child? Can't anyone teach her manners?" The "anyone" was, of course, not just anyone: it was Mara. Mara looked at her daughter and silently pleaded with her to keep quiet. But it was not beyond Mosa to spring back from Ali's reach just to ask another question. All other children knew what questions not to ask, but not Mosa. She just seemed to be unable to stem the tide of questions constantly swirling in her little head. And if it was not questions she was asking, she was trying out something.

Mosa looked at Nnana as her beautiful hair fell off over Ali's hands. Instead of being angry, she marvelled at the swiftness of Ali's hand. She held the baby in her left hand and the razor blade in her right. It almost seemed as if she had not put down the razor blade to deliver the blow. Her slaps hardly hurt, so Mosa just rubbed the area and continued to watch Aunt Rinah at work, always shaving babies' heads and piercing girl babies' ears. When she did these things, she was careful and tender. But, it seemed, after this initial welcome, she could not abide these babies.

Later, Mosa believed, without anyone ever having told her so, that the baby's hair was shaved not because it was itself offensive but because it reminded the women of what had framed it as it emerged into the world. Shaving the baby's head was a kind of tampering with evidence to hide very private and secret things. That explained, she had decided, why men were not allowed into the house for at least two months after a baby was born. It also explained the ribbon she was not supposed to mention. Thus baby Nnana emerged from the hut light brown and bald, and with a regular belly button two months later, and the women's secret remained protected. Mosa decided that these were thoughts she was going to keep to herself. Even Uncle Rich might not be too happy about these sorts of questions. It was unlikely that he knew much about these matters anyway.

Mosa knew that Uncle Rich did not know everything. For example, he confessed to being confused by the surgeon-general, who kept on writing the ridiculous message on cigarette packages that "smoking is bad for your health". He was disappointed, he declared, that America, the land of freedom, would tolerate interference from an army man in that way. He could understand a sergeant-general in Africa just writing his own messages on someone else's product: African army generals were known for their brutish behaviour, and ruining someone's business would not be any big thing for them, he said; they often ruined much more. But he was confused that a general in America could get away with such behaviour. "It just goes to show," he said, blowing his smoke into the air, "that you cannot trust army men, even American ones."

Mosa thought that the American general was not as bad as her uncle made him out to be. He did not take over the government; he just played a prank on cigarette makers, and no one took him seriously anyway. She had never heard of anyone not smoking because of what the general had written on cigarette packs. Uncle Rich had started smoking at the age of sixteen because he had too much blood in his body and was prone to nose bleeds. His mother offered him his first cigarette for this malady. She, of course, had known nothing about the surgeon-general, because she could not read; she just asked for the cigarettes that had a picture of a camel on their pack.

Mosa also remembered her brother Stan as being an inquisitive, happy and generous person. She was twelve when she first felt this ball of unhappiness in her. She could not point to a particular source for her melancholy. As long as she could remember, she did not like her name. Why could her mother not come up with a nicer, more optimistic name? she wondered: Mary; Gwendolyn; Sylvia; Elizabeth – something English and sophisticated. Even a Setswana name like Naledi or Boitumelo would have been preferable. Then she could have changed the name to Star or Gladness; she knew some people who had done that.

Instead, she was called Mosa, short for *mosadi*: woman. Her mother, when being affectionate, called her *Mosadinyana*: little woman. She could not possibly go by the English meaning of her name: woman. It would be ridiculous to be called woman. She had a friend who was called Magdalene. She was such a lucky girl: her grandmother shouted with pride, for all to hear, "Maggieeee!" And it sounded so special.

And while her own mother was working in the fields, carting water and being a rural woman, Magdalene's mother was in Johannesburg, working there. When asked where her mother was, Magdalene would announce, proudly, "She has gone to the place of the white people." The only drawback was that she did not come home until Christmas time, and sometimes not even then. Magdalene sometimes did not see her mother for close to two years. She did not, however, stop boasting that her mother was cooking lavish meals for a white family that had white children in a white house who slept between white sheets in Johannesburg. Mosa sometimes felt she could not possibly compete. But on some days, she thought she sensed sadness in Magdalene's proud voice. Her eyes were not as happy as her mouth. At those times, she was certain she would rather have her mother close by, even if it meant no parcels of secondhand clothing and dried bread from Johannesburg.

One day she asked her mother why she had named her Mosadi. Her mother answered rather proudly that after two boys, who she expected to grow up and fly away, she knew her daughter would always be there for her in her old age. "Surely you know that *mosadi* means 'she who remains at home to ensure that the fire will never go out'?"

Mosa did not share this sentiment: she wanted a name that told the world that she would go far and beyon', like Uncle Rich had predicted. Her oldest brother's name was *Thabo*: joy, and clearly he brought lots of joy to their mother. Her second brother, *Pule*: rain, must have been born on a rainy day or during the rainy season. Then there was her youngest brother, Stan. Not only did he have an English name; he was named after their mother's father. He was often called *Ntate*: father, or when the family was being particularly affectionate, *Monnamogolo*: old man. Everyone but she, it seemed, had a special name. Was it not a common saying that a name was a self-fulfilling prophecy? How could her mother have hoped for so little for her? How could she have had such limited expectations about her potential? She wanted to be more than just a woman; she wanted to achieve. Had she been asked,

"Achieve what?" she would not have been able to answer the question. But she knew that she had a yearning in her heart.

Sometimes Mosa was honest enough to admit to herself that she was afraid of ending up like her mother: poor, unmarried and struggling to raise a family alone. She could never forget her mother's brief but painful time with Solomon Moloisa, her most recent lover, who had been a violent, loud and disruptive drunk.

As the only girl, she saw herself as more likely to follow in her mother's footsteps. She felt that the boys had a certain freedom she lacked. They seemed to have longer play hours, and could venture further away from home than she. They could sit any way they pleased, but her mother was always at her about how a girl should sit. "The chickens are eating the malt," her mother admonished whenever she caught her with her legs apart, and Mosa would obediently bring her legs together. Her brothers were not reprimanded as often as she, though, for "letting the calf get out of the kraal"; in fact, if truth be known, Stan's calf spent more time out of the kraal than her chicken did eating the malt.

Whenever their mother spoke of their future, children featured more in Mosa's future than in the boys'. If a visitor showed up, it was she who was called from play to come and make tea. If a visitor came with a younger child who needed minding, it was she who had to do the job. If the child decided to squat and do its business during the visit, it was Mosa who had to deal with it. And she had to be quick; otherwise, the chickens would get to it before she did and then she would be in trouble. There was a particularly quick hen, and she had long made up her mind that that was one bird she was never going to eat. In general, however, her personal policy was that if it were before Friday, and if no one were watching, she would let the chickens help her clean up. That saved her the trouble of scooping up the mess and disposing of it. If they were going to have any chicken for lunch, it was most likely to be on a Sunday, and she had long decided that at least a full day should pass between the chicken feeding on baby shit and her feeding on the chicken.

Sometimes her mother even offered her to the old woman who lived three homesteads away. Then Mosa had to spend a Saturday there fetching water, stamping sorghum and cooking for Grandma Mma-Naso. It was at times like these that she really doubted her mother's love for her. How could she happily consign her to a day of hard labour just like that? The old woman was not even nice to her. The sorghum was never done just right, and the water was never enough. She was an unhappy, horrible old woman who seemed bent on making all those who came into contact with her unhappy. That explained why her own son had taken his wife and children away to establish an independent home. Nor did she have kind things to say about Mosa's mother, for that matter. She was always making comments about the morals of unmarried women and what they were likely to teach their headstrong daughters. Mosa was tempted to retort that it was better to be unmarried than to marry and then kill your husband. That is what it was whispered Mma-Naso had done. But of course she bit her tongue. One could get into serious trouble for answering back an adult, even a mean and nasty one.

"Mosadinyana, she is only a sad, unhappy old woman. No one else will help her. She has had a tough life," her mother explained.

"But why me?"

"Because a good heart brings rewards to the owner's heart."

But that was then. Now her two eldest brothers were dead within a year of each other. She had dropped out of school for a term but was now back with a fierce determination to finish. She was not going to allow her name to dictate to her what she could or could not do. She was not going to stay at home to tend any fires: she was going far and beyon'. Her mind wandered to the pregnancy and the abortion. She recalled the loneliness she felt during those three months. Although she felt that she had been responsible for her condition, she also felt that responsibility should have been shared with the man responsible for the pregnancy. But she was quickly accepting the special place of men in her society: they were responsible for very little. If she wanted to go far and beyon', she would have to start with accepting that basic reality.

Mosa had enjoyed Ntate's stories and was hoping for more. But Stan was quiet and contemplative.

"When is Rre-Namane coming, Mma-Pule? I feel tired and would like to go to bed?" she said to her mother. The question brought a rustle from where Stan was sitting; he was listening for the answer as well.

"As soon as the village becomes a bit quieter. It is still too early for him: he has to come when it is too late for us to have visitors."

"What exactly is he going to do, Mma?" Stan asked, trying to keep his voice as even as possible. He did not want to seem disrespectful, but he was not looking forward to yet another encounter with a diviner: as far as he was concerned, they had caused more problems than they had solved. They were always blaming some relative or friend for the misfortunes of their clients. No names were ever given, only vague descriptions for the clients to decipher.

"Ntate, how can you ask such a question?. You speak like you are not a Motswana child. Surely I do not have to explain such obvious things to you."

"Mma-Pule, I think we should talk before this man comes. Let us agree about what I am willing to submit myself to, ahead of time. Please do not force me to do things I do not believe in. I can tell you right now that I will not be cut up with any razor if that is part of the plan. You force me to answer back to you, mma." There was an apology in Stan's voice.

Before there was much more talk, the traditional doctor arrived: a portly man in a khaki safari suit, carrying a bag of soft leather, smoothed by years of handling. In his right hand he carried a fly whisk.

"Wake the child up," he barked without preamble. "I do not enter the yard of sleeping hearts when I come for business. The hearts of all I come for must be awake. Even a child's heart must be awake. A sleeping heart is a wicked heart. Wake the child, I say."

Mara scrambled to shake Nunu, rather roughly. Nunu opened her eyes, sat up and looked up, rubbing her eyes. She sensed tension and instinctively moved on to Mosa's lap. And as if for extra protection, she reached out for Stan's hand.

Everyone moved into the house on the instructions of the diviner. Once inside, he ordered that the door and the window be closed. He wanted to know if anyone else had spent the night in this house over the past week. The answer was no, and that seemed to satisfy him. He mumbled something about some people being able to leave their powers behind for weeks after they had left. He opened his bag.

Nunu was clutching at her aunt. Stan looked positively hostile, and his mood did not improve as they all took off their clothes, except for their underwear, on Namane's instructions. Mosa seemed indifferent to what was happening. With her eyes, Mara pleaded with Stan to just give the whole thing a chance. From his bag, the doctor brought out four tiny twigs, a small metal container and a box of matches. Stan opened his mouth to say something, but the diviner raised his hand to stop him. Namane arranged the four twigs with their four points meeting at the centre. He opened the metal container, scooped out a thick, black, oily mixture and placed it at the points where the four twigs met. He reached back into the bag and took out a mirror. Unlike the diviners before him, Rre-Namane used a mirror instead of bones. Pointing at each twig individually, he announced, "This is the mother, this is the girl, this is the boy and this is the child. Your lives and futures are in there."

He took out a box of matches, and lit the twigs at the point where they met. Immediately the house began to fill with fumes. The diviner looked into the mirror at the smouldering twigs and at the four people in front of him. Frowning, he murmured to himself and shook his head.

"You have known great suffering. You have known death. Mother, is that so?"

"That is so, *rre*," said Mara.

"You have known great suffering. You have known death. Girl, is that so?"

"That is so, *rre*," said Mosa.

You have known great suffering. You have known death. Boy, is that so?"

"That is so, *rre*," Stan answered, to his mother's relief.

"You have known great suffering. You have known death. Child, is that so?" he addressed a now fully awake Nunu.

"Yes, *rre*," answered Nunu.

Stan smiled despite his mood.

"The mirror tells me of great sadness. But I see a lifting of the sadness as well. I see two ancestors who need to be appeased. You must slaughter a pregnant cow. It must be a first pregnancy. You must also brew traditional beer. Not from store-bought sorghum; the sorghum must come from your field or the field of a relative. You have been in this cloud of misery for a long time. I can see it right here. But you will come out of it strong. You will triumph because you have a white heart." Rre-Namane looked up at the four pairs of eyes, studying each pair in turn. The fumes continued to swirl around the room. The smell was not unpleasant, but the group members were beginning to cough and rub their eyes. Nunu turned her head away, hoping for relief.

The diviner asked her to look his way, and in a kindly voice assured her that she would be able to go out soon. The diviner returned to the smouldering twigs for a while and gazed back into his mirror.

"There is love in this room. I sense a need to rebuild. The child is the glue that bonds you together. Your ancestors and your God are happy she is here. But you need to appease the ancestors because some were not consulted when the child was brought here." Rre-Namane put his mirror back into the bag. By now the twigs were completely burnt out. He took out a razor blade and unwrapped it. Stan looked sharply at his mother, but she looked straight ahead, pretending not to be aware of her son's anxiety.

"I hope you have four razor blades, for the four of us," Mosa ventured before Stan could say anything. "If you do not, I took the liberty of buying three more, just in case."

The diviner frowned, not knowing whether to be angry at this girl's presumptuous behaviour.

"And how, may I ask, did you know that I would be needing razors tonight, young girl?"

Stan had wanted to ask the same question.

"Well, sir, my mother said you would be coming here both to divine and to *phekola*. Is it not standard procedure to use a razor at strengthening rituals?"

"You are right, my child. And as long as your razors are all new, I will be happy to use them."

"Uhm –" Stan began. But before he could say anything, Mosa stood up, walked over to her brother and whispered in his ear, "Please do it for mother; please. Can we talk about this afterwards? Please?" Without giving Stan a chance to respond, she reached behind him, and from a bag, brought out not three but four razor blades. She was not going to trust this man even with a supposedly new razor blade if he had not had the sense to bring one for each of them. For all she knew, he had re-wrapped the one he had after using it on his previous customer.

Rre-Namane received the razor blades, and silence returned to the room. He motioned for Mara to come forward. He made two quick, small cuts in both elbows, the chest, the back, the knees and the ankles. After every cut, he rubbed in the ashes from the four twigs. When he was done, he motioned to Mosa to come forward.

Without comment, and clearly not inviting any from the diviner,

Mosa pushed forward a bowl of soapy water for the diviner to wash his hands. He looked up at her, but she pretended that there was nothing amiss. No one had even realised the bowl was there until then. When his hands were clean, she sat down for the razor. By this time, Nunu was on her grandmother's lap, clearly scared. She had seen the blood and knew that her turn was coming.

After Mosa, Stan submitted to the strengthening without comment. Once again, Mosa made the diviner wash his hands, this time using an extra pitcher of water for rinsing. This went on until all four had been strengthened against evil forces. Stan was not able to watch when Nunu was under the razor. But Nunu was so frightened that not a peep came from her. A mixture of water, herbs and some other unrecognisable materials was placed in a bowl. The diviner dipped his fly whisk into it and swished it into the air, splashing all four of his patients, entreating the ancestors of Selato to enter the house and protect the family. He ordered all evil forces out, and directed that the senders of the bad omens get back their evil ten times over. The diviner was a very energetic waver of the whisk, and sometimes stung one or two of the patients.

Afterwards the group members went outside. The diviner asked them to stand in a row, from oldest to youngest. By now Nunu was tired, but she performed as asked. In this order, the group walked the perimeter of the yard, while the diviner walked alongside, raining his potion on them. At the four corners of the yard and at the entrance, he dug tiny holes in which he buried some or other strengthening medicine. His job was done, and he promised to return soon to discuss the date for appeasement of the ancestors. Mara handed him his payment: P600, the equivalent of two months' salary for her.

The cuts began to sting, but everyone was under strict instructions not to wash for twenty-four hours. They went to bed, Mara wondering what Mosa had said to Stan that shut him up. Stan, for his part, wondered what it was in his sister's voice that had made him keep quiet earlier. Mosa resolved that from now on she would work for reconciliation in the family as long as her destination – far and beyon' – were not compromised. She would talk to her brother tomorrow. They had a lot of catching up to do.

Nunu was too tired to think, and was happy to be in her grandmother's bed.

CHAPTER 9

Mosa had been back at school for two months, when, going to school one morning, she decided to take a short cut, which took her past Mma-Queen's yard. There she saw Sakanye, leaning against a wall, watching her as if he had been waiting for her a while. His sly smile suggested that indeed he had been. Mosa responded to Sakanye's greetings with a brief "Ahee". She hurried on, her mind on the Geography test she was going to be writing later that day. She wanted to go over her work later, and hoped she could get to the library to look up some information during lunchtime. But seeing the San man Sakanye had made her mind wander. She thought about the many stories she had been told about the San people when she was growing up. Of course, she had believed most of them and, to be honest, still believed some of them. She looked back at Sakanye, taking in his tattered clothes, his bare chest and feet, his bronze face with slanted eyes. How, she wondered, could she possibly have believed him capable of turning himself into a lion? Sakanye, in response to Mosa's sly look, smiled and blew her a kiss. He was as usual drunk, even at this early time of the morning.

Sakanye was hardly to blame for his condition. He lived a poor existence, carrying wood and water for Mma-Queen's beer-brewing business. His pay was liquor, old clothes, a bit of food and a place to sleep. Mma-Queen was always trying to regulate how much beer he got, but there was no way she could ever succeed: he was always sneaking away with extra jugs of the brew. He was not happy with his lot, but he had no home of his own, so he was unlikely to quit. No one remembered where he came from. He had been brought to Monamodi village when he was a small boy, and

84

had over the years been passed on from family to family.

Although he drank up as much of Mma-Queen's beer as he could, he was unhappy about some of Mma-Queen's bizarre brewing practices. One speciality of hers was the soaking of her teenage daughter's dirty underwear in the beer. Occasionally she used her own. He would have been none the wiser about this if he were not forever sneaking into the brewing hut for his extra jugfuls of beer. Her underwear, he believed, had no real effect on him. But her daughter's did, and it was creating personal problems for him: desires he had no chance of satisfying. Well, he did from time to time resort to self-help measures, but he wished he just did not have the problem in the first place.

As far as Mma-Queen was concerned, the panty-brewing technique yielded the desired results. Her business was booming: not only were more men coming to drink; they were also bringing along droves of thirsty women. And Sakanye observed that men in the company of women drank more than usual. Women, he noticed, drank quite a bit but pretended not to be drinking at all. And as darkness fell, couples disappeared into the acacia bushes nearby, where the effects of the panty beer were quickly satisfied. And these brief disappearances seemed to lead to the need for more alcohol.

Sakanye considered Mma-Queen to be the smartest of business-women, if not the kindest of people. There was the time when she came up with a successful scheme to have the customers pay in advance of their beer consumption. First, she told a few key customers that free beers would be served to the unfortunate men whose cattle had died from eating *mogau*, a poisonous plant. Of course, it was not lost to Mma-Queen that these men, having just sold meat from the dead animals, would have extra money to spend. The word went out. The men made their way to the watering hole. A trap, the wives said: you must resist, shaking their heads and trying to dissuade their husbands from venturing near the cunning Mma-Queen. Few succeeded.

When the men did arrive, Mma-Queen was ready with *mokaikai*, a plant one chewed to confuse the people one was speaking to, in her pockets. She chewed liberal amounts of *mokaikai* as free beers were being ladled out, and the unsuspecting men never had a chance. The stage was set for their entrapment. The chill in the air drew the men to the fire, and it was not long before the *mokaikai* began to work. After the second bucket of free beer, most of the men had happily accepted the wisdom of parting with a few *pulas* as advance payment for beer to be consumed in the weeks to come. One or two got more than just a jug of beer from Mma-Queen that night; they were offered some "black", as the men put it.

Mosa knew about all this because she had on occasion helped Mma-Queen with hauling water from the neighbourhood communal tap, for beer brewing. Her mother received a bit of money for these services. This was when her family had first moved from their grandparents' home, at Namane Ward, in the centre of the village, to set up a home of their own in New Town, a collection of cement-brick-walled, tinned-roofed, two-roomed structures on the outskirts of Monamodi village.

Mosa was unable to see Sakanye without thinking of the panty-brewing and black-offering antics of Mma-Queen. It had taken her a while before she quite understood what the men meant by being given a piece of "the black" by Mma-Queen. She was rather surprised how that alone could make even the smartest of men part with their hard-earned *pulas*. She could not look at Sakanye without thinking they shared some dark secret. His kiss, gallantly blown through the air, made her uneasy, as if it were somehow linked to Mma-Queen's secrets. Unlike many who hardly gave him much thought, she knew that Sakanye was a very intelligent, if abused, man. She avoided him more out of not wanting to acknowledge what they both knew than for any other reason. They had both seen men tumbling into the bushes with women they had not had any business tumbling into the bush with. She did not care to be reminded of all this, and hurried on to school, trying to block Sakanye and Mma-Queen's secrets out of her mind.

Mosa walked on with greater purpose. She knew that she was sometimes called proud just from her bearing and her walk. It did not seem fair to her: she was hardly responsible for her straight back; her long neck; her long, slender legs. She had been back at school for a few weeks now and was aware of the whispers behind her back. No doubt she braced her back in response, seeming even prouder. She was very much aware just how mean students, even friendly ones, could be. The reason for her absence from school was fairly well known: it was not easy to hide a pregnancy and an abortion from all these inquisitive boys and girls at Bana-Ba-Phefo.

Mosa thought of the English composition that she was still to finish, entitled "My Family". She was convinced that all teachers, especially the ones who taught English, had a rather unhealthy interest in students' personal affairs. The topic presented for her, as it had done almost throughout her school life, particular problems.

"Bring your brothers and sisters and parents to life in this composition. Write about what you do together. The outings! The games! Your feelings for one another! Let me read it and see your father. Give me a picture of your mother," said Ms Valley. Excited and excitable Ms Valley, with her English accent, constantly pushing back her ever falling, whitish hair. Mosa had learned that the colour was called blonde; therefore, she had learned, Ms Valley was a blonde. Mrs Matthews, on the other hand, was a brunette; this, just because of the colour of her hair. Strange people white people, sometimes.

As for her family, which Ms Valley wanted so much to hear about, it had expanded and shrunk and expanded and shrunk over the years so that she felt a time period had to be given to make her composition possible. She was positive that her idea of family was quite different from Ms Valley's. Mosa started living with her mother and her brothers five or six years ago, that is, after her mother slapped a few mud piles together into a rectangular structure and placed a few corrugated iron sheets on top. They called it home and moved in with great optimism. Not that it was a unique structure: unmarried women were staking out claims to lots on the fringes of the village and collecting their young from relatives to create "Female Headed Households". Not that her mother knew there was an English expression to describe her and her family. Mosa herself had come across the expression recently in a newspaper. Then her Social Studies teacher mentioned it in passing as well.

Before they had become a Female Headed Household, they lived with her mother at their grandparents' yard. Mosa's grandmother had died before she was born, her grandfather when she was three years old. When they lived there, the place was populated by aunts and uncles and cousins, both close and distant. Some stayed for short periods, departing upon getting married or establishing an independent home, whereas others stayed until their death. Some had left children to be raised there, only to come for them years later. There was Aunt Rinah, who had eventually married a childless widower and moved with him to Serowe village. Mosa's own two elder brothers had not always lived with them. The eldest, Thabo, lived for a significant chunk of his youth with an uncle who had no sons, so that he could do "boy" chores for the family. Pule, on the other hand, lived with an uncle who had many sons, so he could learn how to be a man. "Are all these people members of my family?" Mosa wondered. Sometimes she felt that even a simple question such as, "How many sisters do you have?" was not easy to answer. Is Sis' Koki her sister or her cousin? They call each other sister, and that is fine until you have to write a composition for an English teacher who is actually English. Then you have to try to keep two sets of thoughts, and switch them back and forth, depending on whether you are at school or at home: you have to remember to say "Koki and I" at school and "Me and Koki" at home. Sometimes things got confused, what with trying to think with a school brain during the day and a home brain after school. Mosa thought, My grandmother and Koki's great-grandmother were sisters. So according to Ms Valley's rules, Sis' Koki is a distant cousin. Making little, beautiful Nnana, Sis' Koki's daughter, even more distant. Her mother would be very surprised to learn that she was describing Koki in her composition as a distant cousin. But Ms Valley, not her mother, would be grading the composition. She just had to keep the two lives apart to avoid low marks on the one hand and resentment on the other.

She decided that she would limit her composition to the years between the age of ten and thirteen, and pretend she was writing about the present. Thinking about it, Mosa wondered who had been the head of that household. Sometimes it had seemed like there were sub-households beneath the main one. Had she lived in a Multi-Headed Household, she wondered, or was there in fact such a thing?

Mosa wondered what her Uncle Rich would have thought of Ms Valley: of her gnarled rose bush behind the school library that refused to offer even one flower; of her extra-short shorts and her English accent, which she was trying, unsuccessfully, to impose on all her students; of her chicken that ate the malt rather too often for a woman of her age!

Uncle Rich had had views about almost everything, and seemed to know what went on in every corner of the world. He had known, for example, that white people never filled their tea cups for fear of scalding the tip of their nose. Just as he had known that King George had been insane.

Yes, Mosa had no doubts about it: Uncle Rich would have had something to say about Ms Valley. Mosa could not think of Uncle Rich without feeling deep loss.

She was still feeling her way back into the routine of school. Of the many problems she expected, dealing with uninvited and unwanted advances from teachers was not one of them. She considered her abortion to be protection, because she would be regarded as unclean for at least a year. The main reason, though, was simply that she thought she was seen as too headstrong by most of the teachers. The targets were usually the quieter, politer and academically weaker ones. Thus Mosa was not at all prepared for what took place in the photocopying room later that morning. She had decided to use one of her free periods to copy some maps from a *National Geographic* magazine she had come across in the library. She was in the middle of organising her papers and stapling them together when Mr Merake, her science teacher, came into the room and closed the door behind him. Mosa looked up to offer polite greetings to Mr Merake, but before she could say anything, he strode forward rather aggressively. Within seconds, Mosa found herself wedged between Mr Merake and a photocopier. She was cornered and anxious. Her first reaction was to lean back, but as she did, her dress rode up her thighs, providing no protection from the lecherous eyes on her. Leaning back exposed more of her legs, but leaning forward to lengthen the dress brought her face closer to her teacher.

"Mosa, I have lots of books to take home after school. I want you to help me," Merake said. "After afternoon study, I will be waiting."

Anger welled up inside her, but she had to tread carefully. She hesitated before answering. There were rules against visiting teachers at their home. But he knew that already. She could not simply say "No": that would be suicidal, earning her beatings under all kinds of pretexts and low marks in tests. It was the surest way to a miserable school year.

"I also have dishes to be washed," he said. "It will not take long."

For a brief moment, Mosa wondered what would happen if she were to "tell it like it was": that she had no intention of having sex with him. Of course, if she said that, she would regret it as long as she were a student at the school. The special friendship between Bones, for that is what everyone called Mr Merake, and the headmaster, Mr Kgaka, was well known. The two engaged in sexual relationships with students with impunity. There was even a rumour that when Mr van Heerden, the new Dutch teacher, was transferred from his previous school for sleeping with students, he asked to be sent to this school.

"Sir, . . . I . . . well, I have to look after the baby. My mother . . ." stammered Mosa.

Mr Merake's eyes flew up to Mosa's from her exposed legs. There was genuine surprise in his face. "What? You had the baby? But I thought . . ."

"No, no, no, sir. I did not have the baby. Well, I mean, I have no baby. What I mean is that my brother died, leaving a child. My mother works, and I have to take care of the child after school." Mosa cursed the English language for getting her into this embarrassing situation. Why does Bones always have to speak English? she seethed.

"Are you saying no, then? Are you giving a teacher a no answer?" Bones asked, anger in his eyes.

"No, sir. I am not saying no, sir. I cannot say no to a teacher, sir. Perhaps I can ask Johannah to come with me to your house. That way, we will finish fast, sir." Johannah was a classmate, and her name just popped into Mosa's head.

"I am asking you, not Johannah. Do you think I am so stupid that I would not know if two people were needed?" he retorted, glaring angrily at her. He was so close she could smell his beer-flavoured breath. She wanted to spit at him, and he must have seen the look of hatred in her eyes.

"Sir, my brother has just died. My mother says we must be inside the yard before sunset to avoid *sefifi*, I mean bad luck," she pleaded.

Just then, Ms Bontsi came in. She looked at both of them, and without any sign of surprise, told Bones to leave the child alone. The laughter in her eyes showed that she did not really care how the matter was finally resolved. To her, and many other women teachers in the school, being pressured into sex with a teacher was just one of the many hurdles of attaining secondary education. She'd probably had to deal with similar encounters in her days as a student – and even as a teacher. Bones stormed, out and Mosa breathed a sigh of relief. A bit prematurely, as it turned out later.

The following day, during the science lesson, Bones made a great effort at ignoring Mosa. He looked right through her raised hand. But he engaged the class in lively discussions and made a show of being happy with the entire class. Happy to have escaped from the man's lecherous clutches, Mosa did not feel too hurt by this attitude. But at the end of the lesson, Bones had his revenge.

"Sadidi," he asked a girl sitting in front of Mosa, "will you help me carry these books to the staffroom, please? I would ask Mosa, but she has a problem. She cannot carry books because she has a baby. That is what she told me yesterday when I asked her for help. Or do I have the story wrong? Perhaps she said the baby died. What did you say, Mosa? Can you explain to the class, please?" His eyes flashed with triumph; his voice dripped with meanness.

Mosa looked down and said nothing. First there was a hush, then a snicker from Khumo that rolled around the classroom and exploded into a burst of laughter. Mosa was mortified. She looked up enough to see Sinah's sympathetic glance; otherwise, the class was lapping up Bones's ridicule, being part of it. She knew that it was partly self-preservation on the part of most of them, especially the girls. She also knew that no one believed she had refused to help a teacher carry books to the staffroom; they all knew what it was she refused to do.

"Well, Mosa, am I making all this up? Tell the class. Let it not be said that I made up a story about you. Tell the class about the baby," Bones taunted, an evil grin playing on his lips.

"No, sir, the child is not dead. It is the father who died. My brother . . ."

"Oh, I see. I had it wrong. It is the father who died. Class, the child did not die. I apologise for the confusion I have caused." He frowned with mock concern and sympathy, taunting Mosa. "The child is still there and you have to take care of it: is that right?"

Mosa was fuming with anger and a feeling of helplessness. "Sir, my brother is dead. He left behind a daughter. It is that daughter I am talking about. I do not know what is funny about my brother being dead. I do not know how you all can laugh at something like that. And I am sorry, sir. Excuse me, sir. I do not feel well. I need to go outside." Without waiting for a response, Mosa stood up and left the classroom, determined not to cry in front of Bones.

The class grew quiet. Bones tried to make fun of the situation, but even Khumo could not bring himself to respond to the weak jokes. All hung their heads in shame. Now the teacher's pleasant mood turned nasty as he issued harsh commands, threatened and waved his stick about, which he called *senwamadi*: the blood drinker. When the lesson was finally over, everyone was happy that Mr Mitchell would be the next teacher: he was funny and nice to everyone, if a bit silly at times.

Bones left the class seething. He did not understand why Mosa, after the open secret of her abortion, could possibly think she was too good for him. The arrogant slut: he had expected her to surrender to his advances; she was damaged goods anyway. Here he was, willing to mess around with an unclean girl, and she thought herself too good for him. He promised to make her life hell in class.

Mosa went back into class but hardly participated for the rest of the day. She was angry but felt impotent. At the end of the school day, to avoid having to be part of any of the many streams of students walking home, she decided to use her precious P1.00 to pay for a taxi home. But once in the taxi, she asked that she be taken to the centre of the village, a direction opposite to that for her own home. She had made up her mind to go to Kagiso Law Office.

The Kagiso Law Office was housed in an old building squeezed between the village post office and a primary school. The building was an old granary converted to office space. The office provided counselling and legal advice to women and children. It had been established two years previously, and although Mosa had done research there once for a Social Studies assignment, she felt nervous about going there. Going there had a certain risk to it: there were all kinds of rumours about the office, and being seen entering its doors could cause speculation about the nature of one's problems. There were many who believed that family problems should be solved within the family and that involving strangers was a foreign idea that should be resisted at all costs. With uncles, brothers, fathers, headmen and the chief providing time-tested structures for dealing with any problems women and children could possibly have, the law office, staffed by young women, was seen as not only unnecessary but dangerous. Before you knew it women would not be listening to their husbands, and talking about rights and other strange ideas.

Mosa was aware of the outrage the setting up of the office had caused in the village. Theirs was perhaps the fourth in the country, but the resistance to the office seemed to gather momentum whenever a new one opened its doors.

She knocked once, and walked in before she had time to change her mind. She wanted to talk and felt that perhaps there would be someone to talk to there. She wanted to talk about her dead brothers, her pregnancy and her abortion. But above all, she wanted to talk about Mr Merake and his behaviour towards female students. She felt wronged, but could not even clearly articulate her complaint.

Across the room was a bored-looking young woman, perhaps her own age, licking stamps and sticking them on to envelopes. Just then, another woman emerged from one of the offices.

"*Ao*, school child, you have come to visit us?" she said with a broad smile. "We welcome you: sit down. I will be with you shortly."

Although feeling a bit patronised by the address, Mosa felt comforted by the warm welcome. She wanted to tell the woman that she did not want to see a lawyer: she had heard that the office had a social worker, and she just wanted to talk. She had never met a lawyer, and was apprehensive about meeting one. She was not sure whether any law had been broken by anyone, and did not want to seem ignorant before a lawyer. So she would prefer a social worker. Her Social Studies teacher had told them that a social worker was a person who listens to your problems, tells no one about them and gives you advice. That is the kind of person she was looking for today: like the Guidance and Counselling teacher at her school was supposed to be. Except that she did not trust the Guidance and Counselling teacher not to tell the rest of her colleagues if she confided in her. But before she could tell the smiling woman this, she had ducked back into her office.

Mosa settled down and began reading a pamphlet about property rights of married women, which she had found on the couch beside her. Then another woman emerged from yet another office and called out for one of the waiting women. Mosa looked up and froze. In front of her was a woman she had seen over the weekend in the company of Mr Merake and Mr Kgaka, laughing and sharing a drink at a local restaurant. Immediately she felt betrayed: how could this woman work here and dispense all manner of advice when she was a friend of the likes of Bones? As the woman retreated into her office, Mosa stood up and left. As she walked out through the gates, her eyes clouded over with tears of frustration. She willed the tears to stop, straightened her back and walked proudly away.

Mosa decided she was going to get out of the Merake mess in the same way she had survived her problems of the previous school term. It had taken her a whole month then to realise she had been a fool. By that time she was pregnant and alone. No, she was not going to go through that again. She was never going to be a fool again.

The foolishness had begun, ironically enough, at a one-day seminar for students, addressed by nurses, the police, a church group and some well-meaning teachers. Ms Wilson and Mrs Makhikhi, two really nice teachers, had wanted leading community figures to come and talk to the students about peer pressure, teenage pregnancy, HIV and other dangers in the life of young people. As the students filed into the hall, they chattered and dragged chairs noisily.

Mosa remembered the day vividly. She was walking through the door when she felt a piece of paper being thrust into her hand. She looked up to see a young police officer smiling at her and winking. It was not until she was sitting down that she got a chance to read the short note. Her heart began to race. She looked up at the podium to see the speakers being led to their chairs.

First, two nurses took their places. Then Reverend Modise of the High Mountain Apostolic Church of Christ the King – in his trademark purple robe – and his wife were led to their seats. There seemed to be a bit of confusion as to whether the wife should be seated at the head table, seeing as she was not one of the speakers. But in the end, that is where she stayed, simply because no one had ever seen Reverend Modise in public without his wife. She was not called Mrs A. S. – Apron String – for nothing. The joke was that there were not twelve but thirteen ribbons to his apron, representing the twelve disciples and Mrs Modise.

When the police officer strode on to the podium in his smart uniform, Mosa began to wonder whether she had imagined he gave her the note. He was followed by a tall, big man, also in police uniform. The younger office stopped, turned to the older one and saluted. He took off his hat and put it under his arm. Then, in a voice that filled the hall, he called out, "Your chair awaits you, sir," and waved his superior to his chair.

During the opening prayer, Constable Kamane, for that was the young officer's name, searched the room for the girl. He had brought three notes, and if he did not catch anything with the first one, he would try again with a second, after the tea break. The third would be handed out after the lunch break if he failed with notes one and two. Then he spotted her: the girl with the searching eyes upon him. It had to be her.

Mosa, for her part, was confused but elated. The words of the note were "You are very beautiful. I know I should not be sending you this note, but your face is like the moon and your eyes are like stars. I fell in love with you last week." Mosa clutched the note and felt her palm sweating. She imagined the words melting off the crumpled page: all that love, all those beautiful words, being absorbed into her hand, travelling all the way to her heart. She did not know how to respond, so she looked down briefly.

The seminar passed in a blur of words. The pain of the death of her brother Thabo was eased somewhat. The knowledge that Pule was dying was somehow less painful. Someone had noticed her in a crowd and chosen her. She was afraid and happy at the same time. A police officer, in all his magnificence, thought her beautiful. He was not the first man to show interest in her, but no one had ever done it in such style, with such beautiful words.

Mosa was to learn later, from Constable Moreki, a friend of Constable Kamane, that Constable Pako Kamane had left the police station vowing to his colleagues that he was going to get himself a small steenbok – their name for a student girlfriend – at the school. He had not wanted to accompany the boss because he, Detective Superintendent Basha, loved to be saluted in public even when it was not necessary, just to humiliate juniors. The younger man had decided that if he were going to suffer his boss's company, he would set up a steenbok trap and hope for the best.

By the time she found out all this, she had had unprotected sex with Pako and was pregnant. She had not even realised she was having sex until it was too late; that was how naïve she was. If she had not been so angry with him, Mosa would have admitted that the guy was a great actor. When she found out she was pregnant, Mosa disappeared from home and went to live with a girlfriend, Karabo, in Morwalo, a village fifty kilometres away from her own. It was through Karabo's help that she had the pregnancy terminated. She knew she owed Karabo a lot, but how does one thank another person for something like that? Everyone thought she had been living with

Pako, and she saw no reason to correct the error.

Mosa was determined that next time she went into a relationship, if ever, it would be on her terms. No one was ever going to make her do anything she was not willing to do. As for Bones, she was going to get him, she promised herself. How this would happen she did not yet know, but she would make sure he got his just deserts.

Mosa had convinced the headmaster to admit her back into school despite having been absent for more than twenty days. Before then, she had been racking her brain, trying to find a good reason for her long absence from school. Then her mother had asked her to go and collect the death certificates for her two brothers from the local births, deaths and marriage office, six kilometres away, in the centre of the village.

"Why do you need the death certificates? It is not as if they ever had any birth certificates to start with." Mosa was not too keen on going into public just yet, because she was not ready for looks from people who knew about the loss of her brother or about the abortion. It had been a week since Pule's funeral.

"Can someone show me just one child these days who will do what she is asked without turning the whole thing into a political debate?"

Mosa apologised and went down to the local administration office to fetch the certificates. As she walked, only one thought occupied her mind: how to get back to school. She acknowledged friends' greetings by hardly glancing at the friends: her earlier concern about being seen in public was not in her mind at all now.

"At the rate young people are dying, schools are going to end up empty," the young clerk said as he handed her the two certificates.

Mosa stood there stunned, not by the young woman's callous remark but by the idea that it suddenly brought into her head. She asked the clerk to make photocopies of the certificates, and the young woman obliged without hesitation.

The following day, Mosa found an opportunity to carry out her plan. It was late in the morning. Stan had gone off to school, her mother had gone to work, and little Nunu was having her mid-morning nap. Mosa fetched a writing pad from her school satchel, which she had not opened in ages, and sat down to write. After three or four attempts, which she tore up and crumpled on the floor, she finally read the final version:

Dear Mr Kgaka,
Bana-Ba-Phefo High School

I write this letter in the hope that you will find it in your heart to listen to my plea.

My daughter, Mosa Selato, has been absent from school for an unusually long period. I am aware that, according to the rules of the school and education department, my daughter should not be allowed to return to school. But after you have learned about the reasons for her long absence, maybe you will reconsider and allow her to return.

My two sons Thabo and Pule had died from AIDS. During their long illness, they suffered from chest infections, especially TB. Because of the small house we live in, it was necessary to send Mosa away to live with relatives for fear that she might be infected. At the time, Mosa's brother Stan was living with a kind teacher. You will see from the death certificates enclosed that all this is true.

I sincerely hope that you will find it in your heart to take pity on a family that is in mourning.

Yours sincerely,
Mara Selato

The following day, armed with the envelope containing the letter and photocopied certificates, Mosa set off for the school. When she arrived, her heart began to tug. Walking past classrooms, she saw serious heads bowed, and heard the murmuring of discussions, and answers being called out. Oh, how she missed being there.

She knocked on the headmaster's door. After a short pause, he said, "Come inside."

"Good morning, Mr Kgaka."

The headmaster looked up from a sheaf of documents he had been reading, surprised.

"Mr Kgaka, I am –"

"The Selato girl!" he cut her short. "I thought you had disappeared from the face of the earth."

Mosa smiled shyly and handed him the letter. Within minutes, she emerged from the headmaster's with a letter re-admitting her. She also still had in her hand her successful forgery to Mr Kgaka and the copies of the death certificates. The headmaster had wanted to file them, but she begged him not to: the documents contained confidential information, she had pleaded. "AIDS is everywhere, but people still do not want to talk about it. What would happen if your secretary read this, sir? The whole school would know. I came to you because I trusted you."

All of this was nonsense, of course: Mosa despised the lecherous Seramane. In the end, her sincere tone and pleading eyes worked. She was back at school, and there was no record of how that had happened.

Now, Mosa walked home, looking forward to seeing Stan at home again. Hoping for another story. But more importantly wanting to talk with Stan.

She was walking into the yard with all these thoughts swimming about in her head, like the tadpoles in her drinking water. Then she saw the car, but before she could wave to Mr Mitchell, he drove off in a hurry.

CHAPTER 10

If I were to give violence a colour, what would it be? Stan wondered to himself. He had a thing about colours, and was always trying to give situations, moods and characters colours. Would it be white? The colour of pretence? The colour of "no commitment"? The colour of "see no evil"? No, he told himself: I did see evil, lots of evil. What about red? The colour of blood. Or would I say black, the colour of nothingness? The colour of no light. The colour of death. But then perhaps I should settle for purple, a deep purple. Red, but more than red. A thick, threatening, purplish red. Not quite black, but yet close to the edge. For me, definitely not white, for I cannot pretend.

Perhaps the colour depends on the viewer. I would definitely settle for purple. Had I not stepped in, there would have been black.

But what colour would he say? The "he" was Solomon Moloisa, a man whose name Stan could not say even to himself. He had been his mother's lover for a very short but memorable period.

What colour would my mother say? Surely the colour would be influenced by her feelings for him at the time. A red tinted with blue hues for love, and pinks for hope? And what about him? Perhaps he would have said a strong, dark green, for selfishness, mixed with a thick brown, for contempt for all women.

There seemed to be not a day that his mind did not go back to that night. He wanted to talk with someone about what had happened – like his sister, but they had lost the ability to communicate a long time ago. They had grown apart. He sensed a deep anger in her. Sometimes he felt included in that anger. He wanted to step forward, to reach out and massage the anger out, but he was afraid he would be engulfed, consumed.

Stan was going home for the weekend. He stood up and packed his small bag rather slowly, as if he could delay the departure. But Mr Mitchell was due to arrive any minute, and would be driving him over, as planned. Stan was not looking forward to explaining to Mr Mitchell the reasons for his going away, and a part of him was not eager to go home. As much as he was looking forward to being with his family, he was not too keen on continuing the association with Mr Namane that had started the previous weekend.

Mr Mitchell, Stan's benefactor and mathematics teacher, had, in Stan's view, this irritating habit, of all Americans of asking questions. He never seemed to be able to read a face to realise that questions were not welcome. The more Stan tried to avoid answering his questions, the more he seemed to think he needed to ask them. Lowering his head and shifting his right foot about, a technique that worked with any adult Motswana, just seemed to bring an earnest look on Mr Mitchell's face and the inevitable "You can talk to me, Stan."

Stan had developed various ways of putting him off, but some of his methods were losing their effectiveness. He had learned, for example, that appearing to be in control and happy generally kept the questions away. Another tactic of avoidance was to pretend that explaining in English was too hard for him. But his English had improved over the months, and so he had to abandon that little trick. Sometimes pretending to be lost for words seemed to invite even more questions. Having lived with a succession of three white teachers and associated with even more, he was convinced they were an asking race. Deep down, he knew he could simply tell Mr Mitchell that he did not want to talk about his problems. He knew Mr Mitch would respect his wishes. But he had been raised not to say these things to an adult. For this weekend visit, he had decided that claiming to want to spend time with his depressed mother was his best bet. Bonding was a concept Mr Mitchell would understand.

Stan had just turned sixteen when he moved in with Mr Mitchell, and did not regret a minute of it. Mr Mitchell was kind to him, and demonstrated in many ways that he cared about him and wanted the best for him. It is because Stan was both intelligent and poor that he had been accommodated by these good Samaritans. With a year to go before graduating from high school, he felt fully prepared to write the final examinations that would determine whether or not he went to university.

Living with people from another culture, however, had its small complications. Consequently, he has learned over the years to separate his two lives. At first, he told his benefactors everything about his family. When they told him about weekends at beaches and visits to dentists, he told them about the baby who was buried in his aunt's house and the dead grandmother who came to his mother in her dreams. He told them about his neighbour who could cure blindness by cleaning the affected eyes with his tongue. It was when Stan realised that the stories were received with either scepticism or horror that he began to edit the information.

Now he was managing successfully to live two separate lives, and had even begun to question some of his own stories. He had therefore kept quiet about the details of the previous weekend's rituals at home, and had hidden the physical evidence from Mr Mitchell. The scars were still very visible, and hiding them from Mr Mitchell had been a challenge.

He had finished packing and was lying on his bed with his eyes closed, when he heard Mr Mitchell calling, "Stan! Stanley, are you home?" The first of many questions for the day.

Mr Mitchell had long ago assumed that Stan was short for Stanley. Just like he had decided that Bill's real name was William. No one in the class, including Bill himself, had figured out why until the arrival of a new teacher, Mr William Hunt. Mr Mitchell had promptly begun to call his new colleague Bill, and Mr Hunt had not seemed surprised. The students had since figured out that in America, if your name is William, you get called Bill as well, and if your name is Bill, you also get called William.

"I'm ready, Mr Mitch!" answered Stan with an enthusiasm he did not really feel. "I'll be with you in a sec."

Stan took one last sweeping look at his room to make sure he was not leaving anything important behind. He cast a wistful look at the bed, knowing that he would miss it during the next two nights. He was, however, looking forward to seeing Nunu. He had not realised how much he loved the kid until her father died. He had never really even looked at her before. She was this little person who was always around when he went to visit, but then she had no real meaning for him, until after the funeral. Now he simply adored her. He was also looking forward to talking to Mosa, although he was apprehensive about that. They had not been able to talk last weekend. Other things came up, and before he knew it, the weekend was over. Hopefully, this second weekend home would provide them with an opportunity to be together and talk.

Mosa told him during the week at school that a date had been set for the ceremony to appease the ancestors and that he had to come home for a discussion about that. He expected another night of fumes and razors.

On the way home, Mr Mitchell tried to get some information from Stan about his sister. Is she okay? Will she be serious with school now that she has been given a second chance? What are they going to do with the police officer for what he did? Mitch jumped from question to question like a lizard skipping from rock to rock, but did not seem to be aware of this. Stan really did not have a clue about what was in Mosa's head. He had lost his sister some time during the past two years. The only question he could answer without a problem, but did not, was the one about the constable. The simple answer was: nothing. Nothing happens to these men, and Mitch had been around long enough to know that. Mara did not have the might to go against a police officer, even one of the lowly rank of constable. And what could possibly be done to him? Mosa was eighteen years old at the time: two years older than the age at which the law calls that rape. And even if she had been fourteen, nothing ever happens to these men.

As they drove into the yard, Mara was already home, having knocked off a bit earlier than usual. The sun was about to set, but the day was still hot. Mara was talking to Mma Seileng across the fence. The neighbour, a rather large woman, had pulled her dress down to her waist to cool down. Her large breasts were hanging down almost all the way over her sweaty belly, which she kept on wiping with her head scarf, lifting her breasts with one hand to wipe underneath them.

Mr Mitchell, even after five years in the country, was still uncomfortable in the presence of exposed breasts, and did not know where to look as he walked towards the two women. He had to greet them; otherwise, he would be thought rude. He could not shout at them from where he was because that, too, would be rude. He had to approach, but there were those breasts: what was he to do?

The large woman was totally oblivious to his discomfort. Stan smiled to himself and wondered what it was about white people that made them think nothing of exposed thighs but that made them go red over breasts. To him, breasts were nothing but a source of food for babies. He had never seen white women breastfeeding, and wondered how they could bring themselves to do it if they had such crazy ideas about breasts.

As the embarrassed teacher approached, the neighbour lifted her breasts as if presenting them to Mr Mitchell, and declared proudly, "Me feed six children with them these. Six strong children. Grow strong. Now these tired and not use. Just make me hot all over. How you are, Mr Mitch?"

Mr Mitch said a quick hello and did an even quicker about-turn. Stan chuckled to himself as his benefactor drove off. They had not even agreed on a pick-up time for Sunday. He was still laughing when Mosa walked in from school.

"What's with Mr Mitch?" Mosa asked him.

"Mma-Seileng's breasts," Stan pointed with his head. "They are too much for him. He thinks breasts should be covered at all times."

"I kind of agree with Mr Mitch," Mosa said. "But then it is not as if Mma-Seileng is out in the street; I mean, she is in her yard, talking with her neighbour."

"Well, Mr Mitch thinks that breasts are kind of private."

"But he does not seem to mind Ms Valley's underpants, which she passes for shorts! It is sometimes confusing as to what white people consider appropriate and what they consider inappropriate. I guess we confuse them too," Mosa said, chuckling.

"I guess Mr Mitch would have had little trouble if Mma-Seileng had covered her top and worn a pair of hotpants."

This brought another chuckle from Mosa. The idea of Mma-Seileng's fat thighs exposed was both indecent and simply funny.

With this introduction to the evening, Mosa was already feeling better. She never thought the day would end with her laughing at all. Her mother watched them from the corner of a twinkling eye, too far to hear what they were saying but happy that they were laughing together. This had not happened in a long time. Mosa went next door to Mma-Sadibo's house to fetch Nunu.

Stan picked up an axe and went outside to chop some wood. Some huge logs still remained from the funeral. There was a rhythm of family from these simple tasks that warmed Mara's heart.

Only the following day did Mara have the chance to sit down and talk to Stan about why she wanted him home that weekend. No diviner was scheduled to visit them that night, so after dinner, Mosa and Stan had retreated to a corner of the yard, and under the full moon, talked and talked and talked. Mara had gone to bed leaving them still there. She had persuaded Nunu to come in with her, aware that the two siblings needed time alone. At times, she thought she could hear one or both of them crying, then no: it was laughter she was hearing. She let them be and went to bed. The following morning, they did not get up until mid-morning. Mara had decided to let them sleep, and after dropping off Nunu at Mma-Saebo's, got dressed and went off to the funeral of Mr Mosenki, in the neighbourhood. Sad as it was, it was still a relief to attend the funeral of a person who had died after a full life instead of the increasingly common funerals of young people.

The night fell and the moon rose, the smells of evening meals filled the air, the clank of dishes sounded, and the village settled down. There was the smell of biltong being roasted over coals from Mma-Mogotsi's yard, and the unmistakable aroma of *rothwe*, a popular wild spinach, from the yard next door. Stan and Mosa lay side by side in the open air, quiet, watching the stars.

"Stan, please make me laugh," Mosa said, and so began a conversation that would last until the early hours of the morning.

"First, let us discuss why you are so angry," Stan said, deciding to move in before he lost his nerve: to move forward, despite his fear of what lay there.

"Okay. But only if you promise to tell me why you are so afraid of yourself," countered Mosa.

"Me afraid of myself? What are you talking about, sis'?"

"First things first. Why am I angry? I am angry because you have shut me out of your life, because I am a woman and you are a man. I am angry because she is suffering so much and deserves better than this. I am angry because I am afraid I will end up like her. Now I am really angry because I nearly ended up like her." Mosa was lying on her side, staring straight at her brother. Because of the time of day, his features were undefined, and there was not enough light to see the eyes clearly, but there was enough to see a frown, to perceive a slight angling of the head.

"Do you want to go back to that last bit?" Stan asked gently. "Can

104

you talk about it?" He wanted to have that door opened, but yet he was afraid of what lay beyond.

"Oh, Stan, we used to talk and laugh. We used to be each other's strengths. I used to help you with your homework, just as you used to help me with cooking, even as the neighbours laughed at you for doing girl's work. We used to laugh and talk and even cry together. What happened?"

"We grew up, Mosa. You became a woman and I became a man. Well, not quite, but close enough. Everything around us told us we were different, that we shared nothing. We became secretive with each other, and we grew apart. Also, I went away." This last he said as if offering an apology.

As they spoke, the darkness tried to creep in, but the moon rose to chase it away: an orange, magical disk, floating and suspended. Mosa had not answered Stan's question. She did not know whether she could talk to him about that; she was not even sure she could talk to herself about it. There were painful parts she kept cutting, out even from herself. She was still to force herself to confront the extent of the damage since she had fallen to earth with her mangled, one-wheeled bicycle.

"Tell me about that last time he hit her," she whispered.

Stan was quiet for a long time. He had not expected that question, but when he did speak, he was full of pain and sadness. He told her how he never liked him in the first place. He came in and took over the house. His smell permeated every room. His body filled the house. Even when they sat under a tree, he seemed to take over the entire shade, sucking in the cool, dark patches and leaving Stan with a hotness he could not explain. He was not really a big man, but he had seemed to occupy more space than any other visitor. His voice was loud. What she ever saw in him he would never know. It was not even as if he helped support her or the children. From the children, he had demanded prompt responses to his orders. "Bring me some water, boy!" he would bark. Stan had seen him slap her about a few times and had been filled with rage. He was sure Mosa and the others were aware of this. The walls between the two rooms were thin, so her nightly sobs were audible to all of them. The relationship had not lasted even a year, but the hurt it left behind would last for decades.

Mosa listened. That last night, he arrived when Stan was already asleep. Mosa was staying over with some relative, and the older boys were away at Maruping's cattlepost. He banged on the door, demanding that it be opened. Mma-Pule must have been asleep, because it was a while before Stan, who was awake now, heard his mother fiddling with the door. He was expecting the door to creak open, but suddenly, with a vicious howl that made him sit up in bed, the man kicked the door in. Mma-Pule screamed, and Stan felt his body stiffen with a sudden tension. Next, he heard repeated banging against the wall, and knew without a doubt it was his mother's head hitting against the concrete wall, like a cracking watermelon. He jumped out of bed, ran outside to the firewood area and picked up the axe leaning against a log. He ran back inside, through the door, which was now dangling on one hinge. He walked into his mother's room and, without a word, raised the axe. As he swung it high, the man turned around, arms raised for protection. The axe landed on the man's arm with a sickening cracking sound. Fury. Black. Red. Swirls of deep purple. His heart was now in his head, pounding, about to explode.

"The monster screamed. I screamed. Mma screamed and collapsed. There was blood everywhere. I raised the axe again, but just then I guess sanity came back. I lowered it and told him to leave. I told him if he ever set foot in our yard again I would kill him. And, Mosa, I meant it. I was so full of hatred, so full of rage." Stan broke off and was quiet for a while.

"He whimpered with pain and begged me to give him something to stem the flow of the blood. I felt no pity. It was as if he were not human. I told him once more to leave, and he left. I went over to Mma and tried to stop the bleeding. I could not. Her head seemed smashed in. Her arms looked broken. I walked over to Rra-Noko's to ask for help. He drove her over to the hospital. She was whimpering with pain."

Mosa knew most of the rest. Her mother stayed in hospital for three weeks. She cried every time Stan came to visit. Her attacker was admitted to the same hospital. He never set foot in their home again. The matter was never discussed, and but for the scar on Mma's head, it is as if it had never happened. But the incident left deeper scars. For Stan, it had exposed his own capacity for violence. He would rather have been spared that knowledge about himself. For Mara, it had marked the end of all intimate relationships with men. And Mosa had been left thinking it could happen to her. What had made her mother, a gentle, loving woman, fall for that kind of man? What made the many women she knew fall for and stay with men who abused and injured them? Perhaps her mother had been drawn to Solomon Moloisa because he had no wife, mistress or children to drag into the relationship. And even Mosa had to admit that when he was sober, which was unfortunately not very often, he could be charming and considerate.

Mosa had always known about Uncle Maruping's periodic battering of his wife. She had served tea on countless occasions to family members gathered to hear Mma-Ranko's complaints. It was surprising how much one could hear as one went back and forth between the fireplace and the assembled elders. It seemed that whenever he was home on leave from work, Mma-Ranko ended up running away half naked to one of his relatives. The meetings did not seem to help. Tea was drunk, Mma-Ranko was urged to be a better wife and Rra-Ranko was asked to refrain from excessive chastisement of his wife. Everybody went home, and the best Mma-Ranko could hope for was a few weeks of peace until the next time.

So violence of men towards their wives and partners was not foreign to Stan and Mosa. They had seen plenty of evidence of what happens behind closed doors at night. Still, they had not expected that such a thing would ever happen in their own home.

Stan's story was over, and brother and sister wiped the tears from their cheeks.

"Both died of AIDS," Mosa said without preamble.

Stan's mind raced from the earlier topic to the new one.

Who? he wanted to scream. But he knew who his sister was talking about. He felt that he was being dragged along without an opportunity to slow down the discussion. "I thought you believed all that stuff about them being bewitched. Did you not say that Thabo slept with an unclean woman?"

Mosa arrested her brother with her stare. The moon had risen higher, and was brighter, and they could see each other clearly now.

"No, they died of AIDS as surely as I am lying here. I did not have the courage to admit it because I could not face the truth. As for what mother believes, I see no reason to challenge her just for the sake of challenging her. The part I do not like is blaming someone for your ills. For example, I do not believe Auntie Lesedi ever bewitched us.

107

I think it is sad that mother believes that. That belief broke up a very special relationship."

"I did not know that about Auntie Lesedi. Did mother tell you that?"

"Why do you think they do not speak any more? How can you be so blind, *Ntate*? Where do you think the distance between our families comes from?"

"Remember: I do not live here, so there are things that pass me by. So tell me how you know all this."

"Stan, it is pretty obvious that Mma believes we have been bewitched, right? Hopping from diviner to diviner over the past three years. Sometimes I have gone with her and sometimes I have not. Sometimes you, too, have been there. We have had the ZCC, the Christian Apostolic Church, the Church of Zion, the Church of Saint Peter, all of them coming over to do all kinds of blessings and exorcisms. Some have dug up evil medicines supposedly planted by enemies. Others have declared that baptism in their church is the only way out. Remember how one so-called prophet bit into Thabo to suck out *sejeso*? I think the same thing happened to Pule. And some of the treatments were outright harmful, as far as I'm concerned. But I live with mother, and you don't. You cannot take away her belief without replacing it with something else. If I accepted that they were going to die anyway, how would it help her if I told her not to do any of the things that gave her some comfort?"

Stan was shaking his head. "What part do you believe in and what part do you not believe in, then? Is it really possible to separate these things out?"

"Let's take last weekend, for example. I think it is fairly harmless. The razor cutting is no more painful than a needle at the hospital. Anyway, we all already believed that we needed to get together and work together as a family. Mma wanted desperately to bring us together, hoping that the ceremony would do just that."

"But, Mosa, it cost P600: two months salary! And it's not over yet. A cow still has to be slaughtered! A pregnant cow! Jesus! Be serious!" Stan was almost shouting. This sister of his had dragged him from a comfort zone he had created over the past two years, forcing him to open his eyes, to see, to feel. But he was not sure he wanted to do that. He was not prepared for what was there to be seen, to be felt.

Mosa went on: "Ask your know-it-all Mr Mitchell how much

family counselling costs where he comes from. I bet you he will tell you it is not cheap."

"What has he got to do with this? And aren't you being unfair to him? He has never tried to push his beliefs on to you, or even me! I feel you are being really unfair, sis'."

"Stan be honest, at least to yourself. You are sounding more and more like him. There is nothing wrong with that, except that you have the wrong environment for that kind of thinking. But yes, you are right. I am being unfair. Perhaps even ungrateful. But listen." She took a deep breath as if to slow her own thoughts down – and allow Stan to catch up.

"Mma needs to be helped out of this deep pit of depression she is in. God knows we need help too. Mrs Modisane, the Guidance and Counselling teacher, would agree with that, at least. Mr Namane is a good way out. He is a good way out. I suggested him to her because he is not the kind that blames anyone for anyone's troubles. The ceremony will be good for her and for us as well. It will be something positive after the two funerals. It is a building ceremony. Do you understand? Can you see it in those terms? We have to work on mother to drop some of this negativity. We also have to get her to talk to Aunt Lesedi again. Somehow we have to do it. Who knows? Perhaps the ancestors can help there. What other way is there? My God, life is so confusing! At school, I am taught about science and how the world works from that point of view! I get home, and I have to deal with witchdoctors and ancestors, and somehow we are supposed to stay sane! I read all these books that could be about life on another planet altogether, and, Stan, sometimes I feel like I am losing it!"

Brother and sister half sat, half lay under the bright moon, talking and talking. Stan was amazed at Mosa's sharp mind and sense of purpose. They had not really talked for years, he realised. Then she shocked him again: "I think Nunu is safe. She has never been a sickly child. And she is old enough for us to have noticed by now. I don't think she has AIDS . . ."

Stan said nothing. He had not even thought about this.

"But, I cannot be so sure about myself."

"*What*?" Stan almost leaped off the ground.

"Listen, brother of mine. How can you be both smart and stupid at the same time? Surely you should have been worried by now? I was pregnant. That means that I had sex. That means I had unprotected sex." Mosa was crying. Her words seemed to hang in the air even after she had closed her mouth. She had sounded loud even though she had not raised her voice. There was desperation in the urgent and brutal truth she had just uttered.

"Come here, Mosa. Come." He pulled her towards him and held her. "Listen, I am here. You can talk to me. You know you have always been the most special person to me. Just remember you will not know for sure until you are tested." His mouth was moving but he did not know what he was saying. He felt like he was stumbling forward. He was overwhelmed, by loving his sister and wanting the best for her, by his own stupidity for not realising the extent of her anguish. By fear and hope and a mixture of all kinds of emotions.

"Why, Stan? Why am I so stupid? How could I have fallen for that nonsense? Why?"

"Perhaps because you desperately wanted to be loved when all our mother's loving was going to the dying. Perhaps because I turned to Mr Mitch and material things when I needed love. And he does care about me. He does care, and that eased my pain. I had distractions to fill my time. I had television, football, trips to Gaborone. Perhaps we are all vulnerable at one time or another. You are the smartest person I know, Mosa: if you fell for that, you had no chance."

"No: I did have a chance. I need to accept my own role in this to be able to heal. Victims are rescued. I cannot wait to be rescued. You always have a choice, I think. Choosing the easiest and most obvious way out would be my undoing." Her voice was low, and Stan had to strain to hear her. She was really speaking to herself, coming to terms with her own actions even as she was telling him.

Then Mosa told him about the fear and the loneliness when she found out she was pregnant. She told him of the desperation she felt. How foolish she felt; still feels. The rejection by Pako. The jokes behind her back, which she heard about precisely because she was meant to. She told him of the abortion: the mess, the fear, the madness. The inner conflicts she felt. She also told him about the friend who had stood by her all that time.

Stan listened, tears rolling down his face. He held his sister tight and promised her that he would always be there for her. They both cried and cried. For their two dead brothers. For their lonely mother. For

110

themselves. For love and for the lack of love. For little Nunu, who had sprung from death. They cried for the sad episodes in their life through which they had drifted apart.

When she thought it was safe once more to use her voice, Mosa wiped her tears and said, "What do you think I should do – about a test?"

Stan felt some strength come back to him. He straightened his back to assume a more positive posture. "First, you have to wait until you are strong enough to face the truth. Then you need counselling. I understand there are places where you can go to get pre-test counselling: yes, I think that is what it is called. Then you can take the test. I want to be there with you when you do. You are never, ever going through something like this alone."

Mosa told Stan about Mr Merake molesting her at the photocopying machine and then humiliating her in the classroom. Stan had heard stories about Bones but never anything so direct. He was at a loss for words, and as a male, felt implicated. He would have to tell Mr Mitch about his sister's ordeal and ask him what could be done. He knew that little or no support could be expected from the headmaster, who was an even bigger offender than Bones and Van Heerden put together. The latest he had heard was that he watched the girls washing in the hostels under the pretext that he was ensuring that they did a good job of it. The sad thing was that he was not the only headmaster doing that, according to stories from other schools: headmasters wielded great power, and knew it. There was even a story of an English teacher who had made an under-age student pregnant. When confronted, he claimed he did not think that he had done anything wrong because everyone was doing it. He thought it was the way things worked in Botswana.

As the two swapped these stories, they realised the powerlessness of girls in the face of abuse of power. That people in the system could continue to pretend they were not aware of what was happening was unbelievable. But brother and sister both knew that many of the decision makers within the education bureaucracy had been teachers themselves at one time. There were all kinds of stories, for example, about a Regional Education Officer, a respected man in his mid-fifties. He visited schools within the district, including Bana-Ba-Phefo, but was unlikely to ask the kind of questions that would force him to do anything about the situation lest someone reminded him of his own

111

deeds of, say, ten or fifteen years before. There were always skeletal remains of this behaviour, and none of these men in a supervisory role would dare open any cupboard.

Brother and sister considered all this as they went over names of possible allies: teachers they could go to for help. But no matter how they looked at it, they both agreed, the students were alone. Even good Mr Mitchell could not possibly do anything – even with the help of the small group of sympathetic teachers. He had a contract to renew, and getting involved could jeopardise his chances of staying on in Botswana.

"I am going to stay in that school," Mosa said, biting her lip, "and I am going to finish. More importantly, I am going to get a first-class pass. You know why?"

"You tell me why."

"Because I am going 'far and beyon'." Mosa mimicked Uncle Rich so perfectly that Stan had to laugh despite the seriousness of the atmosphere. And Mosa laughed too.

"What makes you remember that?" asked Stan, still laughing. Uncle Rich had left for Zambia when Mosa was about sixteen and had since stopped being a part of their life. Both had never stopped hoping that one day he would show, bearing presents and with a story to tell.

"Because that is what he told me once. He said, 'Moose-Moose, you may be a girl, but you are going to go far and beyon'.' You know something? I believed him at the time. I did not always believe him as I grew older, but at the time I did. Well, he was right: I am going far and beyon', and Bones is not going to stand in my path." Mosa rolled on to her back and stared at the stars, as if looking out for her one-wheel bicycle.

"Let's go back to what you said at the beginning." Stan was bringing her back. "What did you mean when you said I'm afraid of myself?"

"Let me see. You're a very intelligent person, but you are also a sceptic, which is good. But you have been straddling two cultures for such a long time that you are torn between them. You see with two sets of eyes. You have two hearts now. When you were younger, you questioned everything around you. That forced you to think. It forced me to think as well. But I feel that you do not question Mitch's truths enough: you swallow everything he tells you. That is not like you."

"Okay, Ms Psychologist, give me some examples."

"Only if you're not going to be sarcastic."

"Sorry."

"Well, let me see . . . Okay: Mitch tells you that not to say 'thank you' is rude. 'It is not acceptable,' he tells you. And you swallow that; you don't challenge it. You don't say, 'But Mitch, what is important is to acknowledge the gift and to show gratitude.' You don't say, 'But Mitch, when I use two hands to receive what you give me, that, in my culture, is as good as thank you.' You don't say, 'But Mitch, that child is a *Mokalaka*. She presented her hands for you to touch: that is a sign of respect.' You don't challenge him. You don't argue for his recognition of how you and yours communicate." Mosa paused, then went on. "Another example: you have been embarrassed, I can imagine, all week, about the prospect of Mitch seeing the evidence of last week's *phekolo* ritual. Why? Because you don't feel you have the words to explain that. Why? You're smart. You can talk up a storm about anything. Why would you hide that from Mitch? You are afraid of who you are, which is, my little brother, African."

"Are you saying I'm ashamed of being African?" The question was almost a whisper. Stan was not prepared for his sister to think that about him.

"No: I said 'afraid'. But you cannot allow yourself to be afraid. Whether or not you believe in witchcraft, it is all around you. You cannot simply wish it away." Mosa's voice was bold, but she was looking at her brother with softness in her eyes.

"Let me ask you a question," her brother said. "What do you think of Seponono dropping out of school? What is anyone with any sense to make of the stories of *dithokolosi* in that family?"

"I would say, 'Let us look at the facts,'" said Mosa. "Fact: Seponono left school. Fact: Seponono has told more than one person that she is tormented by a *thokolosi*. Fact: Seponono has screamed with fright many nights. Fact: Seponono is not eating well and has lost a lot of weight. Fact: Priests who have been called to exorcise the *thokolosi* have declared failure. Fact: Seponono is not well, whatever your definition of wellness. Fact: Almost everyone believes that Seponono has a *thokolosi* problem."

"So?" Stan asked.

"So, who are you to assume some superior attitude and say there are no *dithokolosi*? That in my view is not the point. The point is that everyone else believes there are *dithokolosi*, and everyone else conducts their life as if there are. Either you treat everyone around you as crazy or you respect their views and accept that they are different. Telling Seponono that there are no *dithokolosi* is not going to help her or her family."

"But what about you, sis'? Do you really think some short, human-like creature with a beard rapes Seponono every night, without being seen by anyone else? I mean, do you really believe that things like that exist? I mean, these are days of computers and going to the moon and discovering new planets." Stan was incredulous.

"Stan, you haven't been listening. First, no, I do not believe in *dithokolosi*. I don't know why I don't believe they exist – or why you don't believe they exist. I think that is the most incredible thing here: our not believing, because almost everyone around us does. If anything, we are the crazy ones. But we cannot lose sight of the fact that most people believe. Everyone was in a panic about frogs that were sucking the blood out of people just a few months ago. There are stories of *dithokolosi* showing up at funerals and disrupting proceedings. You cannot just brush the beliefs of other people aside. Mma-Pule's wellness depends on her getting treatment within that belief system. If you take her to the clinic, they will probably pump her full of some pills, and she will end up walking around like a zombie. I am not rejecting that solution, but she does not want that, and she does not believe pills would help her. She will tell you she does not want her brain deadened. Why can't you accept Rre-Namane as the answer, not for you, not for me, but for her?"

"But why do I have to be part of her treatment if I do not believe in it?"

"Well, because you love her? No, seriously: you are smarter than that. How does it hurt you? Who do you have to prove yourself to that you do not believe in divination and *phekolo*? But it means everything to her. She needs all of us to be part of the treatment. The treatment needs all of us to work, for her, for us."

"I think I am scared, when we get right down to it." Stan paused for a moment before he continued. "I've decided that distance from all this stuff is safer. Now you are telling me I should get closer, get involved. But then what if I end up believing in these things myself? I don't want to go through life ruled by the fear of powers I cannot control. I've seen what happens. I don't want to be afraid of failing a test at school because someone may be bewitching me. I want to be free – please."

"But are you free? If you were free, you would not have tried to hide the results of last weekend from Mr Mitch. If you were free, you would not be afraid. You cannot be free if you're afraid, Stan."

"Oh, come now, Mosa," Stan countered. "No one walks around with those marks like some colourful tattoo. Everyone at school has gone through the treatment at some time or another, but nobody goes around saying, 'Look at my marks; look at my marks.'"

"But the reasons for the two are different," Mosa said, determined to make her point. "You keep it hidden from Mr Mitch because it's a part of you that you're afraid of. Everyone keeps it hidden from everyone else because the treatment has to be kept a secret for it to work. If you did not believe in any of this and you were not afraid of anything, you would not hide it from anyone, especially Mr Mitch. So I believe you when you say you are afraid; I even understand that. But remember: you don't owe Mr Mitch any explanation of who you are. Africa does not need to hide from the Mr Mitches of this world just because they would not approve."

"You're becoming heavy on me now: where does all that come from?"

"Oh, Stan, I am just tired of feeling like I am being taken over by all kinds of forces: teachers, men, foreigners, other students. Even poor Sakanye just has to blow me a kiss and that unnerves me. I know it's not fair or even reasonable. But I feel besieged. It probably has nothing to do with what we are talking about at all. Or perhaps it has to do with all of it. I don't know any more. I'm tired. I feel I've gone through some major growing up these past two years. I feel old, Stan. I need a way to survive the pettiness around me." Mosa's voice was so low that Stan had to strain to hear her; her eyes were assuming a faraway look, as if she were fading into sleep.

"You will survive. You are strong; you are strong," muttered Stan.

"I need strength," Mosa continued, as if Stan had not even said anything. "Lots of strength. But I also need my family. Happy and together. I need your old self; your happy, questioning self. I am going to need your support in the next few weeks. I plan to take the HIV test. I have to take it; I cannot go on not knowing. If it is positive, I guess I will not be going far and beyon', will I now, brother of mine?" She tried to make light of it, but it was clearly a matter of great importance. "Not the kind of far and beyon' I had in mind, anyway." She muttered this last bit to herself.

They talked on and on, for hours, about Mosa's visit to the law office. Stan thought she had been hasty in judging the woman. He reminded her that in a small village such as theirs, professionals socialised together and that the woman may well not even know about Mr Merake's exploits; after all, students do not talk about it outside their own group. He also reminded her that although the office was new, there were good reports about similar offices doing similar work in other villages. "Headman Kokana gave an interview on the radio when the office opened. He is strongly against it. That is a sure sign that it is doing good work," Stan argued. Mosa agreed that perhaps she had been hasty in her judgement. Perhaps she would go back for some advice. She still had not decided how she was going to get Bones, but she was certain she was going to.

As the eastern horizon reddened with the promise of a new day, they finally stumbled in to sleep. They had talked more in one long night than they had done in three years. And for that they felt closer together.

When they crawled out of bed several hours later, Mara called them over to where she was sitting: under a tree, drinking some tea. Nunu was playing with Lindie, a doll Mosa had made for her. She had been fed and was happily discussing the story of "The Three Billy Goats Gruff" with Lindie and her grandmother.

Once Mosa and Stan had settled down and poured themselves some tea, Mara informed them that the date of the ceremony for the appeasement of the ancestors had been set. It would be held in four months' time. The reason Stan had to be present was that a cow was needed. And because the ceremony would be during school holidays, it would be a good idea for Stan to come home and stay for two weeks before the ceremony. A ceremony like this meant a lot of work. The cow had to be brought from the cattlepost. Firewood had to be collected. *Leobo*, the bush enclosure for beer brewing, had to be built. All these were male tasks, and it would not look good if relatives came to help while Stan was watching television at Mr Mitchell's house. The ceremony would be bigger than Mara had originally planned because she had decided to combine it with the clothes-sharing ceremony.

Although he would miss a trip to Gaborone to watch a softball match with Mr Mitchell, he decided that the request was not unreasonable. He was happy to have his family back, and would do anything to bring them all even closer together. After the long talk with his sister the previous night, he was not going to stand in the way of the smooth running of this ceremony.

"About the cow:" Mara was saying, "you are old enough to be consulted about these things. The cow I have in mind is yours, and I wanted you to know what I think."

Stan had never taken much interest in the few cattle he knew his extended family owned. He was not sure who really owned them: they seemed to be available for slaughter at weddings and funerals, but generally they seemed to be owned by Uncle Maruping. Although as a child he he used to go to the lands and the cattlepost during every school vacation, he had not been there over the last two years; indeed, this was the first time he heard that he owned cattle, and he asked how this had come about.

"You have always had them, but you were too young to understand. You too, Mosa. The cattle are with your Uncle Maruping. He has taken care of them all this time, and for that I am grateful. But he has also always treated them like his own: killing and selling without consulting me because I have no man to talk for me about cattle. Now Stan is old enough, and he must start taking an interest. These cattle were given to me by your father when he decided not to marry me. They were paid to my family by his family. But you must understand that cattle need care – a man's care: *Ntate*. You must learn to take care of them. Go to the cattlepost with your uncle's children. Find out which cattle are yours. Give them names. Brand and earmark them, otherwise, you will be robbed. And you'll be to blame. Do you understand, son? All three of us: Mosa, Nunu and me need your help if we are to benefit from these cattle."

"Well, yes. But . . . I don't even know about earmarking."

"You'll learn, just as you learn at school."

Stan promised his mother that he would no longer be a reluctant participant.

Pleased with his response, Mara now turned to another matter. "There will be a meeting about the ceremony this afternoon. It is becoming impossible to hold a family meeting on Saturday mornings these days: too many funerals. I went to Old Man Mosenki's funeral

117

this morning. By the way, Mosa, you are old enough to attend funerals now. And you are expected to. I let you sleep this morning. But just remember that your age mates are attending funerals, and if you do not, it does not look good for our family."

"I understand, *Mma*."

They all knew the importance of attending funerals. Two years ago, a young man only a few houses away, Refilwe Morula, was lashed by the ward headman for failing to attend funerals as a pre-condition to having the men dig his father's grave. He and his family had no doubt been disgraced by their son's behaviour. Now they could not attend a funeral without eyes looking their way and whispers going around. At least the men had offered him an option. Last year, there was the scandalous case in which people simply refused to dig the grave of Rra-Matlho. The two sons had to toil unassisted the whole night. When the burial took place the following morning, it was found that the grave was too narrow. The coffin had to be set aside while the grave was widened. The embarrassment and shame! It is an experience no self-respecting family ever wants to have.

"*Mma*, you have made your point. We understand." Mosa said.

"And don't forget: your cousin Mimi is getting married in a few weeks' time. Make sure you go over to help. Her future husband's family will be coming for the first meeting. Make sure you are there. Both of you."

Both promised to be available.

CHAPTER 11

Mosa wanted to get as much information about HIV and AIDS as possible before actually going for a test. She had listened to the radio as much as she could, but still felt that a face-to-face discussion with a professional would be best. She decided that one of the local health clinics, the Borwa Health Clinic, would be the best place to go for information. She had chosen Borwa because it was within walking distance of her school, but more particularly because she did not know any of the nurses who worked there. She felt that she needed anonymity. But even after she had made the decision, three times she had set out to go to the clinic and three times she had turned back. The first time she had gone no more than three hundred metres before returning to school. The second time, she had received permission from her school to be late, but she had gone only as far as the gate of the clinic. She had seen a woman she knew, so she had passed by, pretending to be going some place else. The woman, Mmasethebe, had clearly been a patient, but would definitely have asked Mosa, out of concern or politeness, about her reasons for visiting the clinic. The third time had been a Wednesday afternoon, after school, and Mosa had found the clinic conducting some kind of class for mothers. It was then that she decided that the next time she visited, it would be a Thursday and as close to closing time as possible, to avoid running into any other patients. It was for that reason that on her fourth attempt, she arrived at the clinic at about 4 p.m.: thirty minutes before closing time.

As she walked towards the clinic, she noticed that the door to one of the offices was open, and she could see a nurse, in white uniform and maroon epaulettes, sitting on a chair and slumped over her desk. She was obviously asleep. The zipper of her uniform was down for some relief from the hot, lazy afternoon.

Perhaps she would be happy to have the boredom broken, Mosa hoped. But she was wrong.

"*Ko, ko, ko,*" Mosa said out loud, to announce her presence at the door.

The nurse sat up and rubbed her eyes with both hands. She contorted her face as she tried to stifle a yawn. When she looked at the visitor, there was displeasure whereas a moment ago, there had been sleepiness.

"We are closing. Don't you know we close at 4.30?" She pulled up the zipper of her uniform, and with her hand, wiped the sweaty patch off the desk where she had been sleeping. The left side of her face was creased.

"I just need some information," Mosa said, still in the doorway. "It will not take long. Please," Mosa added hastily.

"This is a clinic, not a place to get information. It is a place for sick people. You are not even carrying a clinic card. Are you sick? What is wrong with you?"

A cleaner popped her head in from a storeroom and gave Mosa a sympathetic look. She mouthed the word "lazy", pulled a face and made a rude gesture with her fingers. She disappeared back into the room and resumed her work, humming a song rather loudly, to warn the nurse that she had been listening.

"Come in; come in, quick. Will you people ever learn to respect time? This clinic is open from 7.30 a.m., and you come at the end of the day. Hey, you cannot teach a Motswana time. Sit down. What's wrong with you?"

But there was no chair to sit down on. Mosa decided to get straight to the point. "Well, I came for information. I am thinking of taking an HIV test, but I need to understand a few things first."

"Do you think you have AIDS? There is a lot of AIDS around, and even young people like you have it. Why are you people so careless? And you are a young girl. You should be concentrating on school, not getting AIDS. The radio is always teaching about AIDS. Government money is being wasted but people do not listen. They wake up too late. Too late! What do you want to know? We do not do tests here. You have to go to the hospital for that. But you must know that if you have AIDS, there is no cure: you simply die. So if you are positive, please do not spread it." With that, the nurse was clearly done, her face almost purple with annoyance.

Mosa considered herself dismissed. But she tried one more time. "Do you have any pamphlets for me to read?"

"What do you want to know? Is there really anything anyone does not know about AIDS? It is transmitted through sexual intercourse. And blood transfusions, of course. So the first clear message is 'Do not have sexual intercourse.' You are too young. Now I am really closing. We have no pamphlets here. Check the hospital." She reached for a bundle of keys and her handbag.

"Do you know anything about pre-test counselling? I mean, do you know where that is done?" Mosa persisted.

"How can we do counselling if we do not do tests? Are you deaf? I said check with the hospital." She stood up and pushed her feet into her shoes.

Mosa turned and walked towards the door. The cleaner gave an apologetic shrug. Mosa mouthed a thank you and walked out. What is going on in this country of ours? she wondered. It does not matter whether one is buying a postage stamp or seeking medical help. The arrogance of the people who have the power to serve or not to serve is appalling. Is there no pride in one's work? she wondered. Will I end up like that, too, one day when I have my office and my desk?

She doubted that she would get any better service at another clinic. A cousin of hers had lost a baby and almost died in childbirth only six months ago because the midwife on duty had given strict orders that she not be interrupted during her tea break. No amount of pleading by the ambulance driver could sway her. The nurse had her tea; the baby died; the mother was torn up and had to go for extensive repairs. The nurse was, of course, still proudly wearing her nurse's uniform. The system had responded in her favour, protective and furious at the people who dared question it. Medical reports had either been doctored or gone missing. Not that the family could really have done anything more than raise a tentative question.

Now all she wanted was some information, and she was subjected to abuse. Only the week before, she was at the village's Omang office to check whether her ID was ready. She had taken a seat at the end of the queue, joining nine other people seated on a long, wooden bench. An old man was standing in front of a large old desk, listening to a clerk, a young woman in braids.

The old man had been told that a new ID had to be made because the picture on the old one had been unclear. Because it was the Omang-office photographer who had taken the unclear photograph, the old man could not possibly be blamed for the need for a replacement ID. Mosa listened as the young woman behind the desk demanded the old ID from the old man before handing over the new one. She had the new one in her hand. The old man explained that the office had taken the old ID from him during his previous visit. He also explained that he had had to walk to the office from Seloje, a neighbouring village, where there was no Omang office. This visit, he had added, was the fifth one. He needed the Omang to be able to collect his old-age pension. He had walked because he had no money for the bus, he explained. Mosa had taken in the stooped figure with its torn jacket, worn obviously out of respect for the office, because it was too warm a day for anyone to be wearing a jacket. Her eyes went to his feet, which were barely contained in old, under-size sandals. His feet were caked in dust, and his shins, visible from below his ill-fitting trousers, were like thin twigs. Conscious of her examination of the old man, and afraid that her actions might be interpreted as disrespectful, Mosa raised her eyes to the old man's face: lean and angular, with friendly eyes. His head was covered with neat, short, grey hair.

"Old man," barked the clerk. "I have a lot of work here. Do you want your Omang or not? Do not tell me your life story." She placed her elbows on the desk and rested her chin on her interlaced hands. Her eyes blazed with contempt. Above her, an inadequate fan turned lazily, hardly stirring the hot, stagnant air.

The old man used his hat to wipe the sweat from his forehead. "Like I was saying, you took it. Maybe not you personally, but who-ever was here last time. She took it." His voice shook with shame at being talked to with such contempt by one so young. Shame born out of powerlessness.

The woman swept her braids back, dropped the old man's ID in a box and announced, "This old man is here to play games. Let me tell you our rules. We do not take the old Omang cards without giving you the new one. So please, if you do not know why you are here, just let others who are busy come forward. Next!"

Other people in the line moved forward with some embarrassment.

But they said nothing. There were young and old people, male and female. All had listened and watched, but not one of them had said anything. Mosa was ready to burst. "Why are we suffering this abuse and not saying anything?" she seethed. But she, too, said nothing. No one would have listened anyway. No one listened to anyone in a school uniform.

The old man sat down at the end of the line, confused, not knowing whether to leave or stay. The clerk's colleague, an even younger woman, who must have been looking for the old man's old Omang during the exchange, silently placed it in front of her barking colleague. Without batting an eyelid, the woman called the old man forward and warned him never again to surrender his old Omang before getting his new one. No apologies. Nothing. And still no one said anything as the old man shuffled away, crushing his hat between his hands, not in anger but in shame.

Thinking about all this, Mosa wondered why she had not challenged the nurse about the treatment she had given her. The answer was obvious enough: a challenge would have ended up being no more than angry words back and forth, nothing more. Besides, there was no place to complain, really. And, more importantly, she had a bigger problem weighing on her shoulders: she went to that office for confidentiality, and speaking up might have involved other people and closer scrutiny about why she was there in the first place. She decided that she would just have the test without seeking any more information. Could one just show up at the hospital and ask for an HIV test? Perhaps she would have to pretend to be sick and then ask for the test. She had no idea. Good service often depends on who you know on the other side of the desk. This was a case in which she preferred not to know anyone. Not that she knew too many civil servants, though.

With mission not accomplished, and with some time to spare before she had to be home, Mosa decided to go back to school to watch a traditional-dancing practice session; the school was on her way home anyway. She was not part of the group, but she loved watching them practise and perform. There is nothing quite as soothing, Mosa thought, as the roll of drums, the clapping of hands and the clatter of leg rattles. She was once a good dancer herself. She was not quite sure why she had stopped dancing, but she still enjoyed watching it. She had not danced for more than a year, and it dawned on her that she had not had any real fun for at least that long, watching but hardly taking part in anything, even as she had become pregnant.

When she walked into the classroom, the group was trying out some new dance steps. She took her usual seat. A few eyes were cast her way, but she was mostly ignored. After a few minutes of trying this and that, the group sang *Dikgomo Kwa Kudumane*, an old favourite about old times in Kudumane, where black people used to own land and big, fat cattle. She, too, loved this piece.

Without having planned it, she rose from her seat, kicked off her shoes and joined the two dancers. She borrowed a set of foot rattles from a singer and tied them to her feet while the players looked on bemused, but the singing, drumming and clapping continued. It had been so long since she was part of the group that most of its members had never seen her dance.

With the rattles in place, Mosa began to dance; at first tentatively, but within seconds she had picked up the step, swaying and stomping to the rhythm. She danced like she had never danced before: turning, twisting, using up all the space in the room. Before long, the other dancers moved aside, preferring to watch her. She danced with fury, with joy, with pain. With a feeling that welled up from deep within her. The drummer beat his drum until beads of sweat formed on his forehead; the singers sang with their heart. Soon the room could no longer contain the thrill, and someone called out the door, "Mosa is dancing! Mosa is dancing!" Students ran towards the sound of the music. Mosa, oblivious to all this, danced on as if she had never stopped dancing. When the song came to an end, there was first silence, then a burst of applause. She looked around her, exhausted, surprised to find so many eyes watching her. She gave an embarrassed little laugh, shrugged her shoulders and went to sit down. She took off the rattles, put on her shoes and got up to leave. Then the members of the dance group were all crowding around her, speaking at once.

"Mosa, you must join us. Please: you must join us for the next competition."

"No, no: I do not think so."

"Please: you are the best. With you, we would surely win."

Lilian, the leader of the group, short and muscular, stepped forward and said, "Okay: everyone back to your places. Let me talk to Mosa alone." She turned to Mosa. "Why have you not danced with us before? I heard you were good, but no one ever told me you were this good."

Mosa merely shrugged her shoulders.

"So, what do you say? Will you join us?"

"No: I do not think so," Mosa said, shaking her head.

"Why not? You are so very good. Why did you just dance with us if you do not want to do it? Surely you do want to dance. You love it. Everyone could see that. Please, Mosa."

"That is different. That is for –"

"For?" Lilian wanted to know what had moved Mosa to dance in a relatively empty classroom when she would not dance to a crowd and applause.

"No, listen: I have to go. I will think about whether I want to join the group. I will let you know soon." Mosa gave Lilian a pat on the shoulder, and left. She had no plans to join the group, and had promised to think about it only to get out of the room.

Was it rude to do what I just did? Mosa wondered as she made her way home. The group probably thinks I'm a show-off. But how could I have possibly explained to Lilian why I suddenly got up and danced today? She did not even have the words to explain it to herself. The closest she could come is that she had danced as part of a personal ritual to regain herself. She needed to go backwards so that she could go forwards. She needed to pick up a thread she had left behind. She had danced as a way of gaining a measure of freedom. She had danced for no one but herself. Would that explanation have made sense to dear, bewildered Lilian? Perhaps Stan might understand.

Walking by Mma-Queen's yard, she saw Sakanye, as usual chopping firewood. She waved and called out hello. Sakanye waited for her to come closer so that he could blow her one of his many kisses. But when she waved and shouted first, he found himself upstaged. So he mumbled a hello and went back to his wood chopping.

"Aha!" Mosa said to herself with a chuckle. "I have that one solved forever."

When she got home, she went next door to get Nunu, bathed her and cooked her some soft porridge for supper. Nunu wanted a story, so she told her about *Koronkopele*, the girl who fell in love with a horse and cried when her parents would not let her see the animal. She was in the middle of the story when her mother arrived. Together, the two women sang the song part of the story while Nunu clapped happily. The story was one of Mosa's favourites, despite its sad ending, and she loved the song.

CHAPTER 12

"Mosa, can I talk to you, please?" Sinah had been following Mosa for a while before summoning up the courage to call out to her. It was the end of the school day, and the road was blue with school uniforms as students streamed home. Mosa stopped and turned to face Sinah. Although in the same class, they had hardly ever talked before. Sinah was reclusive and quiet, and Mosa was surprised at the girl's approach. She looked expectantly at Sinah, who seemed to shrink under the scrutiny. Sensing the girl's discomfort, Mosa smiled encouragingly.

"Come: let's walk together. We can talk as we walk. I am sure we both have to hurry home to cook. What did you want to talk to me about?"

Sinah hesitated, then blurted out, "It's Mr Merake. He is bothering me. Really bothering me. He will not let me alone. And look; look; look." Frantically, she pointed at a car speeding by, causing students to jump off the edge of the tarred road. "That's him going by. He is going to wait for me by Mma-Koketso's yard. I have to go by there to get home! I do not know what to do any more!" With a ball of tissue, she wiped her forehead desperately.

"Have you told your mother? Anyone?" Mosa asked, knowing the answer to the question already.

Sinah shook her head sadly. "You know I cannot do that. She cannot do anything about it, and that would worry her and make her feel useless. She might even blame me for encouraging him. What can my mother do? As it is, she has to deal with Bini's problem. What am I going to do?"

"What exactly has Bones done so far? Do you want to talk about it?" Mosa decided not to ask about Bini. Sinah's fourteen-year-old sister had to go and live with an older sister in Gaborone. Sinah seemed distressed, and getting her to recount yet another problem did not seem a good idea.

"Last week, he sent me into the storeroom and then came in after me. He pretended to be getting books from a shelf above me, but he just wanted to lean on me and rub himself against me. He does that with many girls, so I can kind of live with it. He's not even the only one doing it. But a few nights ago he dragged me into his car and insisted he was taking me home. I jumped out as he got into the driver's seat. Since then, I do not come for evening studies. And look." With a furtive look around to make sure no one was looking, she raised her skirt a bit to expose raw flesh, made to look even worse by the gentian violet on it.

"What happened?" Mosa said, trying to hide her shock.

"I was trying to sneak out of the school by jumping the back fence. I am in the Wildlife Club, and we went on a trip on Saturday. We got back late in the evening. When the bus came in, I saw him lurking behind the library, and I knew I was in trouble. I tried to jump over the back fence, and that is how I got hurt. I thought I would bleed to death: maybe it's the fright that made it look and feel worse. Well, I can't spend the whole year jumping over fences to get away from that man. But . . . I don't know what to do."

Even though Bones had humiliated Mosa in class, at least he had since left her alone. Now it was poor Sinah's turn, and she needed help. Of course, things were still rough for Mosa, because Bones was still ignoring her in class. He was also marking her tests strictly and refusing to discuss the matter.

Mosa was fuming. Bones had no right to make Sinah's life so miserable. None of them had that right. But she knew that there was no one within the school, or anywhere else for that matter, to go to for help. Some "big men" – men who had money and influence in the village – were known to prowl the grounds at the end of the evening study session in search of young girls. There was even a rumour that the headmaster ordered Jane, a Form Three student, to come for evening classes because, he claimed, she was behind with her work, just so that one of these prowlers could get her. The evening study sessions were not compulsory; they were intended to provide the day students with a place to do homework and to study for tests and examinations. Most day students did not have good lighting at home.

In any event, everyone knew that Jane was not behind in any work and that evening studies were optional. When Jane did not turn up, she was whipped. Since then, she had been seen on many occasions being picked up after evening studies. Whereas she had the sympathy of the students before, she now had their contempt. She was giving herself to a sugar daddy, they said.

The girl had changed in many ways. Whereas most girls had their hair braided at home, hers was done at the village's only hair salon, of which most of the customers were working women. The teachers who had to share hair dryers with her resented her presence. The girl was now sporting Nike shoes when almost everybody else was making do with P50-a-pair pavement specials. And to go with her school uniform, a pair of expensive Bronx. And she had an extra uniform. These days, she was the headmaster's favourite, always being sent on this and that errand within the school. But there were already rumours that the same "big man" had his eyes on someone else.

That Sinah had attracted the attention of Bones would not necessarily earn her sympathy. The girls would be resentful that she was being made special. As if being cut up with wire while escaping a near-rapist could ever be considered being special.

The boys, too, had their issues. They hated what they considered to be special treatment given to girls, and felt excluded and ignored, and blamed the girls for the teachers' behaviour. They particularly hated the fact that they got beaten in class no matter what but that a girl could escape beatings if a teacher was hoping for a positive response to his advances. They overlooked the fact that a girl might also get a beating because she said no.

"Are you going to help me, Mosa?" Sinah pleaded.

"But how? I don't know how I could possibly help. You know Bones hates me as it is. If he even smells my involvement in this, he will get worse. I might even fail the end-of-term science test. You know how he is."

"Please, Mosa. You are the only one who has ever stood up to him."

Mosa laughed. "You call that standing up to Bones? The man chewed me up. He humiliated me in front of the class. He made Khumo's day."

"Yes, but you did not cry and hang your head. You answered back, and you left his class. Have you ever known anyone to do that and not get a taste of his stick? He is afraid of you. You can see it. He doesn't know what to do with you." Sinah gave a wan smile, and her eyes filled with tears.

"I don't know that he's afraid of me, but let's both think of what we can possibly do, okay? Come: I will walk you home; it's on my way anyway."

That seemed to mollify Sinah somewhat. The pair walked together in silence. Sinah was desperate for Mosa's friendship. Mosa was only one year older than Sinah but seemed much older. It was not just her height; it was the way she walked and talked; the way she carried herself. Sinah had heard her being called proud behind her back, but Sinah was sure that "proud" was not the correct way to describe this self-assured young woman. She had a resolve that seemed to radiate from her eyes. She seemed wise beyond her age.

When they reached Sinah's home, Mosa squeezed her hand and said, "We'll talk some more tomorrow."

"Thanks, Mosa," she said and this time, her smile was warm and happy.

Konkoronkokoo! Mosa sat up in bed and yawned. She knew that today would be a day of yawning. She and the rooster were engaged in an undeclared competition. Most mornings, Mosa woke up seconds before the rooster let out its throaty greeting to the new day. Then she declared herself the winner. But with Sinah's story churning in her head, she had found sleep elusive.

She stumbled out of bed and out of the house to find that one of Ramositsane's donkeys had managed to knock off the water-drum lid and drunk most of their water. Even though there was still some water left, she did not find the prospect of washing with water mixed with donkey saliva very appealing. The donkey was standing quietly in the middle of the yard, unperturbed. She gave it an angry look, but it returned her glare with its gentle eyes.

She grabbed a bucket and ran to the tap to get some water. There was still a uniform to be ironed and shoes to be polished. At least her mother had put the iron on the fire before she left for work.

But Mosa's hectic morning had only just begun. When she searched for her bar of soap, all she found was a pathetic piece in the yard: she realised she had left the soap outside the day before and that the chickens had eaten most of it. It was supposed to have lasted the rest of the month, and there were still two full weeks to go! The soap her mother used was homemade from pig fat, and she swore by it. Mosa was convinced that the quickest way to a pimply face was using her mother's special soap. But she was going to have to before the month was out. And now she had to hurry if she was going to be on time for school. She was in no mood for lashes from the headmaster for being late. He would surely be guarding the gate with his stick, ready to deal with all latecomers, a duty he performed with obvious relish. The thought that another human being had the power to inflict violence on her filled her with fury.

She still had no clear plan for how to tackle Sinah's problem, but something was beginning to form in her mind. She needed to talk to Sinah a bit more to find out how strong she was and how prepared she was to carry this thing through. It would not help if Mosa herself charged forward only to find that Sinah had decided to give in to Bones because that was the best solution to her problem.

Having dropped off a sleepy Nunu at the neighbours, with the child's usual bowl of porridge and the not so usual bit of meat to go with it, Mosa hurried off to school. She herself had not eaten, and would have to wait for the ten o'clock tea offered by the school. She hoped that that malicious boarding master, BM, would not be supervising the tea break. He was an expert at giving out thin slices of bread topped with films of peanut butter. The matron was much nicer. She always ordered more milk and sugar to be put in the tea, and made sure the bread was sliced thickly with liberal amounts of peanut butter.

The students loved the matron and hated BM. He called them pigs and she called them angels. The students were always at pains to behave themselves when matron was on tea-break duty, by standing in orderly lines and leaving no litter in the area. When BM was supervising tea, however, they charged forward in a wild stampede to get their share, spilling tea and indeed behaving like pigs.

Mosa was just entering the school gates when the bell rang: she had escaped the first possible punishment of the day. Who will be in charge of morning assembly? she wondered. It turned out to be Triple B: Boring, Balding Ball, a round, short, balding teacher who was always berating the students for not making Jesus their personal saviour. Most teachers did assembly duty precisely because it was a duty; otherwise, they hated it. But Triple B, whose real name was Mr Moses Mosime, was different: he preached, sang, shrieked and shouted the word of God. Despite their cruel nickname for the man, the students liked him. He was good to them, and listened to them, and did make Religious Studies, the subject he taught, interesting and fun. Whereas most of the teachers carried sticks for lashing at students, Triple B did not. They did not even really consider him to be boring; it was just that "Boring, Balding Ball" had sounded nice, and it had stuck. When he first came to the school, the more experienced teachers repeatedly warned him that he could not possibly manage without a stick. He responded that if the good Lord had not needed a stick for the ass that carried him, he saw no reason why he would need a stick for minds that just wanted to learn. His colleagues laughed at him and gave him a month before he saw the stupidity of his ways. His form of punishment was to have the students write out and analyse a Bible verse as punishment, with never any suggestion of spite or malice.

One day, Mr Mosime wanted to know what Triple B stood for. Quick Mouth Thomas, the class clown and prankster, answered without hesitation, "Big, Bigger, Biggest, sir. Because your faith in the Lord is so great, sir." Mr Mosime beamed and made it clear that if that was the case, he did not mind being called Mr Triple B to his face.

Even with the Lord's Prayer said by the six hundred or so assembled students, the voice of Triple B could be heard above them all. He bellowed the prayer so loudly that Mosa thought God might just be offended by the man's pushiness.

As the students dispersed and headed for their various classrooms, Mosa fell into step with Sinah and whispered that they meet during the tea break.

"Okay," Sinah nodded, pleased that after a night's sleep, Mosa had not decided to back out.

By tea break, Mosa was sure that her stomach had begun to digest itself as she listened to it rumbling. Still, she suggested to Sinah that they go to a private corner to talk before getting their tea.

"What's the use of wasting time in the queue? We'll join it later as it shortens. Matron is in charge, so there will be plenty for everybody."

They chose a bench under a tree from where they could watch the slow-moving food queue.

"The way I see it, some kind of confrontation is called for," Mosa began, watching Sinah's face. "Are you prepared for that?"

Sinah seemed worried. "What do you mean a confrontation? I cannot go directly against Bones, you know that."

"Not a confrontation by you alone, but with you included. I am willing to face him in some way or another. But I have to be sure you are prepared as well. Perhaps there are other girls who would join us. But what I am saying is that we cannot fight this by jumping over fences and running away from him: there has to be a more direct and effective way." Even as she spoke, Mosa was trying to convince herself as well.

"Well, I want it to stop, and I want to be part of those who will stop it, but I am so afraid. The headmaster could just recommend our expulsion to the Ministry of Education if we cause trouble." Sinah had a worried frown on her face.

"Listen, Sinah, I am not recommending that we burn the school down or anything like that – although burning Bones might not be a bad idea."

Sinah gasped.

"Come on: that's a joke," Mosa laughed.

"Oh. So what do you have in mind?" Sinah asked, smiling hesitantly. She did not want to do anything that would end up in public or have her mother called to the school about any of this. She believed that the teacher would always be favoured if matters developed into a confrontation. Teachers never got punished: maybe transferred, but not punished. She knew of at least two girls who had dropped out of school pregnant amid rumours that teachers were responsible. The two teachers were transferred on promotion to other schools.

"To tell you the truth, I don't know. I know silence is not the answer. I also know that Bones will pester you until you either give in or drop out of school. He might even rape you. No one will call it that, of course. You might call it that the first time it happens. But after a while, the abnormal becomes normal, and suddenly you have convinced yourself you are in a 'relationship'. He will then give you some money, and you will buy new socks and do your hair. Of course, you will not buy shoes, because he will not give you enough, and even if he did, you would not want your parents to know. Perhaps there will be enough left for a can of Coke. The rest of the students will hate you and envy your Coke. If you are lucky, you will not become pregnant. Or perhaps you will be lucky and become pregnant but not get AIDS."

"Mosa, please do not say that. I will not give in to him. I hate him.

I hate his bony, slimy, sneaky face. I hate the way he cannot give me a book without making sure he touches me. I hate his sweaty palms. Oh, God, I hate his breath and the way he leans forward over all the girls. Mosa, you have to help me. Really, I just might kill him after all." Sinah was surprised by her sudden, uncharacteristic vehemence.

Mosa was silent for a moment. "Let's do this. Don't kill him – not yet, anyway. Let's walk together after school. Perhaps with more time we can think of something. We need to think a bit more of what we are prepared to do and what we can do. Okay? Let's go for tea. I'm starving."

"Can't we meet at lunchtime? Matron will let us take our food out here if we ask," Sinah said.

"Oh, I'm sorry, but I'm already meeting my brother Stan at lunchtime. I have already promised him. We do not get much time together."

Such confidence, Sinah marvelled. Very few students will admit to being hungry for the school tea. They gulp it down and tear at the bread hungrily, but they will never admit that they need it for their survival. That goes for the school lunch as well. For many, the two meals represent the bulk of their daily sustenance. But still, there were even students who claimed not to eat porridge or beans or anything traditional. Sinah admired this new friend of hers, who both inspired and frightened her with her strength and sense of purpose. She had a lot to think about until the afternoon. It did not help that they were having a double period of science immediately after tea: an hour and a half of Bones.

The double science period was fairly normal. Bones strode in brandishing his "blood sucker", kissing it as he did every time he started a lesson. He told them that some of them were going to fail, just as some were going to pass. That speech, too, was usual enough. Some of the girls, he warned, were being distracted by boys, and the boys wanted only one thing from them. Most of the boys would end up as thieves. All this they'd heard before. Thus Bones was his usual self. At the end of the lesson, only three boys and three girls had been lashed: two girls for passing a note between them, one boy for looking outside the window, two boys for asking stupid questions, and one girl for whispering to her neighbour. Of course, no one dared to point out to Merake that according to the rules, all beatings had to be entered in a register. Talk such as that would have earned the student a beating –

which, of course would not be entered in any register.

Mosa, as usual, had been ignored, as if she were not even part of the class. She, however, continued to raise her hand whenever Bones asked a question, refusing to acknowledge Mr Merake's behaviour. Like everyone else in the class, Sinah watched as this cold war continued. She figured that Mosa was not prepared to give Bones the satisfaction of seeing her defeated.

But Sinah could not understand how Mosa could be so cool in the face of the treatment meted out by Bones. She herself did not raise her hand in Bones's class, hoping that he would not notice her at all. It was this show of strength and confidence that had drawn Sinah to Mosa in the first place.

Even with the Bones problem still to be dealt with, she wanted to tell Mosa about Bini, her little sister. She badly needed someone to talk to about it. In a way, she agreed with the solution to the problem, but she still wanted Mosa's opinion. She understood that it was not because her family loved her sister any less than they loved her uncle. Or even that they were not hurt or disappointed. She had seen the pain in her mother's eyes. It was just that they loved the family more than they loved any one member. It was because of the special position in the family of a maternal uncle. No celebration of birth, wedding or death could be undertaken without a maternal uncle. How could her sister possibly benefit from the exposure of the family to public ridicule or the removal of the uncle from the family? How could her needs ever supersede those of the family and the many other members? She understood that it was in the greater interest of the family for nothing to be done. Well, not quite nothing, but nothing public. That explained the small gathering of a few select relatives who spoke in hushed tones, urging the uncle to leave the child alone. That explained the sending away of Bini to Gaborone to spend the rest of the school year with their oldest sister. It explained Bini's tears as she packed her little tattered bag, leaving her friends behind to go to a strange school in a strange town. It explained why her mother continued to cook, wash and clean for her brother as he continued his important role as the uncle. Sinah understood. But still, she wanted someone to talk to about it. Perhaps she would raise the matter with Mosa some day. She had more-pressing problems at the moment. She just hoped Bini was adjusting to her new life in Gaborone.

After the double period of science and abuse, there was lunch, and then the class had Mr Mitchell, another teacher who did not carry a stick. He punished in strange but effective ways: making a student stand inside a small circle for an hour whilst working out maths problems. During his lessons, the absence of a constant threat of violence made for freer discussions and more class participation. Most students agreed that Mr Mitch was a good teacher, who treated them with dignity and respect. They loved him, and worked hard in his class.

It had taken a while for some students to know how to deal with Mr Mitchell. At first, they had abused what they thought was a lack of firmness. But they quickly realised that there was no lack of firmness at all, just a different style of dealing with people.

Khumo, however, remained one of the few students who refused to change his view about Mr Mitchell. Mosa recalled an incident that took place the previous year. One day, the final bell rang. Mosa packed up and walked out. Her classmates called her and told her to help with the sweeping.

"It's not our turn yet. We have four more weeks before our turn comes again," Mosa explained.

"But it is our turn." A classmate pushed a timetable under her nose. "We were on four weeks ago, and this week we're on again."

"You're wrong," Mosa said. "Just look at that timetable again." She turned on her heel and went on home.

The following day, Mr Mitch, the class teacher, called Mosa into his office.

"Well, Mosa, it is not like you to just ignore your duties. But I was told that you did not take part in class cleaning yesterday. I have to say I was really surprised. And disappointed! I am told you gave the excuse that it was not your turn yet. I have looked at the timetable, and it is here in black and white. This week you are on class cleaning duty. Do you want to explain why you behaved like that?" Mr Mitchell knew that the class would be curious about how he dealt with Mosa. It was no secret that her brother was living at his house, and a whiff of favouritism would not go down well with the rest of the class.

"If that is really the case, Mr Mitch, I am very sorry," Mosa replied, returning his seriousness in full measure. "But may I see the timetable, please? Somehow I do not think I am wrong."

Mosa examined the timetable with a frown, and Mr Mitchell began to think this whole thing was an act.

"Mmm: Mr Mitch, there is something wrong with this timetable. Look, I have the class list here. There are forty students in our class, and only eighteen have been assigned cleaning duty. Must be a mistake somewhere: look."

"Mosa, you know that this class list includes boys as well." And as soon as he said it, he knew that that was exactly the point Mosa was making. He studied Mosa, who was looking at him with amusement in her eyes. "I get your point. A new timetable will be drawn up, and everyone will be taking part in class cleaning from now on."

"Thank you, Mr Mitch. I knew it was a genuine mistake on your part." Mosa left the office with an irrepressible smile on her face.

From then onwards, to the consternation of the boys, and some girls, all students of Form Four (H) took part in the cleaning of the classroom. Khumo was so mortified by the prospect of holding a broom that he even missed school a couple of times just to avoid it. As for the Friday floor scrubbing, polishing and buffing, he made it clear that he would rather be expelled from school than do that. The thought of going down on his male knees, like a woman, repelled him. A female student offered to do Friday cleaning for him, and so his participation was limited to moving desks and dusting the chalkboard: tasks he was more than happy to do because he considered them to be male tasks.

Khumo had never forgiven Mosa for reducing him to the status of a girl. And even some girls were angry with Mosa for forcing boys to do things that are against Setswana culture. And, they felt, boys were disturbing a previously girls-only activity. It was a special time for them to gossip and laugh and tell each other secrets. Now all that had been lost just because Mosa had gone to complain. And as if that was not enough, their class was now the laughing stock of the other Form Four classes. Mosa ignored all this as if there were more important matters concerning her.

Khumo continued to seethe about the matter, and Mosa acted as if he did not exist at all. Khumo was particularly disagreeable during Mr Mitch's class, accusing the American teacher of being weak, as he saw it.

At the end of the day, the two girls walked home together. When they finally parted, they still had not come up with a scheme for solving Sinah's problem. They agreed to meet the following day.

CHAPTER 13

It was only two weeks later that Sinah and Mosa agreed on a plan for Bones. During this time, Sinah had avoided meeting Mr Merake by not attending any extracurricular activities that involved walking home alone or late after school. She had even dropped out of after-noon choir rehearsals.

Mosa and Sinah approached Lilian, the head of the traditional-dance group; Naledi, a key member of the drama group; and Tebatso, a member of the art club. Lilian was also the head girl, so her support was important to give the activities legitimacy. Mosa and Sinah told the other girls that their plan was to expose the abusive behaviour of some of the teachers, at the annual prize-giving ceremony. Their idea was to put together a play, poems and artwork to tell the audience what was going on at Bana-Ba-Phefo High School. Tebatso, who had been suspended from school for five days only the previous term for refusing to submit to corporal punishment, needed little persuasion. Lilian and Naledi, although excited about the idea, were at first sceptical about its success. Why would they allow us to present the play? How can we keep the whole project a secret? What if we are expelled from school? Who would dare do anything about the abuse anyway? But finally, they were won over. After all, except for the artwork, what they were planning was nothing new. What was radical was the content of the play, songs and poems. As long as the other participants they would need kept the secret, no one would be any the wiser until the main day.

"Working in private need not raise suspicion," Mosa argued. "After all, Naledi, you never allow other students to watch your group rehearse before a major event. If Bones, who, as our luck would have it, is this year's chairman of the prize-giving ceremony, wants any details, we can send Lilian to assure him that everything is okay."

"That is true, but Ms Mogome, our adviser, always wants to watch the final version of the play a few weeks before any major event. She will definitely want us to perform for her before the prize-giving day. She takes her job very seriously," Naledi said.

"I have an idea!" Tebatso piped in. "You are right now finalising the play for International Day of the African Child: June 16, right? You could tell her you will be performing the same play at the two events! It actually makes more sense that you would do that: they are only a few weeks apart!"

After a lengthy discussion, the group decided that as long as they could convince the other necessary participants, the plan was workable. Then Mosa suggested that it would be best if they invited the Minister of Education to the event.

"That sounds like a great idea, Mosa, but I cannot imagine the Minister of Education attending our event just because we invited her. I mean, last year we had to do with the ward headman, not even the chief!" Tebatso threw her hands in the air. She was a tall, very pretty girl who had beautiful eyes. When she got agitated, she waved her hands about and rolled her eyes.

"Okay, girlfriend: before you give up, remember what Mr Mitch always says: 'If you don't try, you will surely fail.' I say we listen to Mosa. How can it hurt us to try?" Lilian suggested.

Tebatso shook her head and asked, "But how could we persuade her? Every school in the country must invite her every year! Headmasters invite her, not students, and she turns them down! I want to believe this is possible, but I just don't see it happening!"

"Perhaps the very fact that students, as opposed to the headmaster, will be inviting her would make a difference. Like Lilian says, how can it hurt? Let us try." Mosa was looking at Tebatso.

"You are right, of course," Tebatso said, "I just get frustrated sometimes. It is at times like this that I understand how students at Dikolo Kgolo High School rioted and burnt down the staff offices!"

Sinah coughed to indicate that she wanted to say something, and when the other girls looked at her, she said, "Perhaps we can all draft the letter to the Minister. Perhaps we should start with a list of ideas we want reflected in the letter."

"I agree with Sinah," Mosa said. What is it we think would persuade the Minister? Of course, we should first say who we are and why we have taken this unprecedented step of writing to the Minister. Then I think we have to emphasise our achievements during the past two years. We should –"

"We should mention that some of us are approaching voting age!' Tebatso interjected, without waiting for Mosa to finish.

"We won the district and national debating competitions last year! Thanks to you Mosa, in fact."

"And our football and softball teams have been national champions for the past two years!"

"And we have never had any riots, only God knows why not!"

"And last year, our June 16th play was voted the best in the district."

"And, of course, we have something special to present to the Minister at this year's prize-giving ceremony," Mosa added.

"Let's try to put all these ideas in a letter now," Lilian suggested.

After a few drafts, the five girls finally came up with the following letter.

6th May 1999
The Hon. Mrs Lesego Molalane,
The Honourable Minister,
Ministry of Education,
Private Bag 092
Gaborone

Dear Honourable Minister,
We would like to start this letter by introducing ourselves. We are students at the above-named school. All five of us are leaders of clubs or special-interest groups in the school. We are all Form Five students and will thus be writing our Cambridge examinations at the end of this year. We have come together to write this letter because we believe that the students of Bana-Ba-Phefo have something very special to show you and their parents. We explain what we mean below.

As you are aware, during the next two or so months, all schools in the country will be holding a prize-giving ceremony. As you can imagine, every year, headmasters hope to get the most inspirational of guest speakers. Of course, every school hopes that the Minister of Education will honour its event by her attendance and be that very special speaker. And, of course, it is not possible for you attend all the events. We write this letter, however, in a bid to persuade you to be the guest of honour at our school. The event will take place on the 2nd of July from 8 a.m. to 2 p.m. This year's chairman of the prize-giving committee is Mr Merake, and we are working closely with him to ensure that this year's event is a special success.

In preparation for this event, we have planned various activities, not just to entertain the audience members, but to inform them. Thus this year's play, poems and songs will have special messages for both the young and the old. A special feature of the event will be an artwork display. One of the reasons we are putting a special effort into this year's event is that we know it will be our last. We would like to make one last major and memorable contribution to the school, before we write our final examination and leave, hopefully for further studies.

We believe that our school's record of academic, sport and extra-mural achievements should be enough to impress you. You will note that during the past three years, our senior school has been ranked among the best five schools in the country. Our junior school has had impressive results over the past three years as well. This past year, it was ranked number one nationally. We have also won trophies for sports and have been the unbeaten champions at the national debate competitions. All five of us have been involved in some way in bringing glory to our school.

Even though we have such an impressive record, we have not had the honour of hosting a high-ranking official from the Ministry of Education. We feel that this honour would encourage all of us to work even harder. We know that yours is a busy schedule, but we do hope that you will be persuaded to honour us with your presence.

Mosa offered to type the letter the following morning, during the Computers class. Mr Selby's head was always buried in one book or another, so it would be easy to type and print the letter without detection. The girls agreed that the letter would be signed by all five of them. They would then mail it by registered post, to ensure delivery.

Three weeks later, Mr Merake, the chair of the Prize Giving Committee, was delighted to get a letter from the Ministry of Education, addressed to the 'Chairman of the Prize Giving Committee', accepting 'such a genuine invitation'. At first, he was sure that the letter was meant for another school, but when a tentative phone call confirmed the Minister's acceptance he was truly ecstatic. As soon as he was certain the Minister was indeed coming, he started to boast about his coup. He posted the information on all the noticeboards and made a special announcement about it at one of the morning assemblies. He even called a few of his colleagues at other schools to spread the good news: he knew that chairs of prize-giving committees around the country would be biting their nails waiting for confirmations from guests of honour.

What he actually assumed had happened was that the Ministry of Education, receiving, as it did, numerous invitations to the annual prize-giving ceremonies throughout the country, had simply pulled a name from a list at random. Or perhaps there was a political motivation for the choice of his school. A school was lucky if it managed to get a regional education officer to attend its prize-giving ceremony, and most schools instead looked to other government departments for their guests of honour. The Minister's choice was always a political decision motivated by the need to maximise election votes. During the previous year, for example, the Minister of Education had been the guest speaker at Thapama High School, in Thapama village, a month before a council by-election was to take place there.

When various groups asked to be on the program, he was convinced that he was a genius putting together the best prize-giving ceremony ever held in the school. Without any effort from him at all, there would be an art exhibition, poetry readings and a play by the traditional-dance group. And he did not even have to oversee their activities. All the groups, including the Scouts and the Scripture Union, were giving him weekly reports about their rehearsals and meeting with him for weekly briefings. He was certain it was because he had secured the attendance of such an important guest that there was so much enthusiasm. *Magic!*

Mr Merake knew that most parents did not attend the annual ceremony; that was a yearly lament all over the country. Generally, only the parents of students who received a prize attended. He had to find a way to attract them. Food. Plenty of meat. A cow or two would have to be slaughtered. He knew he had to persuade the headmaster to give a bit more money than had been given in the past. He would write to all the parents, urging them to attend and inviting them for lunch.

With a week to go before the prize giving, a staff meeting was called for the final planning.

The meeting had been going for about an hour and a half, and there were two items still remaining on the agenda. It was a late-June afternoon, and the sun was not warm enough to keep the room comfortable. But Mr Kgaka, the pompous, domineering headmaster, had a small heater at his feet. In a recent circular all heads of schools had been renamed heads, but he insisted on being called a headmaster.

"I am the head and master of this school, and no circular is going to change that," he retorted in response to a teacher who suggested a new nameplate for his door. The students called him Headless Master behind his back. His idea of chairing a meeting was to control the discussions and reject any suggestions he did not like. He had, as usual, drawn up the agenda having not consulted with anyone. The teachers could raise issues under AOB: Any Other Business. But at this point, Kgaka rehashed earlier items or tossed in matters he had forgotten to put on the agenda. And he called upon only some teachers, ignoring the rest.

"The next item on the agenda is School Drop-outs. I have to report on this item at the prize-giving ceremony. The minutes of the previous meeting indicate that we had then lost five students. Three girls dropped out due to pregnancy, and two students absconded: a boy and a girl. Since then, two more girls have dropped out, both pregnant. The floor is open for discussions and comments."

Mr Kolo's hand shot up.

"Yes, Mr Kolo?"

"Like I said last time when this topic came up, I do not see what we can do about the problem of girls' falling pregnant. Girls will always fall pregnant; that is just the way things are. That is nature. So I say, we have heard the figures: let us just pray to God we do not lose any more girls, and let us go to the last item on the agenda."

There were nods because some teachers agreed with Mr Kolo; the rest look bored, waiting for the end of the meeting.

Mr Merake was invited to make a comment. "I have to agree with Mr Kolo. If these girls are loose, there is nothing we can do about it. Maybe it is even best that the really bad ones become pregnant and leave early, before they corrupt the rest of the school. You know what they say about a rotten apple."

Those who did not agree had long given up trying to put their views forward. These meetings were about hearing the same voices saying the same things over and over again. There were people who would readily vote for the scrapping of staff meetings; people considered the meetings too long, too boring, too controlled and too ineffective.

The headmaster was satisfied that the matter had been adequately dealt with. He moved on to the next topic: the annual prize-giving ceremony. Mr Merake was invited to report about the progress. In his report, he hardly mentioned the hard work of the other members of his committee. Although he had already announced to all the teachers on three occasions that the Minister would be attending, he reported about the matter yet again. "It will be the first time ever that a Minister has ever graced a school occasion with her presence. I have secured the attendance of not just any Minister but the Minister of Education herself. I think that calls for an applause."

"A round of applause, please!" The headmaster ordered. There was a reluctant clapping of hands.

Under AOB, Merake reminded the meeting that due to his heavy responsibilities, he would not be teaching on the Friday before the event: he could not possibly be expected to teach on the eve of such an important occasion, and he invited volunteers to stand in for him. No hands shot up, and he could not understand why there was no stampede for the privilege of helping the man of the moment. The headmaster volunteered the services of a new teacher without even glancing at her. "There being no further business, I declare this meeting closed," he intoned: a phrase he had picked up from some regional education meeting.

CHAPTER 14

" "What did they say to him, the old men? What did they say to Tshepo?" There was an edge to the question that made Stan look up. He sensed that his sister was in one of her dark moods: a mixture of anger, frustration and belligerence. It was a Saturday afternoon and the two were walking home, having spent the day at their cousin Mimi's wedding.

"What do you mean?" Stan said, as if delaying an answer would somehow make it go away. He knew exactly where Mosa was going with the question, but he was tired after a long day, and would have preferred a lazy stroll back to Mitch's.

Mosa glared at her brother. "The instructions given to the new husband by the other married men: what were they?"

"Mosa, how am I supposed to know? Those instructions are given in private. You know that. Only married men are allowed to be present when they are given."

"Don't give me that. You were there. I saw you. You were serving them tea and beer. And I know you have long ears." They both knew that Stan, just like Mosa, was always eavesdropping when children were being excluded. And listening in was never hard anyway, because all adults seemed to think that children were too ignorant to hear things. And they were always asking for tea and water, so children came and went during their adults-only meetings.

"Mosa, you know I was not supposed to be listening, and I am definitely not supposed to be talking about what I heard. I could get into trouble if you got it into your head to go around repeating what I tell you."

"Come on: think about it. Why should these instructions be private anyway? We should all know what marriage is all about long before we go into it. Then we would go into it with full information."

"Oh, come on, Mosa. We both know that you want me to tell you so you can get more ammunition in support of some view you already hold. I am even willing to say I agree with you. But still, I do not feel right about repeating what I heard to you. It is supposed to be private, for the new husband's ears only." It was at times like these that Stan wished he had a nice, quiet sister who did the dishes and swept the yard without analysing everything to death.

"Listen, I will trade you. I will tell you what the bride was told if you tell me what the groom was told."

"That is not a fair trade, and you know it. Not that I am willing to trade anyway! But you want from me information available to men only. The bride gets her instructions in the presence of the groom, and both men and women. And any idiot can listen to any wedding song to learn what you are offering as a trade." Stan was smiling now, despite himself. He loved this tricky, charged sister of his.

"Okay; okay. Forget the trade. But you'd better tell me, because otherwise I will pester you to death; you know that. So why are you prolonging the suffering?"

Stan tried a new excuse. "If I tell you what I heard, it will make you angry. I am not sure I want to be the one to tell you. I would rather we ended this day in a happy mood. Can't we discuss this tomorrow?"

"Do not worry: I will not kill the messenger. Go ahead: I am listening."

"Like I said, I heard only a small part of what was said. I cannot say that what I heard is representative of the entire advice given to Tshepo. I only heard what Uncle Maruping said. You know how he is."

"I am listening."

"Well, Uncle Maruping did advise Tshepo to try to avoid hitting his wife. He said . . . he said . . . if he ever had to hit her, he should never do it in public. He also advised that he should not hit her around the face." Stan stopped, his body tense as if he were expecting an explosion. Mosa said nothing, but her look made it clear that she expected the whole story.

"And Rra-Masu added that he was never to use his bare hands to hit his wife: He said a belt or a switch, but never his bare hands. He said a man who uses bare hands could get into trouble because he could easily kill his wife. Getting a belt or a switch allowed for the cooling of a husband's temper. I am only repeating what I heard, okay? Do not look at me like that." When Mosa said nothing, Stan was forced to continue. "He also advised that the first year would be critical in establishing his authority. He said that if a man failed to show a woman who is the head of the family within the first year, he would never succeed after that."

"What did Tshepo say?"

"He did not say anything! He was not invited to say anything. He just sat there listening. He had no chance to say anything. He was being told, not asked. He looked embarrassed. I even felt sorry for him." Stan was waving his hands as he spoke.

"What did Rra-Kubu say?"

"I did not hear what he said. Like I said, I was not there all the time. I also had to pretend not to be interested; otherwise, I would have been thrown out, even lashed, for having long ears. I might still get lashed if you start repeating what I am telling you now."

"Did anyone talk about love? about respect? friendship? companionship?"

Stan stopped and faced his sister. He looked wounded and angry. "Mosa, you are treating me like I am implicated here. You are interrogating me. That is not fair!"

Mosa did not acknowledge her brother's anger but simply repeated her question, with a controlled, steely voice: "Did anyone talk about love? about respect? friendship? companionship?"

Stan felt defeated. He fell in step with his sister again, and continued. He told her that Tshepo was advised that during the first year of marriage, his love for his wife would blind him to her shortcomings: the worst dinner will taste great. He was reminded, however, that long after the love had evaporated, the marriage would still be there. It will be his duty, as the husband and head of the family, to make sure that the marriage, which was a relationship between two families, was not jeopardised by his love for his wife.

"Did they say anything about faithfulness?" Mosa wanted to know.

"He was told that every man went astray once in a while, and that only a fool flaunts his mistresses. He was warned never to eat too much at a mistress's house that he was not able to eat at home. According to Rra-Kubu, that is the biggest insult to a wife: not to eat dinner."

"What did you think as you listened to all this? What do you think?"

"Why me? I am not getting married. I do not care to answer any more of your questions with you in this mood."

"What mood am I in?"

"Obviously you are angry. And you are clumping me together with all these people. You know me well enough to know that I would never agree with all that stuff, but I do not see why you should back me into a corner and demand answers from me." Stan was more dismayed than angry.

Mosa sounded tired as she answered. "I am not demanding, Stan. Well, maybe I am. But I need to know that you are on my side. I need just one person on my side. Will you be that one person?"

Stan looked away with exasperation. "Why do you have to fight every single moment? Why won't you just relax and enjoy life a little bit?"

"Look at me, Stan. Look at me." It was an order, and Stan had no choice but to turn around. He was expecting sparks of anger from Mosa's eyes, but what he saw was something else. A tiredness. Eyes brimming with a plea for understanding. "I am not fighting, Stan. I am thrashing to stay alive. Can you understand that?"

Stan tried to redirect the mood. "Mosa, you were happy eating and singing the whole day. Do we have to end the day on this sad note? Do we have to part in this gloomy mood?"

"So now it is me who is responsible for 'this mood', as you put it." The anger was back.

"No: I am just saying that the two of us need not fight. Not on this topic, anyway. Why can't we postpone this discussion? We are not going to solve it tonight, or ever, for that matter. Why do we have to fight today, of all days, when I have not seen you for a whole week?"

Mosa looked hard at her brother. "Okay; okay. I understand. But you should have heard some of the stuff they were saying to Tshepo and Mimi. It just blew my mind! Can you believe that she was told to expect – to expect – that Tshepo might go a bit astray? And she was told this in his presence! That is a clear licence for him to do so, if you ask me. If this happens, she is told, she must be strong and be good. She must hold on to one of the house pillars before she is tempted to complain about his behaviour. A wife must persevere, she was told. Divorce is a shame, not just to the woman but to her entire family. Mma-Ranko, Maruping's wife, said, 'Tshepo is your father now.' Her father! I mean, Stan, that is outrageous. How do you, Stan, end up being your wife's father? I mean, what gives you the right?"

"There you go again! Stop it, please. I cannot take it when you do that. What have I done or said that makes you direct your anger at me? Why am I the target of your anger? Why do you implicate me?"

"I am sorry, Stan, but you are implicated. We are all implicated. You are right, though: I have no right to treat you like this. But look at all this from start to finish. It has been Mimi as an object. You heard the conversation at the very first meeting of the families. You saw the hoof ceremony this afternoon. How can I not be angry?"

Mosa's mind went back to the first meeting of the two families. Tshepo's family had come seeking Mimi's hand in marriage. Mosa was amongst the girls serving tea and food to the assembled guests. There were at least thirty people there: men and women. Mosa was fascinated by the interactions between the two sets of families. Sometimes the meetings were of both men and women, and at other times the men moved away to meet privately. It was like watching a play in which the script was old and well known to the actors. Some had large parts; some had bit parts. The maternal uncles and their wives seemed to play the biggest parts of all. Mosa poured tea and handed out teacups as if she were not at all interested in the discussions going on around her. No one, except perhaps her mother, could have guessed she was interested.

"Our son has found a water gourd in this family," Tshepo's aunt announced.

"This water gourd: what does your son say its name is?" Mimi's aunt responded.

"Our son says the gourd goes by the name Mimi."

"Oh, Mimi. Does this Mimi have a last name?"

"Yes, Mimi Selato."

"What else does your son tell you about this water gourd?"

"Our son wants to take the water gourd for himself; to make Mimi his wife."

"What does your son say is the condition of the water gourd?"

"As the wife of the uncle of the young man who seeks a water gourd from the Selato family, I do not understand the question."

"Does the water gourd you seek have any cracks, or is it intact?'

"The water gourd we seek has cracks; it has two cracks, in fact."

"Who is responsible for the two cracks?"

"We are responsible for the second crack. But we are prepared to assume responsibility for the first crack as well."

"What are you saying? Please make yourself clear for all of us assembled here to understand. It is a major responsibility that you are tying yourself to."

"Our son tells us that the water gourd has two cracks. Our son is responsible for the second crack. Our son, however, accepts the gourd with the two cracks. We take responsibility for the cracks. We will take the wife with the two children."

"We hear you. What are you offering about the crack you have caused? We cannot discuss whether you may take our child as your wife until we have dealt with that problem. We are not able to answer you until you clean up the path you have littered. What do you say to that?"

"We accept that. We came prepared for that rebuke. We offer our apologies. We beg that you put your hands in cold water before you are tempted to use them against us. We come in peace, and apologise for our son's behaviour in fathering a child in your house without the benefit of marriage. We offer the traditional *tlhagela* cow."

"We hear you. We hear your apology. We note your offer to pay the *tlhagela* cow. But we need time to discuss the matter amongst ourselves."

As the visiting family was led away to a neighbour's yard, Mimi's family met to discuss the offer of the *tlhagela* cow. Mosa missed most of the discussions that followed, but lingered as much as possible, offering more cups of tea and bread, to the gratitude of the people assembled. She caught her mother's eye. Mara was not fooled by her daughter's great show of hospitality. She knew her daughter only too well. Others congratulated her for having such a dutiful daughter. Mothers lamented about the laziness of modern children, whereas fathers accused these mothers of not being strict enough.

The talk went back to Mimi and her marriage negotiations. There was consensus that Mimi's second child was two years old, after it was pointed out that she had been born in the year Grandmother Rankgole died: two harvests ago.

The fact that Tshepo had practically lived with Mimi since the birth of their child was discussed. Some argued that he should be made to pay an additional cow for that behaviour alone; others said there was no basis in custom for that additional payment. Instances were cited in which an additional cow had been levied against the family of a prospective son-in-law; yet others were cited in which only after many years of living together and many more children had been born was the *tlhagela* cow paid. An argument ensued as to what was the real custom, as opposed to modern deviations. Someone suggested that they should not react too harshly so early in the marriage negotiations, and that there was still the *bogadi*, or bride-wealth stage, to come. A tough stand would have to be adopted then to ensure the maximum possible number of cattle as *bogadi*.

An aunt who was on her feet as she was about to go to the toilet made a comment, and was reprimanded. She was ordered to either sit down to make the comment or leave and make it later. At her age and with her experience, she ought to know that speaking while standing would give the marriage bad luck. The marriage would never sit down and settle down into happiness; instead, it would stand up and float about in confusion. That she could have done something like that was just one more example of the erosion of good, traditional practices. It was a wonder that God even bothered to send them rain occasionally, with the rampant disregard for culture and tradition. The aunt offered apologies, and called upon the ancestors for forgiveness. She never got around to making the contribution: the reprimand, it seemed, had knocked it out of her head.

After considering the pros and cons of seeking additional payment for Tshepo's behaviour, the family agreed that a *tlhagela* cow and an axe for the uncle would be sufficient as a sign of an apology from the prospective groom's family. It was also agreed that the cow would have to be an actual one, not the monetary value of one. The other family was called back in, and the matter was settled, with no dissent from anyone. The discussions then turned to other matters.

Then, this afternoon, Mosa observed for the first time the hoof ceremony. Her attention was drawn to a procession of about twenty men from two yards away, where Tshepo's family was staying during the three-day wedding celebrations. The procession had drawn the attention of giggling women as well as excited young men. Leading the procession was the groom's uncle, Rra-Lenong. Immediately behind him was the groom himself. Tshepo looked sheepish and embarrassed.

The uncle was holding up a stick that had a hoof stuck on to it. Slowly, the procession moved forward, attracting more and more onlookers behind it as it went on its way.

The procession made its way into the yard, past the milling wedding crowd, to where fifteen elderly men, all Mimi's relatives, were sitting under a *mogonono* tree. The men made a big show of talking amongst themselves, pretending to be oblivious to the procession. Rra-Lenong squatted on his haunches and announced that he was, on behalf of the groom's family, presenting the hoof. The rest of the members of his party were now squatting as well. The groom's head was bowed, and he would not meet anyone's eyes. Still the old men ignored the squatting line of men and continued to talk amongst themselves. The hoof bearer and his entourage remained squatting for a while, the hoof still impaled on the stick for all to see. The hoof bearer cleared his throat and announced more loudly this time that he was presenting the hoof for examination and approval, lowering the hoof in the direction of the old men. One of the old men reached for the hoof and pulled it off the stick. He examined it carefully, turning it this way and that. After much nodding and muttering of approval, the old man bit into the hoof. The tough skin at first stretched with resistance and then snapped off, leaving a white patch. Mosa expected it to bleed, but it did not. The old man chewed loudly as he passed the hoof on to his wizened neighbour. The hoof was passed from man to man in this way, each examining and biting into it in turn. The old men looked at each other, and finally, with a conspiratorial smile, announced that the hoof met their approval.

"You can see that we give you our daughter with all parts intact. She has two eyes, two ears, two arms, two legs." Then, after a significant pause, "And all other important parts are in place. Or do you know of any missing parts?"

"No, sir," answered Rra-Lenong. "Your daughter indeed has all her parts in the right places. She suffers from no disability."

"Then, if ever you do not want her any more, return her to us with all parts in place. We will not accept her back without an eye or an ear, or any other part, for that matter. She is now yours."

Turning to his entourage, Rra-Lenong declared, "The hoof is now ours. The daughter of the Selato family is now ours. Let us go back to report the good news to the waiting mothers.

The watching women greeted this news with an explosion of ululation. An elderly woman, who had looked too old to move, burst forward. A naked breast sprang from under her blouse. She held it in her hand, rubbed it and proudly offered it to Tshepo, who tried to escape this offer by hurrying past his uncle. But the old lady could not be evaded so easily. She blocked Tshepo's path, dancing, ululating and showering him with praises. His head bowed in unbearable embarrassment, he pushed the old woman away, fleeing from the yard ahead of the rest of his party.

Mosa's heart went out to Tshepo, who she knew to be a jovial and outgoing man. Had he even been aware that he would have to go through this? she wondered. The young know very little until it is too late.

Mosa wanted to go over to Tshepo to talk to him. Hearing his new wife referred to in such crude terms was clearly hard for him to bear. Would he have cared if another man's wife had been the subject? She believed that he would have. But then, perhaps, like all the other young men watching, had he not been at the heart of the ceremony, he might have found it amusing, gawking and snickering and hopping about with glee as the old men had passed the hoof around.

Mosa had felt a depression well up in that space in her heart in which there had been elation before. She continued to serve food and to collect used plates, but a part of her had left for some unreachable place.

Later, she sneaked into a room adjacent to the one in which the groom and bride were, to eavesdrop about the final marriage instructions given by the elders. She might as well get her fill of depression once and for all. Whereas the groom received his instructions privately, the bride was given hers in the presence of her new husband – who was receiving additional advice. The elders were both male and female, and came from both families. All the attendants had to be either married or widowed: divorcees could not possibly be good examples at a time like this.

Because of the size of the room and the number of participants, the door had to be left open, so the group members were spilling into the narrow passage. The groom and bride sat next to each other, he on a chair and she on a mat. From her hiding place, Mosa could see only the top of Mimi's head; even if she had been closer, it is unlikely she would have been able to see the young woman's face more clearly. An aunt repeatedly ordered Mimi to look down, warning that "a bride's eyes do not roam around." But Mosa could see the whole of Tshepo's face, and it looked like he had still not recovered from the hoof ceremony. On his wedding day, he looked forlorn and unhappy.

The young husband was instructed to refrain from spending nights away from home, missing meals, beating his wife. But if he ever did do these things, the young wife was instructed not to overreact. Mimi was informed that all families had problems but that only women who did not heed the marriage advice and instructions went around shouting their problems to the entire world. She was not to expose her house to the eyes of the public, and it was her duty to keep her husband happy.

"A wife holds on to the house pillar for support and comfort before shouting about her problems."

"A wife does not ask her husband where he has been."

"A husband may go chopping in a neighbouring field. Only a wife who has long ears will hear things she does not need to hear."

"A wife must cook, clean and wash for her husband."

"A husband served cold food will go looking for warm food some place else."

"Your husband must never complain of hunger."

"A married woman does not keep the company of unmarried women."

"A married woman must make sure the home fires do not burn out."

"There is no house without a leaking roof, but you do not see women in the streets telling all and sundry of their problems."

Mimi was told that her parents' house was not hers any more.

"We have taken their cattle. They have taken you. You must persevere."

"You do not belong here any more. We did not choose this man for you: you chose him."

Her duty was to her husband and his parents. Mimi was told that if it ever became necessary for her to complain about her treatment at the hands of her husband, she was to tell her husband's family, not her own.

"Your mother is your husband's mother now, not this woman who bore you."

"Do not shame us. None of us have ever been divorced: do not be the first."

Mimi had begun to cry under the onslaught, and her family was pleased at the reaction. A bride who did not cry at the final marriage instructions was stubborn and a disgrace to her family.

The wedding songs afterwards reinforced all these messages, causing Mimi to cry once more: crying as the crowd sang about how she had to go away and face the whip: about how they had eaten the cakes and will be leaving her with the problems of marriage. Another song urged the husband not to hit her, just to make-believe with a branch. And while the new bride was sobbing at all these songs, yet another song told her not to cry, because she was the one who chose him. There were songs telling her that she had been bought and paid for. Even in the songs problems and beatings were not mentioned, Mimi was promised a life of working for other people. The groom's mother was urged to leave the pots because the new cook had arrived. The jubilant crowd sang about the successful buying of Mimi and the acquisition of a water carrier. Hardships were not promised in all the songs, though: in some, Mimi's beauty was compared to that of the stars, and in others she was warned about an evil mother-in-law. They were all old songs, sung over and over again at countless weddings.

It was because of these events that Stan now found himself in a rather disagreeable conversation.

"Can I remind you what you said to me a few months ago: about respecting the ways of others as long as it does not hurt you?" Stan ventured.

"Exactly my point, Stan. This harms me. This hurts me. I am a woman, and I was embarrassed by the hoof ceremony. I was humiliated by the final instructions to Mimi. Do not even try to tell me I was not supposed to be there. That is not the point. The point is that from start to finish, the marriage ceremony was about the degrading of women. It was sanctioned humiliation. Women were portrayed as mere vessels for use by men."

Stan agreed with all his sister had said, but felt that agreeing was not going to be enough to get her out of her anger and frustration. Of late, these discussions seemed always to end with him on the defensive, and he did not think that was fair. He made the error of expressing that view.

"Fair! You talk of fairness?" Mosa responded with characteristic energy. "It might not be fair for me to vent my anger on you, but is it fair for the whole society around me to objectify me all the time? Is it

155

fair that I am described as a water gourd that has cracks? Is it fair that cows are paid to my father in exchange for my labour, both productive and reproductive? Someone else gets paid so that my children will not be mine! Is it fair that I am reduced to a sexual part: represented as a hoof cut off from a cow? Is it fair that I get instructed to obey my husband? To serve him without complaint? To tolerate his beatings, his unfaithfulness? I am sorry that you have to suffer my telling you about it; at least that is all you have to deal with." Mosa's whole body was taut, as if a bend of the finger, an angling of the head, even a creasing of the forehead, any slight movement, would result in a break.

"I hear you; I hear you," Stan said, his voice tired and helpless. "You know that I understand where you are coming from. I could not even bring myself to watch the hoof procession. You know that I feel helpless, but what can I do? What can you do? I cannot change the society around us. You cannot do that either. People have been doing things this way for centuries. They are not just going to change overnight. And Tshepo had no way of getting out of all this stuff. Anyone who wants to get married has to do the whole thing. What can I say? What can I do?"

"I cannot believe we are just helpless. I refuse to accept that. That we must just let all this go on without lifting a finger. People are dying around us because of AIDS. Telling women to expect their husbands to sleep around does not help the situation. Telling them to be passive is a recipe for disaster. Surely everyone can see that."

"I agree." Stan had never really reached that point in his analysis of the issues, but he was not going to disagree with anything now. "But I still do not see what we can do. People know no other way of doing things."

"I have heard that excuse about too many things. I cannot accept that things cannot change just because that is the way things have been done in the past. I just cannot accept that. I just can't!"

Brother and sister walked in silence for a while, until Mosa suggested they go and sit under a big *morula* tree.

"Please make me laugh. Tell me a story, Stan."

"Oh, no."

"Oh, yes."

"What kind?"

"Any funny kind. What about a bush story? A lion-and-hyena

story, perhaps? A story that will make me laugh."

"I cannot make my mind conjure up a funny story after the conversation we've just had."

"That is exactly why you must come up with a story. Get me out of my mood. Please, Stan. You can do it. Make me laugh, please."

The goats eating *morula* fruit ignored the pair, who also gathered dozens of the fruit, and proceeded to eat them. Stan told his sister a story, and she listened as she sucked one fruit after another, spitting out the pips. When they got up to leave, the mood had changed to a happy one. The sun was setting, and when Stan looked at his watch, he noted that it was six o'clock. Having walked his sister home, Stan walked on to his temporary home, with Mr Mitchell.

CHAPTER 15

The sun rose on the day of the clothes-distribution and appease-ment ceremonies to meet an extended family eager to give thanks and make merry. Pule had been dead for six months, and the family members were meeting to make offerings to their ancestors. It had been decided that the trunk could not be left sealed during the appeasement ceremony. There could not be any merry making while a trunk containing the personal effects of a deceased sat unopened in the house.

Unlike the funeral gathering, though, this was not a time for mourning but a time to celebrate a life. It was a time to remember Pule, and to laugh about his follies, and muse about what could have been. It was a time to open the trunk so that Mosa and Stan could share their brother's possessions.

It was time for the completion of yet another circle, Mara thought.

Mosa looked up from the big bowl of dough she was kneading, her face covered in blotches of bread flour. Her mother, sensing Mosa's eyes on her, looked up. Mara's hand paused over the drum of cooking oil she was about to open, and she waited expectantly. There was a twinkle in Mosa's eyes, a sparkle that her mother had not seen for years.

"Thanks for not calling me Nellie or Elizabeth or Mary: I am happy with Mosa. And I love you."

Mara, having long forgotten the conversation about Mosa's name, had no idea as to where this was coming from. She searched Mosa's face for a clue, but all she got was a smile, and Mosa went back to kneading the dough.

"I love you, too," was all she could say in response. Declarations of love were rare amongst children and parents, but for some reason,

Mara did not feel self-conscious about saying it: the strange had a way of seeming normal with her.

With this to start the celebration, the day had great potential for both of them. Mosa was making fat cakes for tea. Other relatives were already busy with other chores.

At ten o'clock the clothes distribution began under the watchful eye of Mma-Ranko, and was carried out by Mosa and Stan. The bulk of the items went to the two themselves, but a few others were given away: a pair of shoes for an uncle, a plate for a cousin. Pule had little, so there was not much to distribute. These, however, were mementoes. Mosa passed a small purse to her mother, for no reason other than that its size meant she would be able to take it any place she went. Her mother looked up with gratitude: this strange daughter of hers could see into her heart.

It was decided that the ancestor appeasement would be performed in the late afternoon. The rest of the day was devoted to cooking and singing, and by mid-afternoon the older women were straining the traditional beer. As the first taste of beer was passed around, the liver from the recently slaughtered cow was also being served. The liver was always the first part to be cooked and eaten, and the fresher the better. Things were on schedule, and the mood was a happy one.

The two deceased grandparents chosen to be appeased by the ceremony were remembered, as stories about what they had done and said were recalled. These were old stories that everyone within the family had heard at one time or another. The grandfather, Rra-Mara, was remembered as a big, gentle man, until he was crossed; then, it was said, he could be as furious as the August wind. The grandmother, Mma-Mara, was beautiful, and had been spoilt with presents by her husband – or so the stories went. Few of the grandchildren had been old enough to be able to now tell the stories first hand. The stories they told had therefore been handed down and, no doubt, embellished during the many retellings. It was said, for example, that Rra-Mara had been a great hunter, who had once wrestled and killed a wounded cheetah. About Mma-Mara, it was said that she was a great storyteller who always had children around her, eager for one more story.

By the time the second ceremony began, everyone was happy. The two beer buckets, for tasting only, because no beer could be served until the ceremony itself, had helped matters a lot. Rre-Namane started the ceremony by calling for prayer, and a priest, Father Mogoma of the Three Apostles of Zion Church, stepped forward in a white robe and blue sash, to lead the gathering.

"God, our father, you who are our salvation. You who are all powerful. Bless all of us. Bless this gathering that has gathered in your name, father. Give us the knowledge of what our ancestors require. Guide us so that we can do that which they require. For, God, Almighty, they sit with you up there, and you know what they want. Bless Mara, father. Bless that breast that has breastfed. Bless her children. Bless little Nunu. Let there be peace in this family, father. Your child Mara has known unhappiness. Only you know why you took her children, father, but we pray that you give her some peace, father. Bless her, father, and give her peace. We ask all these in the name of the Father, the Son and the Holy Spirit. Amen."

"Amen," chorused the gathering.

A woman began singing a popular hymn. Unlike at the funeral, the hymns were happy ones. Some people swayed to the music, and there was even some dancing. This was not an occasion to mourn the dead; it was one to celebrate them. After much singing, Rre-Namane called the group to order. The sun was going down, and the procession to the graveyard was next.

Stan found himself crying, not from sadness but from all sorts of emotions. He had never really thought of his grandparents much until his mother decided to go ahead with the ancestor-appeasement ceremony. Since then, fragments of memories had seeped back into his head. About Mma-Mara, his grandmother, he remembered a beautiful face that had lots of wrinkles, gentleness and grace. An old woman who used their behinds to clean off her hands after eating fatty meat. It was a privilege to have your butt chosen. The mischievous woman would call for snuff. This was the cue for all the kids to come forward giggling, and she would grab their crotches and sniff, sneezing and making a big pretence at having sniffed the most powerful snuff ever. But as he grew older, he refused to offer his butt or his snuff, and his cousins would try to catch him. He recalled an emotional tug between wanting to go forward to offer his grandmother a sniff and refusing, and declaring himself too old for that. Mr Mitch would probably call this child abuse or some kind of perversion, he thought. He did not know what he thought about his granny's teasing now. But he knew that it had been an important and beautiful part of his growing up. How would he react if Mara did that to Nunu? He did not think he would like it. He would have to explore his thoughts about it some other time. Mosa would no doubt have all kinds of ideas about that.

As for his grandfather, the man he was named after, he remembered even less about him. The image that came to mind was of a man who had unclear features, sitting just outside the yard, making huge wooden spoons while a dog lay next to him. The man was happy and humming to himself. Was this picture really a memory? He wasn't sure. Perhaps it had been conjured up through stories told of him: after all, the grandfather had died when he, Stan, was only three years old. There was, however, no shortage of stories about him from other members of the family.

The first grave was their grandfather's. A cow's foetus had been ground into seswaa. A bucket of beer was brought forward. Mara, Mosa, Stan and Nunu were lined up at the head of the grave, and under the supervision of Rre-Namane, each one ate a handful of the meat and took a sip of the beer.

"The ancestors of Selato, may you rest in peace. Give us good luck and blessings. We give you a calf that has known no sins." Each one uttered the words in turn, and Nunu got it so jumbled up that even Rre-Namane had to smile. The remaining beer and beef were left on the grave. This was repeated three more times – at the graves of Mma-Mara, Thabo and Pule.

This done, the crowd went back to the yard, where there was much feasting, drinking, singing and dancing.

The day had been a great success indeed, except for an unfortunate fall, probably due to a bit too much alcohol, which had left Maruping with a broken arm. But still, good things sometimes come from bad things. Maruping's wife promptly became all concerned and made her husband promise to have the fracture set by a traditional doctor. She argued that although it would cost a cow, a broken bone was not something to be taken lightly. Maruping argued that a visit to the hospital, which would cost only two pula, would be enough. But his wife insisted that the traditional doctor be consulted even after the hospital visit.

Mma-Ranko had her own motives. She knew that with a traditionally set arm, her husband would be forbidden to raise his hand to anyone: neither her nor the children. An act such as that would make the recipient of his blows get a fracture which could not be easily mended. Of course, with her husband out of commission, it would be hard: the children needed new school shoes, and there was a child on the way. But it was a small price to pay for about six months of domestic peace.

The four members of the family retired to bed. Mosa, however, was not quite done. She had enjoyed the day for what it had symbolised for them: togetherness. She enjoyed remembering the dead under the atmosphere of happiness and celebration. Even as she had handled her brother's items, she had not been flooded by grief, as she had expected. Yes, she had enjoyed the day, but she had yet one more thing to do before going to bed.

"Mma, let me tell you a story." It was late, and Mara wanted a bit of peace and quiet. The day had gone very well, but it had exhausted her, and she wanted to get some sleep.

"Mosa, it is late: how about tomorrow?"

"No: this story cannot wait. It has to be told tonight. Now."

Before Mara could argue some more, Mosa began.

"A long time ago, there were two women who were great friends. They could pick each other's teeth without fear of harm, as the saying goes. They laughed and raised their children together. Their children played together as if they were children of the same womb. They got involved in each other's joys, just as they got involved in each other's problems. They never said that the private wrangles of one womb could not be entered by people from another womb, as the saying goes.

"They were both poor, these women. Poor only in material things, that is. But they were rich in love and kindness. In the evenings, one would take her bowl of porridge and go to the other's yard. On rare days, there would also be *morogo*. On very rare days, there would be a few pieces of meat. On all days, there was love and caring.

"The two friends would sit and eat from one plate, then another. Sharing. Caring. Loving. Trusting. They would swap stories about lovers and children.

"Then, one day, one of the two friends started going through a series of misfortunes. First, one child got sick. Then another. Her only daughter withdrew into herself, and did not help with her sick brothers. The youngest child became foreign, and took up foreign habits.

162

"Desperate and confused, the friend went from diviner to diviner, from prophet to prophet, from priest to priest. She was told that she had been bewitched. This woman was at first not convinced, but then, two of her children withered away and died. Two strong boys, snatched away in their youth. Her daughter . . . her daughter . . . her daughter went astray. Her youngest son turned his back on his culture.

"This woman, in her hour of need, did not go to her only friend because the friend was responsible for her misery. Yes, her friend, who had been there for her before, who had helped when she was limping with the pains of childbirth, who had helped her raise these very children, was now killing them off.

"The friendship died; there was no more laughter, no more sharing of food, no more love. Instead, there was anguish. The children of the two women were confused. Should they talk to each other? Should they play together? Should they even greet each other? When one offered a pencil to another in class, there was suspicion: perhaps death was being offered.

"Then the witch became the victim. Her daughter fell ill. She, too, like her friend, hopped from diviner to diviner, from prophet to prophet, from priest to priest. But her daughter became worse. There seemed to be no hope. She, too, had been bewitched, like her friend. Bewitched by her own friend. The victim had become the witch. The friend who had first shunned her and turned her back on her was now killing her daughter. The friend was confused: what had she ever done to deserve this? How could someone she had loved so much do this to her?

"But the truth was that the daughter was dying of AIDS. Just like her friend's two sons had died of AIDS. She had not bewitched her friend's sons. Just as her friend had not bewitched her daughter. The sons had died, and now the daughter was dying, just as many other people around them were dying. They were dying of AIDS. That is the simple truth. A painful truth. A truth exploited by many diviners, priests and false prophets, for their own financial gain.

"Then, one evening, the friend who had the dying daughter came to visit the friend who had the dead sons. The friend who had the dead sons had just had a ceremony to appease the ancestors. The friend who had the dying daughter was hoping that there would still be a bit of love where once there had been plenty. The friend who had the dying daughter had no porridge with her: just love and a need to be loved. The friend who had the dying daughter was coming in peace.

"Mma, do you think the friend who had the dead sons would open her heart just a little for the friend who had the dying daughter?"

"Oh, Mosa. Mosadinyana. Mosa. Please, don't," Mara implored, sobbing.

"I asked you a question, Mma: will she?"

"Yes. Yes. But maybe Lesedi will not see me. If she was told that I am the one killing her daughter, how can she want to see me? Don't you understand that you cannot just undo things like that? Oh, how I would love to see and talk to Lesedi again."

"Auntie Lesedi, please come in: your friend wants to talk to you."

Lesedi, who had heard everything from just outside the door, came in. She too was crying. She had been reluctant to come, but Mosa had literally ordered her to.

"I am tired. I think I will go to bed and leave you two together." With that, Mosa went outside, entered her room and went to bed, carefully easing herself into the bed she was sharing with Nunu for the night. Stan shifted in his sleep; kicked a bucket at the foot of his bed; rolled over, causing a creak, and went back to his snoring. Within minutes, Mosa, too, was asleep.

Stan woke up to the sound of his mother singing. At first, he thought he was surely dreaming. His mother did not sing – well, not any more. He could not remember the last time he had heard her singing. He rose from bed, taking in the empty, narrow bed that Nunu and Mosa had shared. He dressed and went to join his family. Already there were some girls who had come to wash up after yesterday's festivities. And boys were wheeling some pots on wheelbarrows back to the neighbours from whom the pots had been borrowed. He was embarrassed for having overslept, but grateful for having been allowed to do so. But then he realised that the good mood of the previous day was still in the air. The children, even as they were doing their chores, were laughing and horsing around.

There was trash everywhere: empty cans, bones, plastic bags and pieces of paper, all over the yard. Mr Mitch was forever asking him about this practice of the Batswana to drop litter anywhere, without apparently thinking of the consequences. Stan had no answer for this, and saw no chance of an end to the habit. Campaigns about litter were, after all, never focused on discouraging people from littering but rather on picking up the litter. When Mr Mitch asked the question in class once, there was silence – perhaps due to a lack of comprehension of the question. Finally, a tentative hand went up, and the student offered the answer that perhaps the person throwing the can or plastic bag from a moving vehicle or at his feet at a bus stop did not need it any more. There were nods from the class. The answer was so obvious that the rest of the class thought it was perhaps a trick question. Mr Mitch seemed perplexed by the answer, even a bit angry. The exchange left Stan wondering about the problem, but he was yet to arrive at an answer that satisfied him, let alone Mr Mitchell.

By the afternoon, all the work had been done, and because all the food had been eaten or given away on the day of the ceremony, there was nothing to keep children hovering around. Food from an ancestor-appeasement ceremony could not be saved for later use. Stan had learned this only the previous day, when he suggested that some food be saved.

Privacy returned to the family. Mara went to check on Lesedi's sick daughter, Cecilia, and took Nunu with her: she wanted to show her off. This would be the first time in more than a year that she walked the twenty-minute or so walk to her old friend's house. She was really happy that their friendship had been rekindled. Thinking about how she had been persuaded by total strangers to turn her back on a very special friend still filled her with anger at herself. When she had raised the issue of the white power that she had been sure she had seen trickling from her friend's palm, Lesedi had at first not remembered. Then, recalling that fateful day, Lesedi remembered that she had been eating some biltong as she had been walking to her friend's house: she was certain it must have been some salt she had had in her hand that Mara had seen. Mara's body shivered with regret as she thought of all the unnecessary hurt that had resulted from the diviners' supposed advice and counsel.

As Mara left, Mosa promised to go over after school on Tuesday. She would be out early, and would go over and help with fetching water from the neighbourhood tap.

"Do you think I should come back home? I want your honest opinion." Stan was taking advantage of the privacy to talk to his sister after their mother had left for Lesedi's house.

They were lying on a mat under a tree. Stan had been reading a novel while Mosa was flicking through a science textbook. She was doing some extra reading to catch up. She was determined to do well, especially in Mr Merake's class. He controlled the term examinations, but he did not control the final examinations: they were set and marked nationally.

The two weeks Stan had spent at home had brought to him the reality of the poverty under which his sister lived. It was clear that the weekday school lunch was the most substantial meal of the day for her. Her room was also a kitchen, even though, luckily, no cooking was done in there except on rainy days. She had to carry water in buckets from a tap outside the yard. He had hardly given any of these matters a thought over the past two years. He realised how lucky he was to have all he had: good light to study by; plenty of spare time to play and do school work. There was no doubt that he would pass his examinations and go on to university on a government scholarship.

Mosa looked up at her brother, and took in the broad face: almost too broad for his thin and tall frame, she thought, as if the face had grown up ahead of the body.

"No, little brother of mine, I love you very much, but I want my bedroom back. I am not sharing it with you. I refuse to wake up to your snoring one more night." Having teased out a ghost of a smile from her brother, she continued: "No, seriously: you know that *mma* could never feed and clothe all of us if you stayed here. Nunu and I are all she can manage as it is. Mr Mitch is helping all of us by supporting you. As it is, if he had not taken you in as he has, I might have had to drop out of school. We both know that if choices had to be made, you would have been chosen to stay in school. So I owe Mr Mitch a lot."

"I thought you were somehow against Mr Mitch."

"No: I am not against Mr Mitch, as you put it. He's a good, kind man. He is giving you a great opportunity. What I think, however, is that you have to realise that Mr Mitch's ways are not always the only ways. Or the only ways that are worthy of respect. He took you in because you are intelligent, not because you are a 'yes' man. You have to challenge him and not just take in everything he says. You cannot hide in his ways. That will not protect you from surviving in this culture." Mosa's voice had taken on a kindly tone.

166

"Where do you get the idea that I do not challenge him? Anyway, you do not know that guy. He asks and asks and asks. For me, just dodging his questions whilst I hold my views has been my way out of the questions." Stan sounded uncharacteristically defensive.

"This brings us back to our discussion of a few weeks ago: your reluctance to explore your own views about your own culture. You were never one to dodge questions. I think, although you will not accept it, the events of the past two years have silenced you in ways beyond just the obvious. Yes: you continued to do well in school, but you lost your confidence as far as broader issues are concerned. You hid from yourself and other people. Am I wrong?"

"I guess you are right. I guess watching my brothers wasting away shocked me into emotional retreat. Especially Pule. Here was this swaggering young man. He played football. He was strong. He was popular. He was just so alive. And then he withered and died; just withered and died. For me, I could neither accept that he was bewitched nor that he was dying of AIDS. I guess I just clammed up." Stan's eyes were wet with tears.

Mosa studied her brother before responding. It occurred to her that Stan must have had a special link with his two brothers because of their gender. Just as much as she often saw herself in her mother. "The back hoof steps where the front hoof has stepped," is an often quoted saying. The gender-specific duties and obligations of the brothers would now be his. Their death had that special dimension for him. He was the back hoof, and was afraid of where fate was due to land him.

Finally she broke the silence. "First we have to accept that both Thabo and Pule are gone. What is important is that we have survived the ordeal intact as a family, or what remains of that family. Look around you: many have not. Families are breaking up; others are being expanded in ways the members cannot cope with. We are the lucky ones. So go on and take advantage of what Mr Mitch is offering you. And if we have not learned from our experiences, we will never learn."

Then Stan tried to get information from his sister about the prize-giving ceremony, but all he got were evasive answers.

"Just wait and see," she said.

"But you seem to be putting a lot of time into it. I am curious."

"Just wait and see."

CHAPTER 16

She used to be a proud woman. Tall, poised, nose slightly turned up. Lips set in a permanent promise of a smile. She had been poor, too. Materially poor, that is. But proud. She used to have a quiet dignity. A dignity some people are born with and others spend years trying to acquire. She did not have any of these qualities any more. She was hardly human any more. Mosa watched her as she lay under a tree, looking like something that had survived a fire, if what she had become could be described as survival under any circumstances. She was the colour of tar, an unhealthy black-grey, and her hair was thin and reddish.

Next to her sat her daughter Bibi, dazed. Although she was about two years old, she had stopped walking months ago and slid about on her bottom. She moved very little. She had nowhere to go. Mosa thought she looked like some strange bird. Her neck was stretched, and her mouth looked like a chopped-off beak. Her neck was rigid. Her eyes occasionally swivelled from side to side; otherwise, they were on her mother, as if she were afraid that if she moved away, or even looked away, her mother might just disappear. It was perhaps a testimony to the power of the maternal bond that the little girl still saw, in this blackened, horizontal remnant of humanity, her mother.

Mosa was sitting on a wooden bench with two other women. They had come to see Cecilia, who had been moved out of the hot, tin-roofed house for some air. Tears welled up as Mosa looked at this human being who was once so full of life. One of the women, unable to hold back her tears, stood up and left without a word. So much pain. So little hope. So many dying. So many children watching as their loved ones waste away and die. Many little faces full of fear and confusion. So little time to love the living because all emotions go into caring for the dying.

"I am sick, Mosa. I am sick," was all Cecilia could manage to whisper.

Mosa had nothing to offer in reply. She could not bring herself to offer any assurances about getting well soon. Her eyes moved from Cecilia's to the little girl's face. In response to her mother's words, Bibi had moved closer to her and was now gripping her thumb. Cecilia's hands were no more than a collection of bones. Bones reaching for bones, thought Mosa as she watched the little girl's bony fingers wrap around her mother's bony thumb. Could the human warmth the child was seeking possibly be found in that lifeless hand?

"Do you want me to take her away for a while? To get her to play with other children?" Mosa asked.

"No; no. I have to see her. Do not take her away. She will not let you anyway. She will not agree to go." Her voice, though low, was clear. She began to cough, her sunken chest heaving and heaving, as if it would just split open right there.

"Can I talk to you, Mosa? I need to ask you a favour."

The other woman left the shade in response, and went to join Cecilia's mother and other members of the family, sitting under another tree some distance away.

"Will you go to Kagiso Office? You know: the office for women and children? I want Bibi's father to pay child support. Before I die, I want to know someone will support her. Do you know anything about these things?"

Cecilia's voice was fading, and Mosa had to move closer to listen. This meant sitting on the mat next to the dying woman. Mosa was quite sure Cecilia had TB, but this was no time to think about personal dangers. Cecilia, lying on her side, grabbed Mosa's hand, and Mosa was surprised, even alarmed, at the power in that grip. For a brief moment, she panicked: what if I cannot get her to let me go?

"I have only been at the place once. But I do not know whether they can help. Yes: I will go and find out for you."

"You have to do it fast. I do not have a lot of time left. But I will not die until I am sure that something has been done. Please hurry." Having made her request, Cecilia let go of Mosa's hand and closed her eyes. Was she dead? Was she dying? But she seemed to be dozing off. Mosa stood up and bid the rest of the family farewell. She looked once more at little Bibi, and then her tears came rolling down. She thought of the saying that one can return to all previous homes, except for the most precious of all: one's mother's womb. Bibi was indeed trying to be as close to that home as possible, laying her head on her mother's belly. Her eyes still closed, the mother winced with pain. But she did not push the child away. As if sensing Mosa's thoughts, she uttered, "Let her be. This pain cannot compare with the pain of leaving her behind."

Mosa hurried away, like the woman before her, leaving the yard with rigid shoulders, trying to hide the anguish she felt. The family had plenty to deal with, and did not have the time to comfort the people who had come offering comfort to begin with.

Mosa's anguish was compounded by her knowledge that similar scenarios were playing themselves out in many homes in the wards, villages and towns countrywide: young people dropping like kernels from a maize cob in the hands of a greedy man. Her own brothers' deaths had gone the same way.

The young girl at the Kagiso Law Office was still licking stamps and addressing envelopes, the same as the last time Mosa had visited the place. Mosa told her she needed to see a lawyer. The young woman gave her a form to fill out, but without even looking at it, Mosa insisted that she wanted to talk to someone. The young woman, sensing an urgency, hurried off, and came back seconds later with another woman. This turned out to be the woman Mosa had once seen with Mr Merake.

"Come into my office. My name is Julia Kenare. I am a lawyer. I am one of three lawyers who work here. Kidi thinks you have an urgent problem." She was looking at Mosa as if trying to remember something. "You were here a few weeks ago, in school uniform. You left in a hurry without saying why. We were all puzzled by that."

"I have come back with a different problem now. I hope you can help me." Mosa was reluctant to be drawn into a discussion about her previous visit.

"I hope I can help you. But perhaps it is important for us to talk about why you practically ran out of this office last time. Is it the reception? We need to know. We deal with many people, and we would not want any of them to think we do not care about their problems. I need to know that you have some confidence in us before we begin." Ms Kenare had an open, sincere face.

170

"Well, to be honest, I do not think I would have come back if the problem I have come back about was not so urgent. I have come back because someone else needs urgent help. I do not want to say anything that might make you not want to help her."

Ms Kenare looked at Mosa for a long time before she answered. "I am sorry, but I have to insist. I need to know not why you came, but why you left. Was it something Kidi said to you? Was it something I or anyone in this office did?"

"Okay: here it is. I recognised you as a friend of Mr Merake, a teacher at our school."

"And?"

"And I do not understand how you can work here and be his friend! I have read your pamphlets, and I cannot accept that you can be his friend and still believe in what is stated in those pamphlets."

"And this is because of his harassment and perhaps even outright rape of students at your school?"

"You know about that?" Mosa was surprised at Ms Kenare's own directness.

"Everybody knows about that."

"Why isn't somebody doing something about it, then? Why aren't you doing anything about it?"

"Knowing is not the same thing as having proof. And people who tell do not always have the courage to do anything about it. You must know that. We clearly have lots to talk about. I think I am going to like you. You are bolder than many your age. But we have an urgent problem before us, according to you. We will have plenty of time for this later. But let me just start by assuring you that I have been in the company of Mr Merake, Bones as you all call him, on several occasions. Those meetings were organised by a friend. I needed to see the devil at close quarters, so to speak. That is all. But we will get back to that one of these days. Let us discuss what has brought you to this office today. What is so important that even after your negative first impressions of this office you still came back?"

Mosa told Ms Kenare about Cecilia. And as the lawyer asked her questions, she realised how little she knew about Cecilia's situation. She knew only the father's first name: Mothusi. She had no idea where he worked or how much he earned. She did not even know whether he had ever supported the child before.

They agreed that Mosa would take a questionnaire from the office back to Cecilia and help her sick friend complete it. Mosa suggested that Ms Kenare go with her, but the lawyer declined, saying it was better that a stranger were not present at the meeting. She would visit after all the papers had been prepared for the final signing. People talked, she said. Cecilia's family might not want lawyers trooping in and out of their yard. Mosa explained that she did not think they had much time: she estimated that Cecilia would be dead within two weeks, at most. Ms Kenare explained that she would file an urgent court application for child maintenance. If the father was co-operative, things might be worked out without the necessity of an urgent court action. The first step remained the supplying of the information sought in the questionnaire.

The following morning, Mosa returned the completed questionnaire. Getting the information was hard: Cecilia tired easily, and the questionnaire had dredged up details of her unhappy relationship with Mothusi. It was an emotional two hours.

After school, Mosa was back in Ms Kenare's office, as arranged. What with the prize-giving ceremony and Cecilia's urgent problem, she had plenty on her plate. But at least there were now professionals in charge of Cecilia's problem.

Ms Kenare's coolness and self-confidence of the previous day seemed to have disappeared. Instead, behind the desk was a flustered young woman, struggling to get a word in on the phone. Sitting beside the lawyer was a woman, who introduced herself brusquely as Naledi Katse, also a lawyer. Ms Katse was trying to listen in on the phone conversation, and she, too, seemed flustered. She kept on scribbling something on a pad and pushing it over to Ms Kenare, who gave it hardly a glance.

"The matter is urgent, Mr Registrar. We need a judge urgently . . . Please let me tell that to the judge myself. Just place the matter before a judge, and I will argue the urgency . . . My client might be dead by then, Mr Registrar . . . Yes, the child is two, but the matter is urgent. Why can't you let me argue that before a judge? . . . No; no; no: that is not what I am saying. I know you know your job. Thank you; thank you, Mr Registrar. I will wait for your call."

Ms Kenare put the phone down and the two lawyers explained to Mosa what the problem was. The Office of the Registrar was being difficult. A deputy registrar had decided that a child-support application could not possibly be urgent, and wanted the application to be registered in the usual way. That would mean more than six weeks before the application could possibly be heard. And even that was a very optimistic estimate. Getting a date for a case was not easy. And unless the case was registered as urgent, the lawyers for the other side would throw all kinds of delaying tactics at them.

"But Cecilia will be dead by then. I am sorry to be that blunt, but that is the sad fact." Mosa was feeling frustrated.

"We have not lost yet, Mosa. While I wait for the phone call from Mr Gatekeeper – that is what we call this particular deputy registrar – please take these papers for Cecilia to sign. Naledi will go with you."

Naledi nodded.

"Pick up Lily from her office so she can commission the oath," she told her colleague. "And Naledi, please take an ink pad in case Cecilia is too weak to sign her name. In that case, have her thumb print the documents. We need to have everything ready for tomorrow morning. My plan is we go up to the High Court whether Mr Gatekeeper calls or not." Ms Kenare was trying to sound optimistic, but Mosa could sense her desperation.

As they left the office, Mosa realised for the first time how young these lawyers were. Although she did not doubt their knowledge of the law, she could not stop feeling that their being young and female was working against them. That some officer, who was not a judge, could stand between a citizen and justice, and have two lawyers panicking and sweating, bothered her. She had never dealt with lawyers before, but still she felt that the two women were at some disadvantage.

Her concerns proved to be justified. The following day, she missed school to go to court with Ms Kenare. She spent most of the morning sitting on a couch outside Mr Gatekeeper's office while Ms Kenare went from office to office negotiating with officials at various levels of seniority. All kinds of hurdles were thrown in her way, but finally, after lunch, a clerk informed them that Justice Mensah-Khan would hear the case. Mosa let out a whoop of happiness, thinking that at last things were moving forward. But Ms Kenare's face collapsed, and Mosa was soon to understand why.

Contrary to standard procedure, Judge Mensah-Khan was hearing the urgent application in open court. Ms Kenare whispered to Mosa that this was not a good sign; in fact, there were several other signs that were not good. Generally, Judge Mensah-Khan avoided urgent applications. They often ended up as long trials, and he tried to avoid messy matters. Ms Kenare had not been expecting to argue the application before Justice Mensah-Khan: she tried to avoid him whenever she could.

Three loud bangs on the door ended all conversation in the courtroom, and all present sprang to their feet in response. The judge entered, walked to his seat, bowed and sat down. Everyone else bowed and sat down as well. The judge was a man who had a stern, unfriendly face and who dressed, as did the ten or so attorneys in the courtroom, in a black robe.

"Ms Kenare," the judge bellowed, "who is that woman sitting next to you? Is that your client? Your papers say she is dying. She does not look like she is dying to me."

"My Lord, this is –"

"I asked you a question, counsel: is that your client? Is that the applicant? Yes or no?"

"No, my Lord."

"Out, woman! You are not an attorney. You have no right to be seated there. Out! Ms Kenare, you should know better than to invite your friends and audience to sit wherever they want in my court. What do you think this is: a playground?" His eyes bored into Ms Kenare with naked fury.

A shocked Mosa quickly stood up and fled the courtroom – but re-entered through another door a few seconds later, and took her place in the public gallery.

"Why is this matter urgent? Just because your client now wants child maintenance, the matter is urgent: is that it? Did she have this child yesterday? Has she just remembered that she has a child with this man?"

"My Lord, the applicant is terminally ill. Should she die –"

"Are you God?"

"No, my Lord. If it pleases your Lordship, I have annexed medical records. They clearly indicate that the applicant has been in and out of hospital for the past two years. And –"

"You people are just confused. You think every woman who comes through your door has some urgent case. That we should just drop everything and grant all these orders. Is that what you want?"

The other lawyers in the Court lowered their eyes in sympathy with Ms Kenare.

"My Lord, this applicant has a two-year-old child who will no doubt be an orphan soon. I submit that the best interest of that child must be the primary consideration in deciding this matter. All we ask at this point, my Lord, is an order directing that the father come to this court on short notice to answer to the case we have set out in the papers. We do not seek any final orders in his absence. We are concerned that any more delays will result in –"

"Your papers are not in order. You have failed to show urgency. The child is two years old. Why did your client wait for two years before bringing this application? You say she has been sick for two years. The urgency, if any exists, is that of your client's own making. Your client must be a stupid woman." Suddenly something caught the judge's eye. "Are you with her?" He addressed a female lawyer who had just come in.

"No, my Lord: I am not with her," she said, sounding positively relieved that she could give this answer.

"Don't deny it. You are all together. Sit down and shut up."

Judge Mensah-Khan ordered that the matter be set down in the usual course because no urgency had been demonstrated. "In any case, there is nothing in your papers to show that the father, if he is indeed the father of your client's child, has the means to support the child. Your papers merely allege that he is working. They do not say how much he makes. This court does not make academic orders just for the sake of making orders. Application dismissed. Call the next case!"

Thus was justice dispensed in the case of Cecilia Malapa v Mothusi Matsumi.

The lawyer who was accused of being with Ms Kenare was next. She was a state attorney arguing for the dismissal of an appeal against conviction brought by a man who was appearing without an attorney. From the statements and the barrage of questions from Judge Mensah-Khan, it was clear to Mosa that the appellant needed no attorney at all: not with Judge Mensah-Khan presiding.

It seemed, from Judge Mensah-Khan's interventions and quizzing of the state attorney, that upon turning sixteen, a female person was deemed to be in a constant state of consent to have sex with anyone and everyone. It was her duty to withdraw that consent on a man-by-man basis. Her withdrawal of consent had to be loud and clear, and preferably accompanied by wild kicks and bites. If some poor man says he did not hear a clear and loud "No", surely he should be excused. Women were never too clear about these matters anyway. It could happen to any man: this pickle that this poor accused man had found himself in. And there had to be "hue and cry", the judge had said.

Upon marriage, according to Judge Mensah-Khan's reasoning, a woman remains in a constant state of consent to have sex with her husband. It seems that she might, in a very rare case, convince a police officer that a slap across the face is an assault. However, she can never convince anyone that her husband's act of forcefully throwing her on to the ground, pinning her down, and forcefully penetrating her with his erect penis, forcefully and repeatedly banging his pelvis against hers, is a wrongful act. It is not even the most basic of assaults, according to the reasoning of Judge Mensah-Khan. And he was simply quoting the law.

The nervous lawyer had tried to argue that the woman had resisted, had cried, had called for help, and that the man had claimed a marriage without proving that it really existed. She tried to argue that the couple had lived together before but that there had been no marriage: just a long, abusive relationship. But Judge Mensah-Khan was not impressed.

"The law is the law, counsel. You cannot change it just because you do not like it. We are dealing with a married couple here. There was no rape here, and if there was no rape, there was no assault. I allow the appeal. The appellant is acquitted and discharged. I will give my reasons later. Call the next case, please."

The road back home was long and at first silent. Mosa thought Ms Kenare might have been secretly crying: she had gone to the toilet immediately after the court session, only to emerge with a wet face and red eyes. As they drove along, neither of them was aware of the beautiful, rolling hills. Ms Kenare's eyes were on the road ahead.

Ms Kenare assured Mosa that she would re-draw the papers and start all over again the following morning, before a different judge. They needed something new to justify going back to court. Perhaps they could get an affidavit from a doctor to support their case. They might even have to come out and state in their application that Cecilia had AIDS. That might elicit some sympathy from one of the more humane judges. She promised Mosa that she would think of something. In turn, Mosa would have to ask Cecilia about disclosing her HIV status in the court papers. "Any other judge would have granted the application. But there was no way Judge Mensah-Khan would have. Mr Gatekeeper knew that: it was a set-up from the start."

"But why?"

"Let us just say that both will use any little opportunity to put a woman down. Any woman! Cecilia is just one of many in a line of victims. If I began to tell you the sorts of things these two get away with, you would not believe it."

"Can't anything be done about it? Isn't there a boss to go to? I mean, I can understand a student in a secondary school being harassed by a teacher, but a lawyer? A professional like you? And that poor woman lawyer! Why do you suffer in silence? I mean, how can I even think you can help me with Bones if your position is hardly any different? My God! I mean, what is going on? And that rape-and-marriage stuff! Is that really the law?"

"Slow down, Mosa. Don't get all worked up. It may not seem possible, but there are a few skirmishes we do win. This was not one of them. It is an uphill battle. And do not forget there are good judges: they are not all like that idiot. Our strategy is to avoid him, but that strategy does not always work."

"There was a time when I thought I might go into law. But no, not me. That bowing and 'My Lord this' and 'My Lord that' are just too much. And don't you think it is ridiculous that you should talk to someone sitting on the second floor of a building, with you standing, *standing*, mind you, on the first floor? You think putting him up there is going to make him closer to being a god? 'As his Lordship pleases!'; 'I pray for the orders.' Pray! My God! That is what you said as he walked all over you! How can you take it? Is he God, or what? How could that poor, trembling attorney take it? How can you all keep on going back for more?" Mosa was furious. She was close to tears, but she did not want to cry. Was there no relief from this constant battering? At home? At school? Now even within the cradle of justice?

"What do you suggest I do? Toss my gown out and never go back? Do you want me to stop this car and do that? Is that your idea of a solution? You think that will help the Cecilias of this country? What choices do I have? You think I like bowing to that sexist beast? You think I have choices? Look at me, young lady. I have been practising law for three years. Three short, miserable years! I am a beginner and a female! I have no clout. I am nothing. No one would listen. That brute can romp all over me, and I just have to take it. If he makes a mistake about the law, I might succeed on appeal; otherwise, I just have to bear it. That is just how things are, my smart friend!"

"Maybe you should start questioning the way things are. Maybe things do not have to be the way they are. Maybe you have a defeatist attitude."

"Maybe," responded Julia Kenare, with a deep sigh. She could not believe she was having this discussion with a nineteen-year-old.

As it turned out, they did not get another judge until a week later. But by that time, Cecilia had died. Then, two days after her mother's death, little Bibi died too. Judge Mensah-Khan had been right to refuse the application: an order would have been purely academic.

CHAPTER 17

When Cecilia did not get better, the family met and decided that she was suffering too much. Her mother needed to let her go. She needed to release her from her heart. She needed not to hold her back. It was too much to ask of a mother. Lesedi cried in response, but she understood that it was the only way. Bathing her with ancestral soil was the only way out of her daughter's suffering. But, of course, there was Cecilia's child. That was part of what was holding Cecilia back from joining her ancestors. Thus, as Lesedi was being persuaded to release her daughter, the daughter was in turn struggling with leaving her own daughter behind.

For Cecilia, court action had been one attempt at giving herself strength to leave her daughter behind. An action brought on by desperation. When she found out about the court's decision, Cecilia suffered a relapse and was unconscious for two days. When she regained consciousness, she asked for Mosa.

"Mosa, I cannot leave her behind like this. Is there any hope with the courts?" Cecilia had not spoken for three days. Her voice was thick and wheezy, as if it were being forced through a thin pipe.

Mosa chose to be truthful. "I do not know. But I do not think so. I really do not know, Cecilia. I cannot lie to you."

"Thank you for trying. I have made my mind up. Be careful. Promise to be careful. Do not end up like me. Please be careful." With these words, Cecilia closed her eyes. Next to her was her daughter. She seemed to be sleeping, though restlessly, her thin legs thrashing and twitching from time to time.

Mosa was aware that the family was whispering about the need for the final bathing with ancestral soil. There was a quiet that came from more than just lack of noise. A deep quiet in which even communication with hearts seemed possible. A glance was enough, and a pitcher of water was passed. A sigh and snuff were offered. A groan, and a pillow was patted for a head to be rested on.

Mosa left for her own yard. She was not of an age when she could be included in those sorts of discussions; also, she was not family.

"You have to release her," Mara said in a whisper.

"Yes," Lesedi answered.

"She has to know you have let her go."

"I know."

"Can you release her? Can your heart release her?"

"It is hard."

"I know. The breast that has fed a child cannot just let go."

"My womb is with pain."

"I understand. Is her uncle here?"

"He has just left to get a change of clothes from his home. He has been on watch with all of us these past three days. None of us have known any sleep for a week."

"Have you discussed getting ancestral earth to bathe her?" Mara asked. She was not a member of the family, and it was not, strictly speaking, her place to be discussing the issue. But sometimes bonds of friendship are as important as those of blood.

"They are waiting for me to make the decision."

"You have to do it, Sedi. She is suffering. She needs to know you have released her."

"I know. It is difficult to finally acknowledge that it is over."

The two women were watching the skeleton that used to be Cecilia, lying on a mattress in the tiny room, motionless, except for the eyes and the occasional grimace of pain. The eyes seemed to be looking around, searching for something. Pleading. Seeking to communicate. This was a difficult matter Mara had just raised with her friend. Cecilia was clearly almost dead, but her soul refused to vacate the body. She was hanging on when no recovery was possible. What was needed was her mother to release her from her heart, to tell her that it was alright, that she could go. To reassure her that her daughter would be taken care of.

Lesedi's brother walked in, almost on tiptoe. Death brought on softness, even from the clumsy. People spoke in soft voices and walked around silently. They had been on a death watch for three days now, and the strain was showing on their faces. They were not always remembering to eat – or lacked an appetite – and so they were also physically tired.

"Mma-Cecilia, we have to bathe her with the earth from her ancestors. We have to release her. She is suffering," whispered Uncle More.

"Yes. Mma-Pule has just been saying the same thing."

"I will inform the others and go over to get it."

"Please take that clay pot over there for the earth: it was made for her by her grandmother."

"I should be back before it gets too hot. I will take my bicycle."

Uncle More left for the family's grandparents' house, across the river. He expected the trip to take about an hour or so. It was the place in which Mma-Cecilia was born, as was her father before her. It was the place in which the spirits of their ancestors still lived, where the soil and the air had been enriched over the years by the souls, departing and arriving, of members of the Malapa family. It was where Cecilia's mother had lost her umbilicus as a baby; it was also where her daughter had lost hers. Bathing with the earth from this place would help release Cecilia's soul and encourage it to leave her useless body. The bathing would get the soul in direct contact with her ancestors, and they would encourage her to join them, to leave her dead body behind.

When Uncle More came back with the small pot of earth, an old woman mixed it with some water, stirring it and removing all sharp objects such as bits of bark and stones. Cecilia, who had not been able to speak for five days, looked up, her eyes watching. As she prepared the mixture, the old woman told Cecilia what she was doing. She told her that her ancestors were ready to receive her; that her mother would take care of her daughter; that it was alright for her to go, to join the ancestors and to watch over her daughter from there. She was preparing to give her a bath with her ancestors' earth to help her on her journey, so she should not be afraid.

"Sleep. Let the pain end," the old woman urged.

Then she began. It was more of a sponge bath because it was not possible to immerse Cecilia in a tub. Moving her brought painful groans that no heart could bear to hear. The bathing was a family matter, and only Mara was allowed in because of the special friendship she had with Lesedi.

Just as the old woman finished bathing Cecilia, Cecilia raised her hand, dipped it in the water and ran it over her sleeping daughter. For weeks, she had not been able to move a finger, until now. As realisation spread from face to face, calm came over Cecilia's own face: it softened and with her hand on the thin, fragile foot of her daughter, she died.

The old woman reached forward. She closed Cecilia's eyes, straightened her legs and folded her hands across her chest. A white sheet was brought, and the body was wrapped in it. The room was cleared of all its contents. The body was turned so that the head pointed to the west: the direction of the end. Two candles were lit: one at the foot of the thin, long, white parcel; the other at its head. It was in this condition of peacefulness that Mosa later in the day saw Cecilia. She had died about midday, so her body had to wait for the afternoon before transportation. In the meantime, word went around the ward, around the village and beyond, that Cecilia was sleeping the last sleep.

No one expected the child to live long; indeed, when she did die, two days later, it was more of a relief than anything. Her mother would not have rested peacefully unless the little one joined her.

At their funeral, the tiny coffin stood next to the larger one, just as the child had stayed at her mother's side for months. Few could hold back their tears. The family was at first torn between burying so small a child in an adult graveyard and burying her in the house. A graveyard as final resting place for so small a child seemed so heartless, but separating the mother from the child seemed equally cruel. It was finally resolved that Cecilia would have wanted the child to remain next to her. The two would be buried in the same grave. But it was a decision that was not reached easily.

After the funeral, Mosa sent a copy of the funeral program to Judge Mensah-Khan. It was a private act of rebellion. She did not think it would change anything, except that it gave her some measure of satisfaction. There were only two more weeks to go before the prize-giving ceremony, and she told herself that she should not be getting angry and distracted, or perhaps that she should be getting angry and charged for the work at hand.

CHAPTER 18

A Saturday morning, early in July. Cold, but a perfect day for crowding people into a hall that had no air-conditioning. There was a buzz as students streamed into the school. Shoes were shining, all buttons were in place, and there was not a belt missing. A few boys had a neater haircut. And a closer look might even have revealed brighter teeth and shorter fingernails. The big day had arrived.

Huge, three-legged pots bubbled, sizzled or boiled over, filling the air with mouth-watering aromas. A tree was festooned with skins, hooves, intestines, stomachs and heads from the two cows slaughtered for the occasion.

By ten o'clock, as the day's funerals came to an end in the village, parents had arrived and taken their seats. Teachers hopped about, issuing orders and reminders. There was an element of excitement and festivity in the air.

And the Honourable Minister of Education, Mrs Lesego Molalane, would be attending! Parents offered their congratulations to Mr Merake: how he had swung that one was indeed a surprise. But there was still nervousness as the receiving party stood at the gate, waiting. Then the black Mercedes-Benz, the national flag waving from its bonnet, rolled through the gates. Ululation, a drum roll and clapping of hands!

Mr Merake and Mr Kgaka, chests swollen with pride, led the Minister into the hall, in which they were met by even louder applause. The Minister was a tall, imposing figure. She wore a blue, ballooning dress and a matching, intricately tied head scarf. When she inclined her head to acknowledge the applause, the head scarf seemed to be about to tumble off her head. She smiled confidently as her eyes swept through the hall. Merake and Kgaka led her to the front of the hall, and the three of them took their seats at the head table on the stage, from where they had a good view of the entire hall. The students were seated on one side of the hall, and all the parents and other adult guests filled the seats on the other side. The teachers sat on high stools placed along the sides of the hall.

Mr Kgaka began the proceedings by welcoming the Minister, other guests, parents, teachers and students, and almost every word received loud applause.

Things began to fall apart for Mr Merake when the Minister began to speak.

"Before I go on to my prepared speech, I want to congratulate the five girls for the courage and initiative they have shown by inviting me to this prize-giving ceremony. Because I believe the letter they wrote me will make all of you proud, I am going to read it to you."

As the Minister read out the letter, Merake hung his head. But when she finished, he applauded hard and loud, and stood up, provoking a standing ovation. He was selling the idea that he was behind the letter, but the teachers could see that it was not so. The parents, unaware of this little intrigue, ululated, and an excited parent sprang from the audience and offered a spontaneous praise poem for the Minister.

During a song by the Scripture Union, Mr Merake leaned over and whispered in the headmaster's ear, "A good strategy, wasn't it: to have the students write the letter? It worked. I knew it would work!" The headmaster had no time to respond: it was time for the next item.

Five girls came forward to offer a poem. "The title of our poem is 'She Walked With Fear, Until . . .'" announced one of the girls. She stepped away from the rest of the group, and began to act out and mime as the other four girls recited the poem. It was about abusive teachers and their student victims. It was a sad, short piece that ended with the following words:

> She walked with fear, until the Minister came
> and heard, and she refused to let it go on.

There was no applause; not a sound. Silence. Some mothers in the audience had their hands over their mouth. Some muttered, "Ao, shame". Some fathers looked visibly angry. Angry at whom, though? They had a Minister amongst them, and did not know how one was supposed to respond to a poem such as that. They waited for some indication from her. But she was frozen in her seat. This was a prize-giving ceremony. It was supposed to be a happy occasion, a time for congratulations and feasting. She was not mentally prepared for this kind of "entertainment". She looked at the program again: yes: it said this was an entertainment piece. How could this headmaster have allowed an item like that to go on the program?

Mr Merake glowered at the five performers as they left the stage, willing himself not to stand up and follow them. His hand was itching for his blood sucker. They would know him later. They had no right to do this to his ceremony. One of the performers was Lerato. Had she not been smiling at him coyly these past months? He had been working on her for months, and was sure they were getting along fine. What had gotten into her? Who had influenced her to be part of this crazy poem? He would get to the bottom of this nonsense. The person responsible would pay, and pay dearly.

The rest of the students were at first unsure about how to receive the poem. But it did not take long for them to figure out what had just happened. One of the performers was one of Bones's victims. When this dawned on them, there was applause, whistling and foot stamping. Even hesitant shouts from the back of "Bones! Bones! Bones!" The hecklers, however, were careful to cover their mouth, to avoid detection for this daring act.

Ms Khan, the gentle Indian teacher, who was always careful with her language and never had a bad word for anyone, looked as if she were going to faint. Mr Merake was fuming. Mr van Heerden, who had elected to come to Bana-Ba-Phefo because he had felt that the head-master "understood", was sweating.

But Kgaka did not seem to "understand" what was happening right now. His usual line of "Let us have a round of applause for this great piece of entertainment," did not seem appropriate. He glared at the five girls as if he would have loved to vaporise them with his stare. In the end, he chose to ignore the performance, as if by so doing he could wipe it from everyone's memory.

"I will now call upon Mrs Nazor to call out the next set of prizes."

Things seemed to return to normal as prizes were given out. Parents ululated and clapped, and the poem was soon forgotten – or at least that is how it seemed. It was an aberration, like a woman sitting on a chair at a funeral. All it needed was a man to smooth out the little bump. The headmaster had decided that he would deal with the arrogant upstarts later.

"Our next item is an art exhibition and competition. I have to say a special word about this item. This is the initiative of the students themselves. The Minister will select the best three pieces of art; there are special prizes for those three. No one has seen the work yet. This country needs people like these students. They have shown initiative, leadership and dedication. Without the assistance of a teacher, they have conceived and completed an entire art exhibition! A round of applause, please!"

During the loud clapping, Mr Merake straightened his shoulders, recovering from the two doses of shock he had suffered.

The crowd trooped out to view the exhibition. The headmaster walked alongside the Minister, and Mr Merake fell into step next to them. Someone was taking a picture, and Mr Merake wanted to make sure that his presence was recorded.

Outside the school library, a large curtain hung against a wall, and ten female students were standing next to the wall. One of them stepped forward and announced, "Honourable Minister, we present to you ten pieces of art. Although we have asked that you grade the pieces and select the best three, now we ask that you do not do so. There are no best three. There cannot be any best amongst what you will see. You will soon understand why, Honourable Minister." The girl was shaking, and her voice trembled. The Minister thought she might even dissolve into tears.

The girls reached for the curtain, and pulled it off. First, there was silence as the crowd took in the paintings. Then gasps, whispers and exclamations of "Ah, a!" "Oh, God", and *"Maria, Mma-Jesu!"*

In the ten pieces of art were depicted scenes that could only be associated with the school. The students were in school uniform, and the men could only have been teachers. In one picture, a horrified girl was being pressed against a corner in a classroom by a man while the rest of the students were bent over their books. In another, a teacher was dragging a girl into a car; in place of the car's registration number was the word TEACHER. In another, a student was sprawled on her back over a photocopier as a teacher leaned over her. In yet another, a student was scaling the school fence as a teacher waited in a car at the gate.

The Minister gave a gasp and stepped back, as if she were afraid that the images might come to life. Angrily, she turned to the ten girls. But what she saw in their faces stopped her. These were not belligerent students spoiling for a fight with the authorities: there was genuine fear on their faces. Fear at the possible consequences of their daring act. Very deep feelings had led them to throw caution to the winds to do this. This was a cry for help, and no covering of the ears would keep the sound out. The Minister looked back at the artwork and noticed a sentence in a neat hand that read:

> And then the Minister came and saw,
> and she refused to let it go on.

Mosa watched from under a tree. Even though it was winter, the sun was letting through strong streaks of light, and she thought her dark skin was absorbing every shaft. Perhaps some of this heat was coming from within her. She watched her friends, willing them to remain strong. One of them threw a look Mosa's way, and Mosa frowned at her in response, silently ordering her to look away: it was too early to acknowledge a connection between them.

The Minister was perplexed. There was no precedence for something like this. Students in some schools, wanting to communicate some view or another, had protested in more-direct ways in the past: throwing stones, boycotting classes or tossing out food, even burning buildings. She knew how to deal with that kind of behaviour. Ringleaders were identified, rounded up and expelled. Threats were issued to other participants. Parents were hauled into the school, and, too petrified to ask too many questions, quickly agreed that their children be lashed to be taught a lesson. Newspapers carried headlines about how parents were demanding that the Ministry take a tougher stand against unruly students. That approach was known to generally settle matters for a few years; that is, until all the miscreants had graduated and left. But this protest was different.

The Minister looked at the headmaster, who seemed to have forgotten that he was in charge. He was looking at the pictures as if not quite comprehending, tilting his head this way and that to see the scenes more clearly. As if there were a secret that might be revealed if he just found the right angle. Or perhaps he thought there was some trick of light. With his long head, he looked like a puzzled lizard.

As for Mr Merake, he looked like he had been punched in the gut. He was in physical pain. His arms were folded against his tummy. His shoulders were hunched; he was rocking backwards on his feet; his face was contorted with anger and fear. When no one said anything, and the silence began to rival the paintings in inducing discomfort, Merake offered an explanation in a weak voice.

"Honourable Minister, you know girls these days. I am sure –"

"Shut up, you!" The Minister's response was curt and loud. Then she looked at Merake as if noticing him for the first time. She looked at his face; then her eyes went up and down his thin body a few times. She did not seem to like what she was looking at. For a moment, Mr Mitchell, standing nearby, thought she might even spit on Merake. Instead, she turned to the girls and gave them a slight nod.

The headmaster continued to stare at the pictures, perhaps trying to see whether his own face was recognisable in them, or perhaps he just did not know what else to do. He was unsure whether the Minister's order for silence extended to him. He found himself hoping that it did. It was easier to shut up than to try to say anything else. He would gladly take a vow of silence for life right now.

Finally, the Minister announced that they had seen enough. She told the girls that she wanted to see them at the end of the program. Yet another quick look was thrown Mosa's way by one of the girls. Mosa ignored it, and seemed no more involved than any of the many students watching.

The announcement that the program would continue surprised the headmaster. He had assumed that whatever else happened today, continuing with the rest of the program was not one of the possibilities. Surely they could not just go on to the next item as if nothing untoward had happened. But the Minister had spoken, and she was clearly not expecting any contradictions. She began to stride in the direction of the hall. Kgaka hopped after her, shouting at bustling and sniggering students to behave and to return to the hall in an orderly way. The brief confusion had provided him with a reason to shout at someone. He wanted to push a head down, to smooth out the bumps. But these were boulders in his path.

Back inside the hall, Mr Kgaka announced the next item on the agenda. But the mood had been seriously affected. The students who came up for prizes were not cheered. Parents came forward to meet their children out of duty rather than joy. They seemed embarrassed to be part of the program, and feared for their children. Even the Scouts' performance, which was a comic display of marching steps, failed to bring out a laugh or a cheer.

Stan, sitting quietly in the audience, had by this time figured it all out. He was sure the worst would come in the form of a performance involving Mosa. He went over to where their mother was sitting, and whispered to her that whatever happened next, things would be fine. He did not know what else to tell her, but felt she needed to be warned somehow. He had no idea how things would be resolved, but he knew that nothing would ever be the same again at Bana-Ba-Phefo High School.

All the students involved were scared. They had planned the whole thing over a couple of months, but having done it, they were not as convinced of the wisdom of it any more. Being involved in the drawings and the poetry in anger and frustration blinded them to the fact that they were dealing with powerful people in a system that tended to be protective of its own.

Now they were clustered together in the back of the hall, like criminals waiting to be sentenced. The anger that gave them energy was now replaced by cold fear as they waited for the consequences of their actions.

To a depressed audience, the headmaster announced with no enthusiasm, "Honourable Minister, invited guests, parents, teachers, students, ladies and gentlemen, we have now come to the last but one item on the agenda. It is a play by the Bana-Ba-Phefo Traditional Dance Group. I will not say much about the play at this point, for I have not seen it either. Bana-Ba-Phefo Traditional Dance Group, the stage is yours."

The group appeared, singing a traditional song in a quick tempo somehow unsuited to the funereal mood in the hall. Despite themselves, people sat up and craned their neck, as the kids in the audience smiled and stood up to see better.

The play was about three happy schoolgirls, dancing and laughing as they went about their business, Mosa among them. The dancing was so good that people were soon drawn from their unhappy mood, cheering and ululating. The group sang a few more happy songs. Then, without warning . . . Mosa began playing a male teacher. The play was about the powerlessness of girls in the face of abusive teachers. About the failure of innocent teachers to get involved or to intervene. About silence from the capital in the face of oppression in a small village. It was a cry for help, an indictment and a challenge all rolled into one.

When Sinah said, "No, Mr Bones. Please leave me alone," there was a gasp. Even Mosa faltered. That was not part of the script. That was too close. The girl has courage, Mosa thought. Or she's suicidal.

By the end of the play, many in the audience were sniffling. A female teacher did not even try to hide the tears rolling down her face. The students were frozen. A thunderbolt was going to strike. Something was going to happen.

The poetry performers and artists joined the cast on stage. Mosa announced that the last segment of their play was a dance entitled "Dignity for the Girl Child", a beautiful but sad dance piece about the girls' transformation from timid and shy doormats to strong, confident, purposeful young women.

Mr Merake watched this with his fingers interlaced over his eyes. The Minister was enthralled.

The headmaster was in total shock, wondering whether a fired headmaster was eligible for the pension.

Mr Mitch wanted to weep with shame for having looked the other way, but also felt like jumping up with pride at these brave and talented young women.

Mr van Heerden wondered whether anyone knew about his little secret involving a fifteen-year-old. He looked around the hall, seeking her out. When he finally spotted her, she was staring at him, tears running down her cheeks. He stumbled out of the hall. He needed some air.

With the last piece over, the hall was quiet, expectant. The headmaster just sat there staring at the empty stage, so that the Minister had to nudge him. "We are running late. Can we have the last item on the program please?"

Mr Kgaka could not believe it: she wants the last item on the program? "Mr Merake, can we have a vote of thanks, please?"

Mr Merake jumped up, but once on his feet, he seemed not to know why he was standing. He sat down again quickly. Then he was up again. The crowd tittered. Merake looked at the headmaster as if he were pleading with him to do something.

"Mr Merake, the vote of thanks, please." The headmaster's voice was flat.

"Honourable Minister, ladies and gentlemen, thank you for coming. Thank you very much. Yes, I thank you." That was all the usually verbose Merake could manage, his typed speech – seven pages in all – forgotten on the table in front of him.

The headmaster invited everybody to stay for lunch, but most of the parents stood up and left, having lost their appetite halfway through the program. The Minister invited the performers to stay behind. But, turning to the headmaster, she curtly informed him that he was not invited. "And I will not be staying for lunch. Tell my driver to have the car ready in thirty minutes." As Mr Kgaka turned to go, she called after him, "Bring these young people some food and something to drink. They must be hungry after all that hard work."

Mosa and her friends looked at each other and exchanged secret smiles.

The headmaster could not believe his ears. He was being ordered to serve students. Girl students at that! By a woman Minister too! Did she actually mean that he himself should bring the food? He did not want to offend her any more, but there was just no way he was going to carry a bowl of food for a bunch of girls. Instead, when he was out of the Minister's hearing, he bellowed at some women to take the food and drinks. They looked at each other and tried to suppress their amusement, even as they hurried to comply with the order.

The Minister promised the girls that a commission of inquiry would be set up and that an investigation would be launched on Monday morning. She assured them that nothing was going to happen to any of them, and urged them to co-operate with the investigators. She also congratulated them for their courage in bringing the matter out into the open.

"Keep that courage. You will go far in life," she said.

"And beyond," Mosa responded softly.

"Mosa, is there trouble?" Mara had been waiting on a bench in the schoolyard. She had many questions to ask, but they all came back to the one she had just asked.

"Oh yes, Mma, there is lots of trouble," Mosa answered with a mischievous grin.

"Are you in trouble, Mosa? Please, just tell me what is going on. I have been a nervous wreck for hours. I cannot take it any more. What did the Minister say to you?"

"No: I am not in trouble, not the type you have in mind, anyway. There is going to be a commission of inquiry set up, and all the stink will be exposed."

"Is that what the Minister told you? Do you trust her? What if she gets back to her office and she has second thoughts about all this? Have you thought about that?"

"I trust her, Mma. I listened to her. I saw her eyes. She cannot possibly just ignore all this." Mosa was confident, but her mother's words set her thinking.

"Listen, I do not know about how these things work, but what I do know is that the Minister can expect to be blamed for allowing things to get to this point. She just might decide not to go ahead with an inquiry after she thinks more about the whole thing over the weekend. Or others in government might not want her to have an inquiry. It might not be up to just her! And the elections are next year!"

Mosa's earlier elation ebbed a bit. Her mother might well have a point. The Minister could easily decide that it was better to keep a lid on the whole thing after the shock of the day had worn off. There ought to be a way to make her keep her promise.

"You are just a group of girls," Mara continued with a worried face. "She can just say she never said anything about an inquiry. Or the inquiry might well focus on you as the guilty ones. She might decide to suspend you during the inquiry. That will cut you off from the rest of the students, and then the rest would not have the courage to say what they know. Mosa, I am worried. You will be writing your final examinations soon. If you are suspended, you will not be able to write."

She sprung to her feet, causing her mother to nearly fall off the bench. She held her mother's head between her two hands as if Mara were a little kid, and said with earnestness, "Thank you; thank you; thank you. You are smart beyond words." She kissed her and told her to go home. Her puzzled mother tried to grab her hand to restrain her. "Everything is going to be fine! Just fine! I'll explain later!" And she was off.

Mosa hurried after her fellow conspirators, and within minutes they were back together again. The Minister had left, and the girls were feeling triumphant. The day had been tiring, but they were elated at the end results and were thanking Mosa over and over for having master-minded the whole thing.

Mosa brushed aside their praises and ushered them back into the hall. She explained the problem spotted by her mother. The happy faces collapsed into misery. Several girls began to speak at once, but Mosa stopped them. She explained her idea of dealing with the problem. It was simple really. Within a few minutes, the girls had drafted a letter thanking the Minister for her decision to set up a commission of inquiry to look into the school's problems: abuse of power, sexual harassment, unfair and excessive beatings, and pressuring girl students to have sex with "big men" from the village. They concluded by stating that although in the letter they indicated that it had been copied to three newspapers, the copies would not be sent until Monday morning, and even then only after they had met with the commissioners. They felt that they needed assistance in dealing with the press, especially because reporters from two newspapers had already indicated interest in the story. They all signed the letter.

Two students were charged with delivering the letter to the Minister's residence first thing Sunday morning. They would take a bus to Gaborone. Lilian knew that all Ministers lived in an area just off the main mall. Finding the residence of the Minister of Education would be easy.

Of course, there was no sign of interest from any paper yet. Only the government press had been in attendance, and it would report only what the Minister directed it to report. Mosa was certain that the veiled threat to go to the media would have the Minister's commissioners at the school first thing Monday morning, if not earlier. Yes, she was half expecting to get a visit from some very important people at home before the weekend was over.

Sinah wanted to walk home with Mosa, but Mosa explained that there was something personal she had to attend to. Sinah did not press her friend: she had come to know that Mosa could not be pressured in that way.

A few minutes later, still at school, Mosa found her brother. "Stan, may I borrow your bicycle? I will return it tomorrow."

"Hey!" Stan said, "don't we have things to talk about? Protest dances and stuff on the stage? Turning the whole school upside-down –?"

"I know; I know; but later. What about that bike?"

"Do you need money for a bus? Are you tired after today? I do not blame you. I can give you the bus fare."

"No, Stan, it is a bicycle I need. Will you let me use your bicycle, please? I need to repair a dream." From her voice and her body posture, it was obvious that she was not going to say any more.

"Okay, and keep it as long as you like. I hardly ever use it anyway."

"Thanks, Stan. I will not need it beyond today. I am certain of that," Mosa answered.

A few minutes later, Mosa was off on her brother's bicycle. Riding, gliding and floating. Recapturing her youth so that she could repair a dream that had turned into a nightmare.

She passed Sinah and waved. Sinah frowned, then smiled and waved back. She shook her head, wondering what mischief her friend was up to this time.

CHAPTER 19

Mosa told her brother that she had something important to share with him. "But we have to go to our melon rock to do it."

Stan, perhaps sensing that resistance would be futile, agreed. They hitched a ride from a family heading to a cattlepost, and fifteen minutes later they were there.

It had been a week since the prize-giving ceremony, two months since Mimi's wedding, one month since Cecilia's funeral and eight months since Pule's funeral. A lot had happened, and a lot was still happening. Mosa's and Stan's experiences at home, at school and on the streets would continue to shape and mould them. What they became and who they became would no doubt be shaped by those experiences. They had grown closer and had been spending a lot of time together.

Now the two of them were at the place of their childhood. Stan took a deep breath as he felt a flood of memories envelop him. He would never have thought that being there would affect him so powerfully. He looked around, taking in the wild-berry shrubs. He saw his shrub and Mosa's shrub, so designated after countless fights of who had the right to pick the first fruit from which bush. Then he realised that he was sitting on his side of the rock. He had forgotten he had a side until just now. They were on the melon rock, as they had called it as children. Their melon rock.

Mosa tapped Stan on the shoulder, dragging him from the past. When he turned to look at her, she handed him a brown envelope. They had not been there together since they were children, and Stan was in a forest of memories until Mosa brought him back. He looked up at her as if to find out what was inside the envelope.

"You have been up here recently, haven't you?" asked Stan.

"Come on: take it out and read it," Mosa said, ignoring her brother's question.

His eyes returned to the envelope. He saw a date stamp of the local hospital. Fear gripped his heart. Mosa had been acting very funnily the whole day. She told him she had news for him, but refused to say whether she had good or bad news. Then she insisted they come to this place. "Stan, one can always return to one's home, except one's most precious home: one's mother's womb. Let us go back together for this piece of news I have to share with you." With that, she had refused to say any more. Now here they were, and he had this brown envelope that had a hospital stamp on it, and he was sweating and afraid.

"What is it?" He really wanted to ask, "What does it say?" but he was afraid of the answer he might get.

"Well, there is one obvious way to find out. Take it out and read it."

Stan reached into the already opened envelope and retrieved a small sheet of paper. His hands were shaking. He felt his breath quicken. He tried to be slow and deliberate to hide his panic. He wanted to be strong for his sister. He flattened the piece of paper, and his eyes flashed across the words "Mosa Selato", "HIV" and "Negative". That was all he needed to see, and he gave a whoop of joy. He choked on the saliva that had collected in his mouth, and his cry of happiness turned into a cough, and then into a cry, and then he was both crying and laughing at the same time. "You went for the test! You went for the test! Oh, Mosa, I am so happy at the results. But I am so sad you had to do this alone. I promised to be with you, remember?" He was kissing and hugging her and crying and laughing all at once.

"Stan, don't strangle me, please. And you are pushing me off the rock. At this rate, I am going to end up dead anyway."

"Please, don't even joke about it. It is not funny." But he was grinning. Then he became serious once again. "But why did you not tell me about the test? I have been worried about your silence. I wanted to raise the issue, but I did not want to push you."

"Stan, I am so happy. But I did need to walk this stretch alone. Perhaps one day I will explain. It is enough, though, that you offered to be there with me. But some roads can only be travelled alone. Not in loneliness, though. I was alone, but not lonely. Do you understand?" Stan did not really understand. Sometimes his sister was too complicated for him. But he did not care. He was too happy to care. "And yes: I have been here before. On the day I had the test done, I came to sit here before I went to the hospital. I sat up on this rock and tried to recapture what I could of our childhood. I wanted to remember. And I did, and that gave me strength to go ahead. I felt the presence of my ancestors around here, and I asked them for strength. Not in so many words. Just being here, and feeling and thinking and remembering. That gave me strength."

"Yes, you are right. You can almost hear the voices from the past. The sounds of the cattle arriving at the end of the day. The barking of the dogs. What is that crazy dog again? The one with one ear?"

"Mrs Rose. That is his name: Mrs Rose." Mosa was smiling at the memory of the one-eared dog that was so crazy that Aunt Rinah was sure it was possessed by some spirit. She could not make up her mind whether the spirit was holy or evil. The dog started behaving strangely after Uncle Rich had taken it to an all-night religious meeting at which people went into trances, as the Holy Spirit possessed them. Of course, possession by the Holy Spirit meant that all kinds of evil spirits were leaving the bodies of the faithful. It was one of Aunt Rinah's theories that one of these departing evil spirits had entered the body of Mrs Rose. Sometimes she maintained that it was the Holy Spirit that had entered the animal, but because he was only a dog, something had happened in there because the body of a dog was not made for that type of occupation. Uncle Rich thought all this was nonsense. He was certain that the dog had been frightened into a mild heart attack by the craziness of all those heathens pretending to be taken over by the Holy Spirit. It was the shock of the hypocrisy of the human animal that had unhinged the dog's mind.

"Only Uncle Rich could have come up with a name like that for a dog," Mosa said. "And it was not even a female dog."

"Remember the fat pig?" Stan said, "How it bit your foot? You ran up a tree, remember?"

"Of course I do. How can I not? I fell down the tree. Then got a cuff from Ali. Should have stayed down to have the pig eat me up, I guess. That woman was crazy. She was probably the one possessed by some evil spirit, not the dog!"

"She was not evil: come on. And in her own strange and sad way, she loved all of us. A girl was not supposed to climb trees was her view. She was always on at you about your 'boy habits', as she called them. Sometimes it seemed you got into fixes just to irk the poor woman." Stan was smiling.

"What poor woman? Get your victims right, or I will push you off this rock." Mosa was grinning, because any bad feelings towards the strange aunt had long evaporated. "And those frilly dresses she wore, and that ridiculous suitcase she kept suspended on a rope inside the hut. Seemed like she was always mending her dresses. What with constantly being caught in branches. I wonder how her life turned out in Serowe?"

"Speaking about pigs, do you remember the pink pig Uncle Rich brought once? I had never seen a pink pig before, and I just could not believe how thin it was: long and thin. Strange-looking creature. Do you remember? He brought it in a bus! How they let him on the bus with that pig I cannot imagine. He was really crazy, our Uncle Rich. He was special in many ways, too. Thanks for bringing me back here, Mosa. Thanks for helping me remember."

"Thanks for being willing to remember," Mosa answered.

They kept quiet for a while. Mosa noted how much higher the rock had seemed when they were children. Scrambling up and down had been a challenge they met with enthusiasm. She looked at her clean legs exposed below her shorts, and remembered how in those days, washing had been limited to weekly scrubs in a shared tub, by their mother. Water had been scarce, and washing during the week had been limited to sponging the face and cleaning the teeth. Even those limited attempts at bodily hygiene had not been daily. How things have changed, she thought.

"Come on: let us walk about. Let us see if anything has changed." Mosa broke the silence. She jumped off the rock and led the way. They visited places in which they had set traps for small animals. Places they went to collect firewood. Places in which they had fought baboons and monkeys for wild berries. Places they had gone to to look for goats and cattle. Places they had fought each other. Places they had romped in with laughter and a sense of freedom only children could know. Even poor children growing up with little food. Children who had to dodge tadpoles in their drinking water and their aunt's swift right slap. Children who had a loving mother and a crazy uncle who brought pink pigs and roasted them for dinner. A precious